ALL OF YOU

CLAIRE CAIN

Army Couple Photography by Rainbeau Decker.

Cover Design by Amanda Walker.

E-Book ISBN-13: 978-1-7327718-8-8

Print ISBN-13: 978-1-7327718-9-5

To those who are working toward recovery, and those who walk with them while they do.

CHAPTER ONE

Whit

The phone lying face down on the couch caught my eye while my head hung in downward facing dog. I grit my teeth and turned back to my mat. This wasn't the time for *that*.

I pushed through two more reps of the yoga routine for my rest days. But the gritting teeth wouldn't let up—clearly, the routine was failing to do what my trainer designed it to.

Arms splayed, body loose, I lay in *shavasana* on the mat, wishing I could stay there and sleep, wishing I could find satisfaction in relaxing into *anything* anymore. Oh, and seeing *him* behind my eyelids.

Again.

As usual, of late.

The relaxing thing would have to wait. Flipping to my side, I crawled across the plush gray carpet of my living room floor and grabbed the phone. Some part of me refused to turn it over until I'd given myself a stern talking to.

If he hasn't responded, you'll find someone else. You'll ask Damon. You'll ask Reese. You'll do something else besides obsess over this man.

Because I had been. Ever since I'd met Lieutenant Ben Holder at my cousin Reese's house two weeks ago and then spent a few hours with him on a tour of the military base after my concert, I hadn't been able to stop thinking of him.

And really, even *that* was a lie, because I'd been thinking about Ben Holder a lot longer than that. I just hadn't known his name was Ben.

I could still see the five o'clock shadow on his face as he slumped over the bar, inebriated by whiskey and grief, over a year ago. The first time I saw him... and that night, that conversation, had played itself in my mind a thousand times.

With ten minutes until my set, I sat down at the bar to wait for a water. My second time doing this—dressed in a disguise to come sing to a late-night crowd, and it had been incredibly helpful. Performing in front of an audience without them knowing me proved to be the best kind of feedback.

"It's just like this, you know? A beautiful woman walks up next to you, and that's gone, too, you know?"

The voice next to me thrummed low, rough, and slow, almost inaudible, but something about it made me turn to look at the man who'd spoken.

He kept sliding an empty highball a few inches in one direction with his index finger, then sliding it back. He sat slumped on the stool, but when I looked at him, he tilted his head sideways, almost peering upside-down, which it nearly felt like since I was sitting straight and somehow towering over him thanks to his posture.

"You know?" he asked me.

"Do I know what?" Somehow compelled by the misery in his face despite its slackened features, no doubt a byproduct of several rounds of whatever he'd had in the glass, I couldn't resist asking.

"I just got back. I been back two weeks. And you're so pretty, sitting there, humoring me, and I can look at you, you know? And he can't. Jones can't. He never will." His head slumped down, and he leaned more heavily on his arms braced against the bar.

My heart ached.

"Why not?" I asked, scared to know, but needing to.

He straightened then, making it obvious just how large he was. He turned and looked me straight in the eyes. His were bloodshot, heavily lidded and ringed in shadow.

"He's dead. I held him while he died. And now, he'll never have a stolen moment like this—not any of 'em."

We'd talked for a few more minutes, and he'd told me of other *stolen moments*, as he'd called them, that his friend would never have.

He broke my heart that night, and he changed me. I'd sung a short set, then raced home, and "Stolen Moment," my chart-topping and supposedly Grammy-contender single, had poured out of me in hours in what had to be the most complete song-writing experience I'd ever had. It'd grown out of compassion and grief and sadness for this man, this shell of a human who'd had nowhere to go with his pain.

Then I saw him again, over a year later, at my cousin's. He'd been standing tall and beautiful and sober and clear-eyed and fairly articulate considering the moment. He'd been fun and charming and so completely different from the man I'd seen that fateful night, and yet, they were the same. I knew they were.

It felt impossible to stop thinking about him. Was he so much better now? Had he put the loss of his friend out of his mind? He definitely hadn't recognized me—I mean, he had, but as me, Whit Grantham. He'd clearly had no idea we'd talked, and based on what I remembered, he'd likely forgotten the entire night.

But enough about that. On a slow, deep breath, I turned the phone over, entered my password, and clicked the app. *1 new message.*

My stomach flipped, and I resisted the urge to break out in a little dance of celebration. Instead, a tap on the little flag brought up my direct messages, and there it sat, at the end of a long thread.

@WhitGranthamOfficial: *I have a question for you, but I'd like to ask over the phone. Could I have your number?*

@TheRealBenHolder: *You want my phone number?*

@WhitGranthamOfficial: *Yes.*

@TheRealBenHolder: *Should I be nervous?*

@WhitGranthamOfficial: *Why would you be nervous for me to call you?*

@TheRealBenHolder: *People don't call each other anymore. This sounds serious.*

@WhitGranthamOfficial: *It's nothing bad. Or, I don't think you'll think it's bad.*

@TheRealBenHolder: *You sound uncertain.*

@WhitGranthamOfficial: *If you don't want to give me your number, it's ok. I don't want you to feel pressured. We'll just proceed as if I never asked.*

And here it was. The newest message, which had popped up in the last twenty minutes as I'd done everything

I could think of to avoid obsessively refreshing the app and stalking his username until he answered.

We'd been messaging back and forth for about two weeks. He'd liked one of the photos I'd taken on the tour he'd given me of Fort Campbell military base and had then started following me. I'd messaged him personally once certain it was, in fact, him, and we started chatting. We sent messages every day, and I wasn't ashamed to admit I enjoyed every interaction we'd had.

So much so, in fact, that I wanted to see him again, and he was easygoing enough that he might be able to handle attending an event with me. He didn't seem to take himself too seriously, and though he'd been shocked to meet me and had done the most adorable little stuttering, awkward introduction when we'd met at my cousin's house, he hadn't been tongue-tied at any point after that.

That was rare.

He'd been a different man than on our first interaction, and I suppose that was his right—it had been over a year, after all. The contrast had proven startling, and fascinating.

Even after two weeks, he hadn't asked me for anything, nor had he tried to pry into my personal life or flirt with me. Maybe some of our exchanges were *flirty*, if you really wanted to call them that, but mostly, they were fun.

Very little fun existed in my life anymore.

Not that being a world-famous Country singer wasn't fun. It *is*. It's the dream. It made me abandon my parents' plan for my life and finally succumb to the call of my passion—I couldn't ignore it. It'd been my dream since I'd heard Patsy Cline's *Showcase* at a friend's house one afternoon around age eight.

I grew up a veritable musical prodigy, if only because my parents were determined I would be, and I got into Juilliard for college. And left after sixteen months, dropping out just before the end of my second year to audition for *SouthernSound*, a TV show that looked for the latest Country star. The producers kept my history of privilege and training a secret, partly at my request, and since then, I'd managed to stay separate from my family and my past by freezing out all questions about all that at every turn and requiring iron-clad non-disclosures from anyone I worked with.

Despite the secrecy and their own anonymity from my fame, if I could have done something more appalling to Cynthia and Stuart Grantham, something they would have disapproved of more, I can't imagine what it would have been.

But my determination to achieve—though it won me a recording contract and had launched me into superstardom with two platinum records in just a little over four years, crazy successful tours, and fame so incessant that I was rarely left alone in a room—kept me reaching, working, *striving*.

Fun had never been natural to me—part of me suspected the Grantham ancestry had done its best to breed out any tendency toward fun centuries ago.

Ben Holder was fun—my opposite in about every way. He was tall—me? Vertically challenged. He was blond and golden—I had pale skin and dark hair. Seemingly laid back outwardly, I did suspect he still had a lot going on inside. Outwardly, I presented as stoic unless on stage or interviewing, and inside, a raging pile of insecurities and dissatisfaction fomented.

So, you know, *fun*.

I thought about what to say when I dialed him and wondered if he'd be awkward, or if I would. Like almost every one of my acquaintances other than my publicist, I hated talking on the phone. But for this, it felt necessary.

I tapped his number, and my phone dialed before I could second-guess the choice. One ring, two.

"Hello?"

Ben's voice made my heart beat faster.

"Uh, hi. Ben?" If I hadn't gotten nervous, I might have rolled my eyes.

"Yes?"

"Hey, this is Whit. Whit Grantham?" *Why do I sound like I'm not sure of my own name?*

"I would have known you by your voice, Whit."

I could hear the smile in his tone.

"Oh, okay. Well... thanks for taking my call."

"I'm unlikely to ever *not* take a call from you, even if I have to walk out of church to take it."

"You were at church? You could have called me back—it's not urgent."

"It's all right. What can I do for you?"

His voice sounded warm and smooth, and I marveled, my stomach plummeting, at his asking what *he* could do for *me*. Assistants and staff, even random people, were always asking me that, but in this case, it felt more genuine than any time before now.

I cleared away the surprise, launching into business mode, where I should have started. "I'm wondering if you're busy two weeks from yesterday."

Silence.

I pulled the phone back and checked to make sure the call hadn't dropped—it hadn't.

Finally, he spoke. "You know, I'm not sure what day that is. Do you know the calendar day?"

Something off tinged his voice, but I couldn't tell what.

"The fifteenth of October."

A low voice murmured on the other end, Ben's response covering it, though it was muffled, like he held the phone against his chest. "I should be free the fifteenth, sure. What am I signing up for?"

"It's a charity event. A fundraiser for a local music school. It should be relatively low-key, though I'm sure you can guess that doing anything with me isn't particularly low-key."

I kept the regret firmly out of my voice. I didn't need pity for my fame—didn't want it, either.

"I can imagine. Do I need to know anything before we do this?"

I crawled onto the couch and sank back into the plush pillows. "I don't think so. Probably just that you should simply nod and smile, and don't worry about answering questions."

That covered the basics. I didn't want to overload him, and the small event should mean there wouldn't be too much press.

"And your boyfriend? What's he going to say about you showing up there with me?"

I smiled to myself, enjoying Ben's casual approach to the subject.

"Since he doesn't exist, I don't expect he'll say much at all."

"Jamie Morris doesn't exist?"

A chill ran through me. So he *did* know a bit about me.

Weeks ago, when we chatted, he'd seemed entirely oblivious to everything surrounding me except my music and a little bit about how I came to fame through the show. Of course, he'd also just found out I was Reese's cousin. Whether he'd talked to Reese about me, which would have been fruitless since I knew Reese wouldn't share any personal details, or Ben had searched the Internet, he'd clearly found out about the gossip and a sliver of my dating history.

"Jamie Morris does exist, but he has no bearing on this conversation."

Another pause. Then, "All right. I'll be there."

CHAPTER TWO

Whit

"This seems like overkill. I don't need stage makeup for this event." I relaxed my eyes as Amanda, my makeup artist, readied my fake eyelashes.

"False."

"How is that false? I'm not going to be on stage!"

This was an age-old discussion. I loved makeup, but the stage-level goop quickly became tiresome. And some part of me wanted to be a little closer to *me* when I saw Ben tonight. People tended to gush over the public me, but he'd seen me for the first time as pretty close to myself—minimal makeup, no big hair, and normal clothes in the comfort of a relative's home.

"You and I both know you're going to end up on stage tonight, so don't even try with me today, Whit. You pay me for this, and if I don't do it right, Nikki will kill me. I'll choose your attitude over death any day, sorry." She didn't look at all apologetic as she gently tapped the edge of the lashes to my lid, then blew on the glue to dry.

Amanda had begged me to get lash extensions, and I'd tried them but hated them, so we were stuck with this.

"Fine. But note my protest." I lifted my chin and parted my lips, knowing she'd need this angle for finishing them, then it'd be back to the eyes.

"So noted. And can I just say, you seem particularly grumpy today."

I cracked one eye open, just barely, and took in her short platinum hair artfully messy with a magical pomade that kept the locks in place, but still made it look soft. Her lids were mermaid colors today—shimmering blues and greens, and they brought out her teal eyes. Of course they did—this was her thing. But still. Her makeup always amazed me.

"No, I'm not."

"You are. So tell me why."

I waited as she brushed color over my lips—I'd be going with an *au naturel* look far from natural considering I had more makeup on now than I wore on any normal day. But the look was one I'd become known for working fairly often at events, and I did like it. My dark hair and fair skin lent itself to this kind of "spare" look on my face—nude lips, dewy skin, dark, smoky eyes for evening, but only in grays.

I waited 'til she'd finished. "The guy who's coming. He's sweet. He's a *normal*. I don't want him to be freaked out."

A shimmer of nerves slithered in my belly, but I ignored it—something I'd become an expert at in the last decade.

"You like him?" Amanda asked, surprise clear in her voice.

She'd been with me through all the mess after Jamie, at which point I'd sworn off men altogether.

"No—nothing like that. He's just... sweet. I don't want him to feel uncomfortable, and I feel like this thing is becoming a bigger deal than it should. It's supposed to be about this little school for the arts, not me."

I took a deep breath and let it out slowly, rolling my shoulders back while staying as still as I could as Amanda worked her magic on my eyes.

Nobody should know my response to Ben Holder was nothing familiar. He made me... stop. It felt odd, and I hadn't figured out how to describe it to myself yet, but I was eager to see if it would happen when we met again.

"Well, it's not like he's going to be surprised by who you are, right? He's knows you're... you?" She sprayed my whole face with what amounted to hairspray for my makeup—setting spray, she'd told me and giving me a side-eye like you've never seen—then leaned back to look me over. "My goodness, I'm good."

"It's the raw material, I'm pretty sure." My words came with a grin.

I loved how she *loved* her job. Despite giving her a hard time, I was incredibly thankful for my team. It seemed odd to have an entire *team* that traveled with me, was employed by me, essentially, and who'd become a kind of family to me. They were, and I cared for them; that made some of the road-weariness, the incessant ambition, and the long days far easier.

"Raw material ain't bad. But I'm a genius." She spun me around to look in the mirror.

I did look good in what I called my *Country singer hair* thanks to Damon, my hair stylist. It was just shy of a big bouffant like the old Country ladies used to wear on top with lift at the crown, sides pulled and artfully pinned half-up at the back into some kind of design I hadn't taken time to appreciate, and the rest long all the way to my ribs. It fell straight, and the combination of the hair, the nude lips, and heavy eyes gave me a seventies feel we'd been using a lot lately.

"All right, go get dressed. You've got ten minutes 'til Ru comes to get you." Amanda shooed me from the seat and began tidying up the makeup.

I did appearances here in Nashville often enough that we had the whole set up for her in my bathroom, complete with bright lights and a chair I could lean back in.

I wandered to my closet and scooched a few things around to find what Damon had suggested. The dusty pink chiffon dress had drapey pearlescent fabric on top that shaped into a halter, though it was full and fairly modest thanks to the more classic Country era look. The bottom fell straight from my waist down in pleats giving it a seventies flair, and only a light pink painted toe nail would peek out as I walked in my platform sandals.

I always wore high heels to events because I was naturally quite short—five-foot-two— finding it tiresome to always be craning my neck up to all the people wanting to talk with me.

That sounded so arrogant, but no point demurring—I was one big reason why they were coming, why the parents and guests were paying a thousand dollars a head. I'd join the kindergarten class for a short song, and that was it. There were two or three other Country stars coming, and someone from the Nashville football team—we were all the willing ponies for the show.

I didn't mind this kind of dog and pony, though, because it was helping a school I liked a lot. If I live in Nashville when I have kids, should such an event occur a long time from now, I would consider sending them to this school.

"Ready, Whit?" Ru asked from the entryway.

Ru worked as my driver when I was in town and often on tour, as well. He was a dad of four and only liked old Country, so we got into it when he felt chatty. But mostly, he left me to myself. Yet another part of this big family I'd cobbled together.

"Yes." The word came between two crunches of the last few nuts still in my mouth. A swig of water and a swish later, a stick of gum then went in. "Let's go."

Damon had left earlier, and Amanda waved me off from where she sat on my couch. If this had been an awards show, she might have come with me, but since it was a smaller event, I didn't need her touching up—I'd learned that, at least, in the time I'd been doing this. A small powder, lip gloss, and my ID and credit card always accompanied me, today in my small, sparkling pink clutch. We were going for very feminine tonight, apparently, though it was just what I'd been in the mood for.

We pulled up to the conference center—the Gaylord Opryland, one of the strangest, most Nashville places you can think of. Upon my exit from the car, only a camera or two snapped, much to my delight. I waved Ru off and smiled at the photographers, chatting mildly while inching my way toward the door. Being kind and unrushed was important, but so was staying in motion. If you stopped, it would be hard to get moving again—learned that the hard way.

Once I reached the building, someone opened a door, allowing me to walk through without looking. "Thank you."

"You're welcome," came a familiar voice.

I'd only heard it a handful of times, but I'd know it anywhere. I whipped around to find Ben smiling at me.

"Oh! Hi." My voice was breathy as I took him in. He was as good-looking as in my memories.

Which was maybe a problem.

"You look beautiful." He smiled softly.

His gaze, notably, stayed on my face, which I found alternately charming and irritating. The dress did nice things for me, after all.

"Thank you. You look very nice, too."

And he did. He really did.

I'd told him he could wear his dress blues, if he wanted, because most soldiers had them, but he'd said he preferred to rent a tux. That couldn't have been cheap, based on the clean lines and close fit—no boxy shoulders or worn sleeves to indicate a rental. It was an effort for him to be here with me, and seeing him all dressed up, his hair just barely long and styled on top, making him look particularly dapper, brought that home. "Thank you for doing this."

"It's not a hardship." He quirked an eyebrow and offered me his arm.

I took it, and we started walking.

Even through his jacket, his warmth radiated under my touch. Strange how for formal events, women ended up in very little clothing, and men always wore long pants and long sleeves. I'd worn some heavy dresses, but almost never felt overheated due to my clothing. Impossible to imagine being layered up in a dress shirt and full jacket, even on a cool evening.

"How have your last few weeks been?" It dawned on me that we'd never shared casual conversation in person.

"Good. Busy, but good."

A little thrill shot through me when our eyes met. He looked like he should be an Abercrombie and Fitch model, all golden hair and bright blue eyes. He certainly filled out his suit perfectly—his broad shoulders and narrow waist tucking into slim, perfectly fitted black tux pants.

Normally, unless they were also in the spotlight, I'd detect a hint of nerves from a date. It had been a few years since I'd tried going out with anyone like Ben—anyone whose life and job were, well... normal.

Shoulders squared, back straight, I could detect no hint of unease about him.

Then again, facing down cameras wouldn't be all that stressful compared to being in a war zone.

"Whit Grantham, come here, baby!" Colton Danes said from the entryway.

Great.

"Hi there, Colton. How're you doin'?"

I tended to lay on the accent a little thick in these situations, particularly considering I didn't have much twang at all when speaking naturally. But something about Colton Danes, notorious playboy and self-proclaimed *good ol' Country boy*, made me want to fling out all my *bless your hearts* and drop all my g's.

"Aw, baby, I'm just so glad to see you here. Getting out already after your tour—good for you." The slimebucket sidled up to me as he ran a hand through his shaggy sandy brown hair, his date trailing just behind him.

"Colton Danes," he said, and shot out a manicured hand to Ben.

"Ben Holder. Nice to meet you," Ben returned, and shook Danes' hand like it was no big deal.

I glanced at him from the corner of my eye while keeping my show smile pinned to Danes—Ben looked entirely unperturbed by Country's favorite bad boy shaking his hand.

Okay. Bonus points for being absolutely unimpressed by celebrity thus far.

Colton Danes had a backlist of Country number ones just shorter than mine. He sang the kind of Country that strongly featured what I'd refer to as spoken word set to a Country twanged background that was so ragingly popular these days. In my opinion, his musical ability amounted to three out of ten, but he had the looks, could get along decently with a guitar, and he'd managed to charm the audience of some other competing television show the year following my win on *SouthernStar*.

Say what you would about the TV show-to-musical-stardom machine, but it worked.

Though, apparently, none too well on Ben Holder.

"So, doll face, when am I gonna see you?" Danes ducked his head and wrinkled his brow in false concern.

I looked side to side, no doubt failing to hide my disdain. "Well, you're seein' me now, right?"

"Oh, sure, but I mean just you and me." He dropped his voice just a bit, like we were in an intimate setting instead of him saying all this in front of both my date and his.

His date, petite and blond and looking entirely out of place in the conversation, making me wonder where he'd found her since he usually went out with fellow celebs, glanced at me when I extended my hand. "Whit Grantham."

"Kaylee. Nice to m-meet you."

Her hesitation told me what I could see written all over her face—incredible discomfort hung over her, and she hadn't been expecting me to introduce myself. I suspected Danes hadn't bothered to introduce her to anyone yet.

"Ben Holder," he said, offering Kaylee his hand.

She took it and gave him a huge smile. I could admit it—

he merited that response. Yes, Kaylee was with one of Country music's hottest young stars, but Ben Holder had him beat by a mile, even before you factored in anything beyond the cover.

Ben was a full-sized man, where Danes seemed miniature next to him. He was shorter, maybe five-foot-nine, but he also just seemed... small. And manicured—his hair expertly disheveled and sun-streaked by a pro, his face suspiciously free of any shine or color variation that only a makeup artist could elicit, and his fingers covered in rings, despite his wearing a Countryfied tux.

In comparison, Ben looked positively refined.

"I'll see you on stage, right?" Danes said, putting a hand on my arm, which made me jerk back.

People touched and pulled at me often, but this guy seemed to think he had been invited to touch me, or that his flirty attempts at getting me alone *in front of my date* would do anything other than annoy me.

Just no.

CHAPTER THREE

Ben

If there existed a person more exquisitely beautiful in this world, I couldn't tell you who it is. The woman walking next to me with one delicate hand on my arm was so gorgeous, she was hard to look at.

I'd had the same response to her weeks ago when we first met, and yet, somehow, I'd let the memory of my response to her dull. I'd had to, because if I let myself remember just how astoundingly pretty she was, I never would have agreed to attend the event at her side.

And even now as Colton Danes, one of Country's biggest young stars, propositioned her in front of his date and me, I couldn't think about anything other than how much I wanted to just *look* at this woman.

Whit Grantham.

If Colton Danes was *one* of Country's hottest stars, then

she was *the* hottest. In every sense of the word. I knew she was big, but she'd landed on my radar after she'd released her latest album last spring titled *After Today*. It had been a bit of a throwback, but with a fresh feeling about it.

New music hadn't filled my ears in years—I'd always liked classic Country, and the new stuff just wasn't my thing. Waylon, Willie, Johnny, and Merle had kept me company in Afghanistan and in the long months after as I'd climbed out of the pit.

But someone had recommended Whit Grantham's album to me, said it was thoughtful and lovely, and so, I'd sampled it. And liked it. And bought it. And I'd listened.

Something about it... affected me. It had felt familiar, like she'd looked at me and knew me, though we'd never met. There were several songs about soldiers, which made a lot more sense now knowing that Major Reese Flint, my mentor and effectively my boss, was her cousin.

So when I met her at Flint's house a few weeks ago, then saw her perform from back stage, then escorted her around Fort Campbell for a few hours after the concert for a publicity tour of the post... well, I'd acted normal.

What I'd expected of myself, who knew, but I'd kept my cool. Other than when first seeing her and stuttering over her and my own name, I think I kept it together.

But after spending that time with her, I'd wanted more. After all, that time really hadn't proven to be all that great an opportunity to get to know her since we just went from place to place in a car with the publicity officer for the post and a photographer her PR person had hired. Naturally, I'd wanted more.

Thanks to social media, I got it.

Not really. But following her on Instagram allowed me

to see pictures of her without being too creepy. And then, yeah, I searched the Internet for her and read some of the stories which recapped what some part of my mind remembered from before I deployed—she'd won a contest on TV and got a record contract, then had blown up from there. She was a crazy accomplished musician, so bands and other musicians loved working with her, and she was stubborn, so record companies didn't, except for the fact that whatever she touched turned platinum.

No one knew much about where she'd come from, and Reese wouldn't tell me anything. He'd been preoccupied lately, though, so I hadn't asked him outright.

I planned to.

When she'd sent me a direct message, I'd never felt such a stupid jolt of adrenaline over a line of words as in that moment.

Nothing had been the same since tapping that little notification to respond to her.

Okay, that might be a little far-fetched, but what do you want from me? I'd been chatting it up with Whit Grantham, Grammy-winning Country artist, whose lyrics and voice made me feel like my bones were melting in the best possible way. I'd progressed beyond the point of playing it cool.

Except now, her world surrounded me, something completely foreign, and yet, I instinctually resisted being impressed by it.

One thing was certain—I was less than impressed with Colton Danes' hitting on my date and ignoring his own.

"See ya, man." I gave him a chin nod. "Nice to meet you, Kaylee."

I could see Whit duck her head out of the corner of my

eye, so I looked over at her—well, down and over, despite the lift her shoes gave her, which had to be at least three inches. She was tiny, and even though she'd worn cowboy boots the last time we were together, I still dwarfed her.

I wasn't even that big of a dude, but compared to her, I felt gigantic. But at the risk of sounding cliché, her presence more than made up for her stature.

"Are you laughing at me?" I asked her upon hearing her snicker.

"No, I'm laughing at Danes and how confused he was by your total lack of response to him in all his glory," she said, her face lighting up in a way that looked completely genuine.

"Should I have done something different?"

She shook her head, her perfectly white front teeth biting into her glossed lower lip. "No. Not at all. You handled him perfectly."

Her hand squeezed my bicep where she held my arm.

I could admit—I liked that. Not like some barbarian wanting to flex my muscles and crow, but because any man would enjoy Whit Grantham's hand on his arm, squeezing his bicep as she complimented him, even if it came at the expense of another guy. Perhaps all the more if that guy was the tool box known as Colton Danes.

"You two have a history?"

A waiter approached, and I took a champagne flute from his tray and handed it to Whit.

"Thank you. No, we don't have a *personal* history, if that's what you mean. We've never even worked together, for that matter. But we see each other constantly, and he almost always says something exactly like what he said just now." She took a sip of champagne. "You didn't want a drink?"

"I'm good for now."

We continued into a reception area that vibrated with the energy coming from the little pockets of people talking and laughing.

"Something like, he calls you baby and doll face?"

"Yes. But don't be confused by that—he's not giving me a nickname because we know each other well. I suspect he calls all women something in that range so he doesn't have to work so hard to remember their names." She quirked an eyebrow and squeezed my arm again. "Ready for some introductions?"

"Sure."

~

Whit

"This is my friend Ben Holder," I said as John Smith Johnson—I know, right? John Johnson? Hence the Smith, I suppose—extended his hand to Ben.

"Pleased to meet you, Ben. How do you know Whit?" Johnson asked, looking fully at Ben in a way that said he expected *him* to answer.

This was the one introduction I'd anticipated, but I'd planned on being the one doing the talking.

"We met at one of Whit's concerts," Ben said with a quick glance at me.

I smiled encouragingly, happy he hadn't mentioned Reese.

My family was a private matter. I had a multitude of reasons for it, but mostly, it was because I didn't want press in their business and didn't want anyone thinking about *them* when they thought about *me*. We had less of an issue with Reese than with my parents, but still. It comforted me that Ben hadn't mentioned the mutual friend we shared.

"Is that right? On her tour?" Johnson asked.

He smiled pleasantly enough, but every interaction with him was an audition—one reason why my gown, though halter-necked, looked extremely modest other than my shoulder blades showing.

"No, sir. She did a concert at Fort Campbell Army Base up in Clarksville—we met there. I was honored to give her a tour of the base and show her a bit of my world, and she was kind enough to invite me tonight."

Ben stood straight and tall next to me, not touching me or making any attempt to put a physical claim on me as we stood there with Johnson. It was almost confusing, except that I'd made it clear we were there as friends.

Johnson smiled broadly. "You're in the military, then?"

"Yes, sir. Army."

"Lieutenant Holder! Good to see you and finally put a face to a name. I'm Nikki Gatlin."

Nikki, my publicist, peeked around my shoulder and smiled at Ben, then turned to Johnson. "Good to see you, Mr. Johnson, Mrs. Johnson."

Nikki was always good at being formal, and she knew Johnson would value that. She was, after all, paid to brown nose, essentially.

"Ah, Ms. Gatlin. Good to see you, too," Johnson said, and his wife murmured the same.

John Smith Johnson was a conservative industry magnate; someone you wanted on your side if you ever wanted anything, basically. My brush with rumors a few months ago had reportedly displeased him. Nikki was all over it, always looking for things for me to do to look angelic rather than, say, human.

"Well, I hate to barge in here, but they need Whit up front. Lieutenant Holder, would you mind escorting?"

Nikki's midnight bob shone under the lights. She wore a simple black sheath that flattered but didn't draw attention to her very fit body—she practiced yoga religiously and was the reason I'd asked Kendra to add it to my Sunday mornings despite the fact that it drove me into madness to be so still and calm. An expert at being present but invisible, Nikki always worked to put me in the spotlight, and always at the best angle.

Ben held out his arm. "Excuse us, sir. Ma'am. Have a lovely evening."

I took Ben's arm and said my goodbyes to the Johnsons, and he steered me in Nikki's wake at her usual New-York-at-rush-hour walking pace.

"Are you running late?" he asked in a hushed voice, leaning down a bit to say it closer to my ear.

"She's not late yet, but we will be, plus I didn't want you chatting too long with Johnson."

Ben raised his eyebrows at me as if to say *how did she hear that?* I shook my head with a grin. Nikki hadn't even bothered to turn around.

Not surprisingly, she'd heard him. She had a cat's hearing. In fact, she was ultimately quite feline—sleek, intelligent, moody, and prone to occasional outbursts of affection that resulted in overstimulation and hiding.

Nikki stopped just in front of a stage door. "This is where you'll come when they start singing the group number—it'll be the kindergarteners. Then, you'll likely just exit unless they ask you to say a few words, etcetera, etcetera."

"Yes, I'm ready."

Nikki awarded me with a curt nod. "For now, please go

sit. You're at a table with a few nice parents and board members from the school. I made sure you weren't near Danes. Or Johnson, for that matter."

Her fingers fluttered over the face of her phone as she did five things at once—I assumed, since that was so often how she functioned. But something had been bothering me.

"Shouldn't I be spending *more* time with Johnson, not less? Doesn't he need to get to know me so he'll want me to work with him?"

Ben stood by me, sturdy, great-smelling, warm, quiet.

"No." She didn't pause whatever she was doing, or even look up.

"Why not?"

"Exhibit A." She flashed me a look I knew too well—the *See, I told you so* look, and I had no idea why she was giving it to me.

"What am I supposed to be seeing?"

"You. You're pushy. Stubborn. I guarantee a man who talks about *traditional values* isn't going to appreciate you bossing him around. I've heard things. I know things. You trust me, right?"

She looked me full in the eyes now, and I could see her concern.

"Of course."

"Then believe me. Some men, evidently like Ben here, do like being pushed around, but Johnson won't. He wants meek. I'll see you after."

I turned to Ben, releasing his arm. "I'm sorry. She knows we're not—"

"I'm not worried."

His easy smile helped me relax immediately, and it calmed my frustration a bit to see he hadn't been embarrassed by Nikki's comment.

"And if you need to boss me around a bit, that's all right. I take orders pretty well."

A shocked little laugh escaped my lips. "Oh. Good to know, Lieutenant."

CHAPTER FOUR

Ben

No one could small talk like Whit. She was, as my mama would say, a whizz.

She could get people talking and keep them talking like no one's business. Almost as deftly as Major Reese Flint's girlfriend Erin Kelly could, though Erin, also my friend, was less practiced and more artless. Whit displayed artistry when it came to the conversational acrobatics it took to avoid saying anything personal.

"Whit, tell us about your young man here," an older gentleman, Mr. Walden, said as he gestured to me.

"Ben and I recently became acquainted, and I'm so glad he agreed to come with me as a good friend. We talked about how valuable early exposure to music is, especially in a school setting. What made you become involved with Music City Charter?"

Or another time, when a middle-aged woman named Rita had the balls to ask her about Jamie Morris.

"I heard you and Jamie Morris had a rough breakup, but you're still rumored to be willing to sing together if the song you two did for that movie gets nominated for the Oscars this year. Will you do it?"

Rita practically crawled over the table to hear the answer, one hand on her husband's arm, leaning around him to see Whit's face.

"Oh, thank you for asking. I loved working on the project, and I'll be shocked if MacKean doesn't get nominated. That scene where he's lying in the field?"

At that, everyone started exclaiming about Jack MacKean's brilliance in the scene—it really was astounding, and the spotlight shifted again.

She did that all night. It was amazing, and yet ultimately frustrating. She gave nothing away—certainly not about herself, not about why I was there with her instead of someone she actually knew and liked. Nothing.

When she excused herself to go get ready for the performance, the table's talk turned to her.

"Gosh, she's lovelier in person than on stage, even," Rita remarked.

"True. She is. And very well-spoken," another woman, Janelle, if I was keeping track correctly, added.

"Did you not expect her to be able to talk?" Janelle's husband scoffed.

"Well, you never know what you're going to get with these people! Just because they're beautiful and talented doesn't mean they know their way around a conversation. Plus no one knows her history—where's she even from?" Janelle asked.

"I thought I'd heard Tennessee. She lives in Nashville,"

Mr. Walden's wife said, folding her napkin neatly in her lap.

Rita had a beat on this. She shook her head even before the other woman had finished talking.

"Nope. No, I heard she's from Kentucky. But no one knows where. And it's really strange she's shrouded in all this mystery." Her gaze jerked to me. "Where's she from, do you know?"

I cleared my throat, buying myself time and likely revealing my lowborn manners to the table of wealthy Nashvillians. "Well, seeing as how we just met a few weeks ago, I'm not acquainted with her biography."

I took a sip of water and watched them all smile, though Rita and Janelle were clearly unimpressed with my response.

"But do you—"

Fortunately, the announcer cut Janelle off before she could grill me for details I didn't have.

The performances were all impressive, especially considering most of them were from elementary-aged kids. The high school's closing number could have been a professional orchestra and choral group. My heart beat a little faster knowing soon, Whit would take the stage.

"Ladies and gentlemen, I know you've been eager for this, so here you have it, Music City Charter's kindergarten class, and the lovely and talented, Whit Grantham."

A guitar strummed, and fifteen five-year-olds scampered on stage. Then came Whit, heading up the line and taking her seat on a stool spotlighted to the left of the crowd of kids. She looked over at them, their attention pinned anxiously on her, and I could see her ask "Ready?" in a whisper, and then, all of the kids wagged their heads, signaling they were.

Her face lit up with a delighted smile, and a pulse of warning shot through me.

Danger.

Whit sang along periodically, but mostly, she accompanied the kids on her guitar. When the song ended, the whole crowd stood, including Whit, and clapped for the kindergarteners. She was beaming at them, and if I was reading her right, she'd genuinely enjoyed the interaction.

The kids filed off, and Whit pulled her guitar over her head and held it by the neck. As she turned to go, the emcee leaned his head toward hers, and they had a short conversation, then she turned and sat back on the stool and adjusted the guitar strap over her head once again.

"A special treat, everyone. Miss Whit Grantham."

Applause and a few whistles filled the room, and Whit smiled easily.

"I wasn't expecting to play by myself for ya'll, so I'm hoping you'll forgive me. Those kids are a tough act to follow." A few chuckles and scattered claps filled the air. "How about we do something seasoned, huh?"

I thought I'd heard the chords to one of the songs from her first album, but then came the bouncing strum of *old* Country, and there they came, the lyrics about chasing big wheels all over Nashville while waiting for a big break to come.

After a rumble of unintelligible exclamations, a few laughs, and some quiet applause, Whit continued. And my heart downright *thudded* in my chest, like it beat in time to her guitar.

Her guitar, strumming the tunes of a song by my all-time favorite Country artist, the late great Waylon Jennings. The song? "Nashville Bum," and it was all I could do not to whistle and clap and shout at her. It left me floored.

Who *was* this woman?

She had the attention of everyone in the room, a crowd so full of people who loved her and wanted to hear her sing, and she sang an old, obscure Waylon song?

Danger, indeed.

"...I'm a Nashville bum."

She smiled with one last strum, and everyone cheered as she stood, nodded slightly as a bow, and turned to head off stage with only an inaudible *thank you.*

I sat down in my seat and reached for my glass of water, my hand shaking from the adrenaline racing through me.

She sang Waylon.

That might not seem like a big deal, but it was. To me, anyway. She could have sung anything—*anything*—and clearly, everyone had expected her to sing one of her own songs. It would have been appropriate and enjoyable.

Instead, she'd showed humor and wit and depth when she chose an old favorite, a song about the city, and though it was coincidence, my feeble little mind was taking it personally, a song by my favorite Country artist.

Next up came Colton Danes, and as soon as he stepped up to the mic, I pitied him. Following Whit, especially after she'd played *with* the kids, would be tough, but following her playing a song by one of the greats... Brutal. Danes didn't look fazed, and in the end, his song turned out fine.

And by fine, I mean it embodied everything I hated about contemporary Country music.

Not everyone did it, but those who did drove me crazy. They sang songs about drinking, tractors, and always name-dropped old Country stars. Such a false effort, especially in stark contrast to Whit's cover of Jennings' song.

When Danes finished, the emcee announced the time had come for the silent auction, and after a half hour, they'd start the live auction. The lights came up in the ballroom, and the crowd began chatting loudly, bustling around.

I saw Whit at the corner of the room and moved to her, pacing myself so I wouldn't seem as ruffled as I was. *What is wrong with me?*

"Why'd you play Waylon?" I asked as I came to stand in front of her. Couples pushed through the double doors that led out into the hallway. I searched her eyes and swallowed back the urge to touch her cheek. Her blue-green eyes stared back at me, too pretty.

One side of her mouth formed a smile, then she said, "I love Waylon. Why not?"

CHAPTER FIVE

Whit

"If you're serious about getting Johnson on board, you'll consider it," Nikki said with one of those stern looks she used when trying to impress me with her wisdom.

"It's sketchy." I shook my head and looked out the tinted window of the town car.

Ru was driving us back to my house after a mildly disastrous meeting with John Smith Johnson's team. He'd popped in at the end, but hadn't stayed. Nikki had declared the meeting an *unmitigated disaster*.

"It's done. All the time. You know this. Get over it, and think about what you want." Her attention, as always, stayed on her phone.

The city blurred by as her words sank in. *Think about what you want.* I knew what I wanted.

I wanted to work with John Smith Johnson. I wanted

him to back me as his option for the lead writer in a new project I'd caught wind of—I'd be writing the songs, but I wanted the score, too. There was no way he could know I'd gone to Juilliard thanks to a name change and burying that history deep before auditioning for *SouthernStar*. He couldn't know I had that level of skill, but everyone knew I'd written everything on my albums, even the instrumentation. Some artists wrote the lyrics, maybe even the melody, but they didn't craft the whole musical set.

The problem was, not being in charge wasn't one of my fortes. It wasn't arrogance to say that I was usually the most skilled musician in the room, nor was it me being pushy when I gave my opinion, stuck to my guns.

Fine. I could admit I was stubborn *and* had a temper. But that wasn't what happened in the meeting. The team Johnson sent to talk with me confirmed their status as a bunch of ill-informed hand-holders in minutes. What they expected me to do, who knew, but when I sat down, I presented them with my idea for the score, the songs, and the feel of the sound. Of course, all of that would change if I actually worked on the film, but I had to provide them with *something* showing I had the capability, the vision.

Johnson's team's notorious inflexibility showed in their stiff necks as I spoke, their subtle frowns before responding.

They took the lead, shaped whatever project, and went for it. Part of the reason no one argued was that they had a track record going thirty years back. Johnson had demonstrated how his instinct never led him astray. But one thing his instinct was always known for: only choosing women who were pretty, conservative, and married.

Yeah.

So he mostly worked with dudes.

My not being married was likely no longer a deal-breaker. It was so old-fashioned, it must be possible to get around it. But my stubborn nature, my *willfulness* as my parents used to call it, and probably most of all, the drama with Jamie Morris, were knocks against me.

So let's talk about that.

I dated the very famous, broody, gorgeous, talented (and on and on and on...) Jamie Morris. We worked on a song for a movie about eighteen months ago and got along well. The stars aligned, and we were both in LA for other things after the recording, and we started dating.

It didn't stay quiet, so people started freaking out. Headlines like *Country Princess and Rock God Seen in Epic Lip-Lock* splashed the Internet after he kissed me *in public* as though he'd never been in a relationship with another celebrity before.

And that's when he told me—after everyone was already predicting I was knocked up with his baby and that he was cheating on me with another woman (his sister, it turned out, who had come to visit him while he was in LA— lovely girl)—that he never had. Not once. He'd never dated a celebrity, and hardly anyone *at all.*

But the press always rages about anything anyone remotely famous is or even isn't doing, so it was no surprise. We went on a few more dates before my return to Nash- ville. Jamie came to visit me one weekend about six months after we'd met in LA. During that time, I didn't date anyone else, and I was fairly certain he didn't date anyone else, either.

But Jamie visited the same weekend my friend from Juilliard came to stay. My male friend. The paparazzi had photos of his car at my front door and of me ushering him inside while looking out warily—they caught the perfect moment. I *was* nervous about people seeing him, but not because I was cheating on Jamie.

Jamie and I were barely dating, so it would have been hard to cheat on him, anyway, but I wasn't a cheater. Second, Sam had never been interested in me, partly because the stars had declared we'd be friends, and partly because I was far too female for his taste.

But I couldn't come out and introduce him. No one could know about Sam, now a cellist with the New York Symphony. That would unleash all kinds of *issues* in that no one wanted to hear about my privileged upbringing.

SouthernStar had suggested we keep that quiet to make me more sympathetic, more of a Cinderella story, and I'd stupidly agreed. Now, it would be an even bigger deal if word got out that my parents were from old money—*old* old, like Dukes and Earls and *peerage* in England kind of old. In fact, I had a cousin who'd come into his dukedom, or whatever you call it, when his father died the week after he turned thirty.

Whatever, the point was, the world thought I'd two-timed Jamie. He'd been exonerated by the same public opinion that had wanted to hang him when he made a statement indicating that the visitor had been his sister, and he wouldn't share her name for the sake of her privacy, but that he had never and would never cheat on me.

Very sweet. But I couldn't do the same.

And thoughtful, sensitive, adorable Jamie Morris (I know, cliché, right? Sensitive rock star? But I'm telling you, he is.) understood. He knew I had secrets I couldn't share, and he also knew I hadn't cheated on him after he spoke to Sam, who was far more interested in Jamie than me.

But we also couldn't stay together. More than anything, it was because we had all the chemistry of a paper bag and a rock, but also because we never saw each other. I'd been prepping for a European tour, and he'd been heading back into the studio. It wasn't meant to be, and we walked away friends.

And I walked away being called all manner of things people like to call women who a.) date men, b.) are suspected of cheating, c.) exist. I won't list the names here. Though I'd braced myself for the backlash and swallowed down Nikki's suggestion that I *suck it up* and deal with the fallout rather than letting the larger lie blow up in our faces at that point—the general perception that I'd come from "nowhere" and worked my way to the stage in Nashville (which was true, except that my *nowhere* had eighteen bedrooms and tea served every afternoon and private tutors).

But words can wound.

And they did.

So I went on tour and kept my head down. Happily, most of the tour went without incident, and other than paparazzi constantly asking me *who I was banging now*, I didn't have to deal with the problem.

But now that I was back, no longer on tour and out of sight of the local paparazzi and the American paparazzi, my apparent indiscretions were surfacing again through quiet whispers and sly looks and pointed questions by bloggers and interviewers.

I had to turn it around—no question about it. I wanted to just walk out one day and tell them where I came from. There'd be backlash, not least of all from Cynthia and Stuart Grantham. But they would deal—whenever it did come out, they'd have to, and so would I.

What Nikki suggested made me feel a little sick. I didn't like the idea any more than she thought I would—she knew me well enough to know I wouldn't be happy about *another* lie to make me look better. Especially considering the problem that started all of this, my supposed cheating, wasn't even an actual thing.

I took a deep breath and let it out to the count of five. If I was doing it, I wasn't going to lie to anyone it might personally affect. That included Ben.

"Fine. I'll do it. I'll call him when we get home."

CHAPTER SIX

Ben

No hope of ignoring the incoming messages.

@WhitGranthamOfficial: Are you around today to meet?

@TheRealBenHolder: Meet? Are you passing me secret information?

@WhitGranthamOfficial: Ha ha. No. I need to talk to you about something.

@TheRealBenHolder: Sounds serious. I won't be home 'til around seven tonight. I can be available then, or I'm around this weekend too.

@WhitGranthamOfficial: Tonight please. I'll come to you. Send me your address.

And just like that, I was going to see Whit Grantham again.

In my house.

"Holder! Eyes up."

Major Flint was in a *mood*, and though I shouldn't have been looking at my phone, when it dawned on me that Whit had messaged, no way could I calmly flip the device over and ignore it until after this interminable meeting.

Yeah, no.

So I checked. And looky there, Ms. Grantham wants to talk. But what about? And why did she want to come to *my* house? Because she didn't want me in her house, maybe? Had she gotten the impression I'd be one of those freaky people who stalked her or showed up at her house uninvited? My deeds hadn't shown that, surely. But I could understand not having some man she hardly knew in her home. She'd probably had to learn to be cautious.

My attention returned to Flint, but my mind was traveling through the apartment—not horrible. I'd vacuumed recently because Thatcher had been over for a movie, and that meant popcorn. I'm not sure if the man had a hole in his lip or what, but when he left, there'd been a blast zone of crumbs surrounding where he'd sat. It was almost as bad as my two-year-old nephew. Guess I could thank him that his sloppiness had resulted in my being at least one step closer to having an appropriately clean house for Whit's visit.

I grew up in a house of women. My mom stayed home, and my two older sisters treated me like the baby of the family, which I happily complied with, relishing being showered with their love and attention. They'd given me advice about women over the years, but I had yet to tell them about my interactions with Whit, particularly because my oldest sister Bridgette would freak out when she heard.

One happy side effect of growing up with women was the habit of keeping things clean. I'd been lectured within an inch of my life about putting the lid down, cleaning up "pot shots" as Bea, my middle sister, called them, and picking up after myself. Honestly, I was thankful I'd learned those habits early. Some of my buddies never had, and going into their houses was like walking into a gas station restroom—ultimately not a place you wanted to spend time.

"Have a good weekend, and we'll see you all back here Monday. Don't be idiots!"

Sergeant Major Trask called out his typical send-off, making eye contact with as many soldiers as possible with his usual ferocity, and the men and women of the Rambler Battalion fled the meeting room like it was five o'clock on a Friday. Because it was.

"What's the deal, Holder? You got a hot date?" Thatcher Wild, in all his tall, dark, muscled glory, sauntered up to me and slapped me on the back.

As much as I wanted to tell Thatch about Whit, it didn't seem right. We weren't dating, and even though he was a good guy, rumors always begin somewhere. Keeping my mouth shut was the only way to guarantee nothing started up.

"No, just messaging my sister. *She* has a hot date."

That was true. Bea had started using an online dating app, which just about killed me, even though I had plenty of friends who did the same.

"Beatrice? I can't imagine her needing a dating app," Thatcher said.

If it had been anyone else, I might have flown into protective brother mode and told him to stop imagining *anything* about my sister, but he was Thatch. And even though he didn't think I knew, he was interested in our friend Bec Jones. There was no chance his statement had been meant in any way other than complimentary.

"You might not think, but she's super shy. Always has

been. Anyway, man, I've got to meet with Major Flint, and then I'm heading east. I'll catch you sometime this weekend?" I waved while walking to Flint's office.

The knock on the door came at five minutes after seven. Thank goodness I'd made it back early and had had a few minutes to tidy up. Most of the people Whit spent time with probably had nicer places than mine, but I wasn't ashamed of my home. I chose to live in Nashville upon redeployment from Afghanistan—partly to have some distance from the base, and partly because it enabled me to drink and Uber home more cheaply.

It hadn't been a great few months.

Once I got a grip, I figured out other benefits of living closer to the city, but for a while there, my motivation had been to get through work so I could get through the week so I could get through the weekend, all as numb as possible.

Enough about that.

I tossed a kitchen towel on the counter and shuffled to the door. The surreality of what was about to happen struck me then, and a twinge of nervousness crept between my shoulders. I pulled open the door, and with it came the sweet, distinctive scent of Whit Grantham.

And then came the sight of her.

She stood on my porch in sneakers, jeans, a plain light blue hooded sweatshirt, and a gray baseball cap on her head. When I stepped aside and gestured for her to come in, she moved past me quickly. Her hair had been pulled back through the cap into a ponytail. She removed her sunglasses as she entered the place, then tucked them and her keys into the front pocket of her sweatshirt.

"Did you find it okay?"

Now that she was here and taking in everything in the room with a sweep of her eyes, I wasn't sure what to do exactly.

"Yes. No issues, thanks." She turned to face me and pushed her hands further into that front pouch. "Could we sit and talk?"

"Of course. Can I get you some water?"

"Yes, please."

She sat on the worn, brown leather couch that took up the majority of the living room while I walked to the kitchen and pulled out glasses, filled them, and returned to her. I set one down on the coffee table in front of her and took a drink of mine before setting it down, all while waiting for her to speak. She'd called the meeting, after all.

Finally, right when I was going to break the silence and ask why she was here, she pulled her phone out, swiped a finger to clear it of a notification, then looked up at me.

Her irritation calmed as she said, "Hi. It's good to see you."

"Oh. Yeah, it's good to see you, too."

I hadn't been expecting that.

"Thank you for letting me come to you. I would have asked you to come to me, but I didn't want you to feel uncomfortable. I have something to ask of you, but I want you to do something before I even ask. Can you do that?"

She smiled brightly, encouragingly, like you might at a child or a Golden Retriever you were willing to learn a trick.

"You'll have to tell me what it is."

"Of course." She smiled down at her lap, then looked up at me. "I need you to promise me that you'll answer honestly to what I'm about to ask you. I need you to promise me that you'll tell me no if it's asking too much, and that you won't be offended I'm asking in the first place."

The worry was clear on her face, her eyebrows pinching and her jaw flexing as she closed her mouth and waited for my response.

"That sounds ominous, I must say."

"It's not horrible." She faltered then, her gaze flickering around the room, then back to me. "Not too horrible, anyway."

"I think maybe you should just tell me what's going on." If she kept toeing around it, whatever *it* was, she'd drive me insane.

She was this tiny person, and she filled my entire apartment. I had no chance of being completely clear-headed with her near.

She took a steadying breath and released the air slowly on a count of five. I recognized the pacing of her exhale because I'd been taught the same method for calming down after a panic attack. Had she also dealt with them?

"I'm wondering if you'd be my boyfriend," she said on a rush.

My back hit the cushion behind me. "Uh—"

"Not *really*, though. Just... pretend to be," she added quickly.

I watched her face, waiting for her to crack a smile or laugh or *something*, but nothing. She ran a hand over her hat and let it slide over the length of her ponytail. She was completely serious.

"Um..."

The blank space that filled my mind was somehow loud. Could she be serious? Had she somehow realized just how magnetic I found her and decided to taunt me? She couldn't be that cruel.

"That sounds strange. I know. And I get it. You're thinking *this woman is crazy*, or that I'm trying to trick you into *actually* dating me, or something else totally weird. But that's not it. And I don't know how to tell you this without it sounding like I'm using you, because that's what this is—entirely and completely *me* using *you* to make me look better."

Her cheeks flushed, but she didn't turn away, didn't curl into herself. She met my eyes head on, no faltering.

"I'm not sure how me dating you makes *you* look good." It was all I could think to say, then took another drink of water as she explained.

"The drama with Jamie makes me look bad. I can't tell you the deal there other than to say I did not, nor would I, cheat on him or anyone. I want to work for John Smith Johnson, who you met at the event last weekend. He is extremely picky about who he works with, and he'll flat out deny anyone with a whiff of controversy on them. Obviously enough, I'm having issues convincing him and his team to work with me." She pulled out her phone, cleared the screen, and shoved it back into her pocket.

"He won't work with you because the press accused you of cheating on Jamie Morris? Wasn't that months ago?" I sat back and ran a hand along the back of the couch.

"Right there shows me you have a perspective most people don't. If the press says it happened, it might have happened. And the possibility, the potential of being a woman with a *reputation*, is all that Johnson needs to point to the fact that I'm not up to snuff." She clenched her jaw, then sipped her water.

"You think that by fake-dating me, that'll change?"

This was ludicrous. Why wouldn't Johnson want to

work with her? The idea that a rumor would keep her from working with anyone she wanted to was insane.

"Nikki seems to think so, and I can understand why she'd say it. You're a soldier, which is one of the most respected jobs in the US. It's very sympathetic. You're very handsome, and you've got that all-American Southern boy thing going for you, but you've also got this angelic, sweet quality that keeps you from being too forbiddingly attractive."

She tossed this out like her saying I was handsome wasn't a highlight of my month.

My eyebrows rose, and a small laugh escaped my mouth.

Whit Grantham thinks I'm pretty!

I bit my bottom lip and pressed my mouth together to lock down the all-too-pleased smile that threatened to blast her. She didn't seem to notice the pleasure coursing in my body, because she kept ticking away the reasons how fake-dating me would help her.

"Me with you would show I'm not jaded, that I'm not out of touch with *normal* people, as though that makes any sense. And having a steady relationship is always better than being single in terms of making women look good." She watched me, squinting a bit. "What are you thinking?"

I gave her a grin. "I'm... I have a lot of thoughts. I'm not sure how to verbalize them."

Good grief, right out of a therapy session.

She chuckled and shook her head. "I get it. This is more than a little odd."

"It is. I guess my biggest question is, why not *actually* date someone?" With my arms crossed over my chest, I leaned back to watch her.

Her eyebrows flashed up and down before she

responded. "Sounds nice. But I'm no good at it, for one, and I haven't met anyone I wanted to date in a long time."

"Well, I guess that answers that."

She pulled out her phone once again, then angrily flew through the process of shutting it down.

"Do you need to make a call or something?" Whatever was going on with her phone seemed persistent.

"No. But listen, what do you think?" She sat up straight, angled to face me.

"I think... sure. I guess my gut response is, why not? But I suspect you've thought about this a whole lot more than I have."

She nodded. "I have, and my team has. And it's not without benefits for you. I want you to understand that. It's going to be a big fat hassle dealing with the press, and essentially lying to your friends and family—because you cannot tell anyone the truth, and I'll need you to sign some legal documents to that effect—but I have some bonuses." She gave me a determined look.

What bonuses and incentives would I want from this woman? That train of thought was a dangerous one...

"Okay. Good to know..."

"So, for one, you'd probably come on tour with me in a few weeks, *if* you can swing that with your work. I know that's not always possible, but Reese usually gets a few weeks at Christmas. He's always traveling over Christmas."

"True. We usually have block leave at Christmas. Since I had last year at home for it, I'm guessing my mom will survive my absence. I was going to go home at Thanksgiving, so maybe we can just celebrate early."

"Think about that. Really think about it, okay? I don't want you to say yes to this and then regret it. My biggest fear is doing something like this and having it come out as a negative for either of us, but especially you because you don't have much to gain from this except a few fun events and some travel."

"I'm sure I'll—"

"Listen. I want you to think about it tonight. If you can, I want you to come to the house tomorrow, and I'll have the contract drawn up so you can see what you'd be signing. And we'll go through *all* of the boundaries and rules or whatever—both mine *and* yours. And if any of it makes you uncomfortable or you feel like it's a raw deal for you, we bag it. Does that sound okay to you?"

She'd stood, and so had I, so we were standing a foot apart. Since she was wearing sneakers, I got to appreciate how small she was, but even though I was staring down at her and she was looking up at me, she seemed larger than life.

"Sure. Okay. Give me directions to your place, and tell me what time. I'll think it over, and we'll figure it out tomorrow." A dazed quality tinged my voice.

Standing up and facing her had sharpened the dream-like sensation of the last few minutes. If it were a dream, I'd probably lean down and steal a kiss, just to see if she tasted minty and sweet like she smelled. But this wasn't a dream, and nothing about our interactions had told me she'd welcome the advance, never mind the fact that I couldn't imagine *actually* making a move on Whit Grantham.

There was that, and the promise I'd made myself. I'd respect myself and women enough not to do the things I'd done when I first got back—when I did anything I could to block out the misery of Jones' loss. Knowing I'd cut the drinking to virtually nothing and never for self-medicating, that I'd given up losing myself in women whose names I never knew—that helped the risk here feel less intense.

But even now, I could guess that just being in a room with Whit would test that promise to keep the physical element of a relationship out of the equation—at least that most intimate act—until I'd committed for life.

"Okay. Good."

She moved to the door with keys in hand and pulled her hat lower over her eyes. "Make a list of questions. Make a list of things you'd want or wouldn't want. Think about what would make this worth it to you, and just... think about everything. I'm sorry I have to go, but this is good. Think, and message me with questions if they come up, and we'll talk tomorrow, yeah?"

"Sounds good."

CHAPTER SEVEN

Whit

A horrible thought had occurred to me at about six the next morning.

@WhitGranthamOfficial: *You don't have a girlfriend, do you?*

I'd heard nothing for hours. Not 'til eight. Then,

@TheRealBenHolder: *I wouldn't have agreed to meet you at my apartment if I did, let alone go with you to the gala last weekend. So no. No girlfriend. Not dating anyone. Coast is clear.*

Something about that made me feel... good and bad all at once. Good that Ben was the kind of man that wouldn't go around meeting with women who weren't his girlfriend if he'd had one. It also made me feel bad, but I couldn't pin down why. Maybe because I hadn't even asked him to begin with before making my proposition.

The rest of that day, my mind went through all he might

say when he arrived. He'd seemed shocked, but open to the idea. Exactly what I'd hoped for, but still, the urge to talk him out of it lingered. For some reason, as soon as Nikki had suggested the idea, a horrible swirling of guilt and dread had started in my gut, but I'd ignored it.

As usual, my determination to achieve my goals had outweighed the potential consequences.

Nikki and I reviewed the documents, and she made some suggestions about parameters for the relationship. I had my own running list of questions, plus a few things that should sweeten the deal for him.

Pins and needles, I was nervous. And I hated being nervous. What a tedious feeling. I'd mastered the ability to tamp down on nerves as a teen performing recitals in front of state politicians and whoever else my parents had brought to their compound—because calling it merely a house made it sound even remotely inviting—to woo for one reason or another.

By the time I pulled open the door to find Ben dressed in jeans and a gray jacket zipped halfway up his chest, a T-shirt beneath, my head was pounding, the beginnings of a cold sweat chilling my skin.

"Thank you for coming." My voice sounded far too somber.

"Thanks for having me," he said as he looked around the modest entryway.

I was proud of my home—large by any standard, it did not look grotesque like so many celebrity houses. It had a cozy country feel, decorated in natural colors and pale blues.

"Can I take your coat?" I asked, and reached out as he shrugged out of the coat and handed it to me.

"Thank you."

He was very polite—good manners, nice demeanor and way of interacting. He'd dealt so well with the event last weekend—hadn't lost his cool or had any issues with the big personalities there. It'd been impressive, and just one more thing that made me like him. And one more thing that made him perfect for this... situation.

"Come into the kitchen, if you would. We'll have a drink and... talk." Awkward about how to proceed, I pulled on my business tone. Keeping it straightforward, instead of trying to act like a new friend *and* essentially an employer, would help.

We walked down the hallway and into the kitchen.

I *loved* my kitchen. White cabinets, white and gray marble countertops, but nicely worn wood floors to warm it up. An island with stools people could pull up and chat while dinner was cooking took up the center of the space. I cooked a bit for myself, though it wasn't my forte when entertaining. I liked to invite friends who could cook and then enjoy the fruits of their labor.

Nikki looked up from her laptop where she sat at one side of the bar. "Hello, Lieutenant Holder."

"Please call me Ben."

He stopped next to me as I pulled out a stool for him. We went through the ritual of asking what drinks he wanted (water) and making small talk for a few minutes (yes, it had been a chilly day), when finally, Nikki was ready for business.

She slid a folder across the countertop toward him. He sat on one side of the bar, Nikki and I facing him on the other side, the seats next to him and on either end empty. Something about her sliding that folder made it feel a little sordid.

"This is the confidentiality agreement. What it says is

that you will not discuss anything about this contract. You will proceed as though you are really dating Whit, and you will not tell *anyone* the true nature of your relationship. You will in no way insinuate that you were compensated in any way, nor will you distribute or sell any information to news outlets, photographers, etc. for your own profit." Nikki paused.

Ben had opened the folder to flip through pages, intermittently looking up to assure her he was listening. When she stopped, he turned his attention back to us.

"At whatever point you and Whit determine to dissolve the relationship, the confidentiality clause will still be in effect."

Ben nodded as she folded her hands.

"How about you read through all of that, and we'll answer any questions you have."

His focus moved over each document, and he stretched his neck from side to side every now and then like it was sore. Nikki received a call and excused herself from the room just as Ben finished his read-through.

"How long are you thinking?" he asked, his voice and face neutral.

"A minimum of six months. It's October now, and I'd need to make sure the relationship has a duration long enough to make a positive impression. There are several events at which, whether or not you appear with me, I would want to refer to you as my significant other."

His brow quirked. "Is that how you'll refer to me?"

"No. Probably not."

He smiled. Just this unabashed, happy smile. I didn't know what to do with him.

"What?" It bewildered me how he could be smiling

when we were in this awkward situation of trying to work out details of our fake relationship.

"You're intense. It seems like you feel guilty about this. Is there something I'm missing?" He leaned on his forearms and clasped his hands together.

He was certainly straightforward, and it wasn't a bad thing. Or, at least, I didn't think it was. But I fidgeted on the stool, wondering whether I could be as honest with him as he was with me. In the end, I had to be.

"I do. I do feel guilty. It's a weird thing to ask someone, and ultimately, you're getting nothing from it." A breath huffed out—his apparent refusal to take this seriously proved exasperating.

He leaned farther over the counter, bringing him a few inches closer so we were only about two feet apart, separated by a cold slab of marble.

"I thought you said there'd be incentives. Why don't you tell me about those? Sell me on it—what do I get out of this? Why should I do it?"

My lashes fluttered as I pulled in a breath and resisted the heat racing through me at the way he'd said those words. I cleared my throat, crushing the physical response to what was, at least in one sense, a logical and business-focused question.

"Sure. Yes. Okay. Good." I pulled out my planner and flipped to a page in the back where I'd made the list. "First, you'd get to tour with me if that works out with your schedule. I'm framing that as a positive because I'd pay for all your expenses, and we're going to some major cities. You wouldn't be obligated to stay with me all the time, so you could explore a bit. Obviously, if you hate traveling, then that's a drawback—"

"I don't. Next?"

"Okay. Um, next, again schedule permitting, you'd escort me to the Oscars. I realize that also may not be something you'd want to do. But that one would be a big one for me, so it's kind of non-negotiable unless you really can't miss work."

The nerves fluttered through me. I'd be singing with Jamie if our song got nominated, which it almost certainly would be. The singing would be easy—the whispers of the audience would not.

"I have no idea, but that's something that, if you have the dates well in advance, I can request sooner than later, and that always helps."

His voice calmed me. Was he staying so reasonable and unflustered to counteract my raging nervous energy?

The cool stone helped soothe my burning palms as my fingers spread out on the countertop. "There's one other thing, but I'm still in talks about it, and it only applies if you like football."

He perked up then, his eyes asking the question for him.

"I may be performing at pretty big football half-time show this year."

He froze, then his face brightened, and he laughed. "Pretty big—no kidding?"

"No kidding. They're trying to do a big Country roundup or something. It won't just be me, so it's not—"

"That's a really big deal." His lips spread into a smile that showcased straight white teeth and, inevitably, dimples in his lean cheeks.

Goodness, he's cute.

"Thanks. Yeah, it is, kind of. But I don't know for sure if it'll go through. If it does, you'd get to go with me, if you wanted."

"I would want," he assured quickly.

I nodded. "Okay, then. So... those are the things you get out of all this. Plus any events or dates or appearances we go on, I would pay for any travel and expense, including the activity or food associated with the interaction."

"You're forgetting something," he said, catching my eye.

"I am?"

"Yes. By doing this, I also get to spend time with *you*," he added, a completely genuine look on his face.

Giddiness and embarrassment crashed against each other in my mind.

"I—that's true. Yeah, you get to spend time with fancy old me." A little laugh escaped me.

"I'm inclined to do it, Whit. But your hesitation makes *me* hesitate. So tell me what you're most worried about." He leaned on his elbows now, his arms crossed on the counter.

Again, no beating around the bush. He had this knack for putting his finger on the most disconcerting details, which made me squirm. This was going to come out fast, direct, a little disorganized.

"I'm concerned you'll feel exploited. I'm doing everything shy of paying you an hourly wage, which we could talk about, if you wanted, but that seems a little bit more toward the escort range of things. And I wouldn't expect anything—you know, not anything like *that*. I just don't want you to feel used, which is messed up because you *are* getting used."

I swallowed, then grabbed my glass and took a drink of the cool liquid to help chase away the sudden overheating caused by that last thought, my light sweater and jeans now sweltering as heat crept up my chest and neck.

Ben took a moment, watching me fiddle with my planner, click my pen open and closed, take another drink.

"I appreciate that—both that you don't want me to feel

like you're exploiting, and that you acknowledge you are using me."

I blinked at his words, about to defend the proposition, but he continued.

"We should probably talk about how this would actually work. I work long hours, and I can only imagine what your schedule is like. I assume we need to be seen out and about in order for this to be worth the effort, so tell me what you're thinking in that regard."

Ben had a curious mix of easygoing calm and business-like practicality. It soothed just as it had me fighting the urge to fidget.

"I'd like us to try to get together once a weekend. There will be times I'm traveling, so that won't happen, and times you will be, so the same. Then, if you can, I'd like you to come on the winter tour. At that point, we will have been seen together a few times over the months prior, and it'll seem like we're taking our relationship to the *next level* or whatever. From there, we'll be in the *serious* phase, and if you can come to the big awards shows, that'd be great. Again, I'll pay for—"

"I'm not worried about the money portion of this, okay? I believe that I won't be forced to fly myself around just to catch up with you." His bright blue eyes pressed into mine to emphasize his veracity.

"Okay. Good."

"Okay."

I waited for him to say something more, but he just sat there, looking at me, all calm and self-assured and comfortable.

"Okay? What do you mean?"

"I mean, *okay*, I'll do it. As long as you're sure you want *me* for this job."

His eyes narrowed just a bit, and I detected a flash of doubt.

"I'm sure." My voice came out steady.

I *was* sure. I felt comfortable with him. He'd done nothing but be friendly and polite in every interaction we'd had. We had Reese in common, and my cousin was persnickety about people, to say the least, so I knew he couldn't be a bad guy. So far, everything I'd learned about him proved appealing.

"You should know, I've had a rough couple of years. If the press goes digging, I'm sure they can find people who'd want to paint me in a bad light." A muscle in his jaw jumped, and he leaned harder onto the counter top.

"No one's perfect."

"Least of all me. But I can promise you that going forward, you have nothing to worry about." His face was as serious as I'd ever seen it.

Most of what Ben projected was that easy calm, the laid-back guy who could laugh with or chat with you and didn't have a lot going on. It was one of the things that made me feel so comfortable with him. Not that he seemed shallow, but if a person bought him at face value, they could easily think he was simple. My very first interaction with him over a year ago had told me how wrong that assumption would be, though the two versions of Ben were hard to reconcile.

"Okay. Yes. And I can't have you dating anyone else while we're together, that would totally defeat the purpose." I brushed an invisible something from the page of my planner.

"Of course. I understand."

CHAPTER EIGHT

Ben

At that moment, Nikki breezed into the room. "Have you come to a decision?

"I have. I'll do it, and I'll sign the forms as they are." I took the pen that had been attached to the folder and signed each of them.

Nikki spoke again as she loaded her things into a black bag that must have been sitting at the foot of her chair. "You'll want to discuss your next few dates, the tour and event dates, and then make sure you cover the physical boundaries and expectations."

She was all business, but my breath quickened at the subject of any kind of physicality with Whit.

"Good. Thanks for the reminders. I'll see you next week?" Whit asked, and stood.

"Yes. I'll see myself out—you wrap up here and let me

know anything I should know," she told Whit, then turned to me. "I'm sure I'll see you again soon, Ben."

And off she went down the hall that led to the front door.

We both watched her go, and then I turned back to Whit, hoping she'd lead the way into this new portion of the negotiations.

"In terms of that..." Her cheeks reddened.

How would she approach this element of the conversation? I was man enough to admit I was eager to see.

"Dates?" I asked innocently.

"Well, no, the physical dynamic between us. Obviously, it needs to be believable that we're together. That you're not just a friend or family member." She folded her hands on the notebook in front of her.

I nodded. "Obviously."

"So we'll need to hold hands, touch, that kind of thing. Maybe a kiss on the cheek here and there. Mostly, it's being seen together, seeming like we're comfortable together, which shouldn't be a problem. Is that okay with you?" She brushed something off her notebook and then looked up at me through her dark lashes.

"Makes sense to me. I'd certainly want to touch you if we were actually dating." The truth of that resonated in my mind.

Yes, yes, I would.

She pressed her lips together in a small smile. "Well, likewise. So, just... do what you'd do if we were, and that should be fine."

She cleared her throat and took her pen, made a little mark next to something on the list in front of her, then looked up at me.

After that, we compared schedules. I had a fairly predictable one this time of year, so the rest of October and really, the rest of the year, were easy enough to review. She wanted to get started right away, so we planned to meet for lunch on Sunday when the after-church crowd would be sure to see us, and we put a few other dates on the calendar.

And that was it. The next thing I knew, her front door was in front of me, and she was handing me my jacket.

"I suppose we'll do the twenty questions tomorrow at lunch?" I asked, pulling on the jacket.

"What do you mean?"

"We hardly know each other. I don't know anything about you, really, nor do you know anything about me. We get along fine, but if we're going to seem like we're really in a relationship, we'll need at least a modicum of emotional intimacy, don't you think?"

Her eyelashes fluttered for a moment, then she nodded. No sound came from her lips for another few seconds, then finally, she spoke.

"Sure. Yes. That makes sense. We will... plan on that."

I decided to tell Thatcher the next day at church. He'd invited me to go about this time last year when my struggle had been evident to everyone. All the questions and emotions that had piled up during the deployment, that I'd locked down hard while we were still in Afghanistan, had hit me like a shrieking car crash when we got back.

After I'd had to ask him for a ride in to work more than once because I was still drunk from the night before, he'd had a heart to heart with me and tipped off Major Flint. Then, the intervention had come in earnest.

And so, I'd started attending church. I'd stopped drinking—fortunately for me, it had just created a habit, not unearthed an addiction, and after the first few weeks, the anger and bereavement had somewhat calmed.

Flint had also forced me to go to counseling. He'd been with me when we'd lost Jones, and he knew what that had taken from me. He'd also known I was working through it, and he was just older enough to make it palatable when it came to advice-giving. We'd formed an unbreakable bond, as odd a pair as we were.

But Thatcher, though much of me couldn't stand him in a similar way to how I couldn't stand myself at the time, had refused to leave me alone. He'd dragged me to church, dragged me everywhere, until I could make my own two feet walk.

So Thatch was the first one to know.

"I can't go to lunch with you today, man." I casually slung an arm over his shoulders as we walked out of the sanctuary.

He waved at a few friends heading in another direction, off to Robbie's Kitchen, our usual Sunday spot.

"You told me Friday you'd be there. What's so important you're abandoning your best friend?" he asked, playing it up with a hand on his heart and everything.

"I'm going to lunch with Whit Grantham."

Thatcher barked out a laugh and patted my back. "Good one."

"I am."

"*Right*."

"Dude, I am." It kind of annoyed me he didn't believe me.

"*Why?*" The disbelief etched on his face was not flattering.

I gave him a look. "We hit it off at the concert in September. We chatted on and off after that. I went with her to a dinner thing last weekend, and today, I'm taking her to lunch."

"You—I don't know what to say." He stood there, his broad shoulders slumped slightly, his dark eyes wide. His bright smile then broke out, and he nodded before flashing his eyebrows. "This is good. I like this."

"That was quick." A chuckle escaped me at his typically positive response. He was nothing if not a Pollyanna.

"I'm happy for you. Maybe a little nervous, because she seems like she could chew you up and spit you out, but... yeah. I can see it." He eyed me as we walked to our cars.

"What can you see?" I asked, twirling my keys back and forth around my finger.

"I can see your appeal to her. To anyone, but especially someone like her."

A car full of other twenty-somethings from the church drove by and honked at us, which reminded me of the time. "I gotta get going, but I'll see you at work tomorrow."

"I'll want a full report," he said through a wide smile.

"You won't get one."

I slammed my truck's door and started it up, taking a moment to appreciate Thatcher's willingness to see me as desirable to Whit. If there was one thing I wasn't sure about, it was that I was a believable counterpart for her.

She was extremely talented, famous, beautiful, and wealthy.

I was extremely broken, uncertain, and generally out of my depth with life lately. But I could be good to her, and I could be kind, and we could be friends.

And the part of me that stood alert whenever she was

near me, the part that thought about what her hair would feel like under my fingertips, or how she'd smell in that sweet shadowy spot between her neck and her jaw... those parts would have to lock down.

CHAPTER NINE

Whit

I walked into our lunch date exactly on time at half past noon, the shiny Country superstar Whit Grantham version of myself readied after some deep breathing in the car on the way, but Ben was already there.

"Is my watch slow?" I asked as he held the door for me.

"I doubt it. I just walked in."

And then, he did it—what I imagined he'd do if we were really dating. What I'd told him to do. He was doing just that.

But my heart still skipped a beat, my breath catching as he leaned down with one hand on my upper arm, pressed a soft kiss to my cheek, then pulled back to look in my eyes.

"Good to see you." His voice sounded somehow deeper, richer, *more*.

"Good to see you, too." Why had the words been breathless?

Just then, the hostess gestured for us to follow her, only hesitating a second when she registered I was me.

We got settled in our seats, the din of the restaurant mostly covering the *Is that Whit Grantham?* and the *Who's the guy?* shimmering around us. She sat us in a booth out of the way, which I appreciated on one hand, because we did need to talk, but on another, we needed to be seen.

"It's October—a nice enough day. We can walk a few blocks holding hands after this and make sure someone snaps a photo," he said quietly over his menu when he saw me looking around. He'd probably realized no one could see us without walking out of the way.

"Good idea."

After we'd ordered, we chatted about our mornings. Both of us had been to church, though different ones. If he was surprised to find I went to church, he didn't show it— after all, I'd had the same thought about him when he'd walked out of church to pick up the phone the first time we'd talked, and I hadn't mentioned it.

And then, the time for the questions came.

"Can I ask you about your family?"

His tone was quiet before he took a bite of his burger. The sight of the big meat and cheese sandwich caused a pang of envy I didn't often experience since most industry people wouldn't be caught dead eating a cheeseburger. A bite of my grilled salmon went into my mouth. Pretty good.

Ain't no cheeseburger, that's for sure.

"I can tell you about them, but probably not *here*, just in case." My tone held caution—would he pick up on it?

Realistically, nowhere but my own house was truly safe. We'd have to save that another for day.

"Well, then, why don't you ask me some questions, and maybe in there somewhere, I can find some to ask you?" He grabbed a fry, ate it, and watched as my gaze followed it to his mouth.

"Okay. Favorite food."

"Burgers. Or anything my mom makes. You?"

"I have a typical sweet tooth. Baked goods. Ice cream. Cobbler. Oh, Lord, do I love cobbler." I never ate those things, especially not anymore, but I did love them.

"Candy?"

"No. Not so much."

"Well, at least you have that going for you," he said with a smile, then grabbed another fry.

"Siblings?" I asked, then took a bite while he answered.

"Two older sisters. Bridgette is thirty, married, one child. My middle sister is Beatrice, but we've always called her Bea. She's twenty-eight, an actual genius, single, extremely shy. And then, me."

"All B names," I said, far too excited by the discovery. "Is your mom Becky?"

He grinned. "Nope."

"Bailey?"

"No."

"Beth?"

"How long are you going to keep guessing?"

"Betty?"

"You're not going to guess."

He did a little half-smile with just one side of his mouth curving up, and if I hadn't been distracted by the hunt for his mother's name, I might have noticed the little flutter in my belly at the sight of it directed at me.

"Belinda? Babs? Barbara? Belle?" The smile grew on my face with each suggestion.

"Do you want to keep at it? Or should I tell you?" He seemed to be enjoying this as much as me.

"Tell me. Please." I was leaning over the table, clutching my fork like a life line, then upon realizing this, relaxed my hold on the utensil and eased back into my seat—how had I gotten so riled up by that and been totally unaware of anything else around me?

"It's Jane."

"*What?*"

"Why are you so shocked? It's a perfectly common name," he said, even as he chuckled to himself.

"You said it was a B name!" I said, far too loud.

He shook his head, totally pleased with himself. "No, I didn't. You assumed."

"So why all B names?"

"I'm not sure there's a reason other than they got started with Bridgette and kept it going. My dad's name is Paul, so... there's really no logic behind it. We all have M middle names, too."

"Really? So all the same initials. That seems annoying."

He was so open about his family. It made me want to tell him about mine, except the few people who knew anything about them likely pitied me—not something I wanted. I'd give him the shortest summary possible at some point and leave out the rest.

"I never knew any different," he said simply.

"So what are the names?"

"Bridgette Michelle, Beatrice Marie, and Benjamin Michael," he said, then bowed slightly to me with a formal flourish of his hand.

"Very nice. Benjamin Michael Holder is a sturdy sounding name," I mused aloud.

His close-lipped smile looked uncertain. "*Sturdy*, huh? I guess I'll take it."

"It suits you." And it did. He seemed solid and comfortable.

"Thanks, I think." The doubt in his voice rang clear.

I threw my napkin at him. "Stop. Sturdy is good. You don't want to be the opposite of sturdy. That'd make you... rickety."

"Well, that's true. I'd never want to be called rickety, so sturdy, it is." He wadded up my napkin and tossed it back at me. "Do you have siblings?"

"I'm one of those dreaded only children, if you can believe it," I admitted. Just that wasn't giving too much away.

"I can't imagine growing up without sisters to boss me around," he said, his face soft like he was remembering something specific.

"Well, my parents did enough of that. Anyway, this is questions for you, right?"

He nodded, his mouth full of food.

"Why did you join the Army?"

He swallowed and took a big breath, one that seemed heavy for some reason I didn't know about yet, and fiddled with his untouched silverware as he spoke. "I grew up wanting to go into the Army. My uncle had been in for most of my childhood, and I thought it was so cool. My dad was a consultant, regular business job, and he'd never discouraged my interest. By the time I got to college, I recognized I had no real interests, no passions, no clear career route *except* for the military. I joined ROTC and commissioned when I graduated."

"So you've always wanted to be a soldier?"

"I guess." His eyes met mine and then flickered away almost immediately.

What is that about?

"Any particular reason you sound... uncertain about that?" I prodded.

His lips pressed together in a regretful expression. "Hard to explain. I'm in an odd place with my career right now."

He seemed like he wanted to say more, but stopped.

"How so?" I asked, hoping he'd tell me. I hadn't been forthcoming about myself, but I wanted to know everything about him.

He hesitated for a minute, his gaze sliding over me, evaluating. "I had a bad deployment, and the year since has been challenging, to say the least. All of that and a large helping of therapy have led me to a point where I'm not sure I want to continue, but I have no idea what else I'd do."

He reached for his water and gulped down several swallows before looking at me again.

"That seems like a really important thing to discover, even though I'm sure it's a hard place to be." It sounded awful. Whatever hardships I faced, at least I was doing what I loved—making music, creating, performing.

"It is. And your cousin isn't going to let me go quietly, if I decide not to continue." He studied his plate, dipped his last fry in his ketchup, and ate it, still not looking at me.

"Are you and Reese pretty close, then?"

I'd wondered about that. For him to show up at Reese's house when I was there meant Reese trusted him. They'd seemed very friendly during my visit, and for my gruff, unsociable cousin, that was rare. It spoke highly of Ben, too—another factor in my choice to move forward with him.

"You haven't talked with him... about me?" he asked, his wrinkled brow showing me his surprise.

"No... not yet, anyway. Is he going to tell me a bunch of

stuff that'll make me regret dating you?" I asked, only partly joking.

In truth, I'd called and left a message, but hadn't heard back. Reese was notoriously slow to return a phone call, particularly after he'd messaged to ask if it was urgent, and I'd said no.

Ben pushed his plate back and leaned on his forearms. He used a low, smooth voice when he said, "I'll tell you whatever you want to know, Whit. I already told you I'm far from perfect, and I mean that. I hope the truth of me won't make you regret it, but we should deal with that soon so you don't."

Whatever it was, he was nervous about me knowing, but sure that I should know. Someplace in me knew it had to do with his deployment, with the loss of his friend—but I only knew about that because I'd stumbled upon him that night over a year ago when he was too drunk to realize he'd been spilling all his most intimate thoughts to me. There was an odd kind of humiliation in the fact that he didn't even remember, though I'd been in disguise and he'd been truly drunk.

"I'm not worried, but I do want to know, whenever you're ready to tell me."

CHAPTER TEN

Ben

It had been the longest week of all long weeks.

Okay, exaggeration, but if I had to read through one more operations order demanding ten soldiers to do something the battalion didn't have the numbers for, I would scream.

But that was a big part of the job, and it would only become more a part of the job as time went on. And that thought had me feeling the same old familiar, bleak sensation as I sat at my desk in the Rambler Battalion headquarters surrounded by the musty scent of a building in disrepair despite it being occupied constantly for the last forty years.

"You need to get out of here," Major Flint said from behind me.

I inched my feet around in slow motion, toeing the line between humor and disrespect by taking so long to address him. "Yeah. Too bad I have another hour of work before I can go."

I sounded like a petulant child talking to his punitive father, but that was me today, at five after five on a Friday.

"Get going. Do it Monday." His general demeanor had much improved in the last week or so. Things must have been going better with Erin, his close friend-turned-maybe-girlfriend, and also a friend of mine.

"Since when are you kicking people out of the office? This time last year, you were sleeping on a cot on weekends." The full edge of my frustration could be heard, bare and loud, in my voice.

Most everyone had fled the building for their weekend plans, so no one would hear me being insubordinate, which I sort of was being.

"Since I've stopped avoiding interacting with real life."

No kidding, he had a twinkle in his eye.

"I take it things are looking up where our beloved Erin is concerned?" I asked, then swiveled to my computer and saved my work.

"As a matter of fact, yes."

I could hear the smile in his voice—a rare enough thing that made me quickly turn to catch a glimpse of it, but he'd already knocked his features back to his resting Major face.

"I'm glad. I am." And it was true.

They were sickening together, so sweet. A combination I never would have guessed at until I saw them together and then saw them torment themselves by staying apart. As the haze of my depression and self-destruction had cleared last spring, I'd begun seeing just how messed up Major Flint was by ignoring Erin, and then all the more once they'd been forced together as she took care of him while he was injured.

"Are you dating my cousin?" he asked, his voice low even though no one was nearby.

I stood and took a breath. I wanted to tell him what was really going on there—if anyone could be trusted with that information, it was him. But even telling him would be a breach of contract.

"I am. I'm seeing her again this weekend."

He looked at me—looked *down* at me, I should clarify, since he was a towering hulk of a man at six-foot-four. Nothing could make a guy feel dainty like standing next to this beast.

"This isn't one of your—"

"No. Definitely not." My voice cut into his insinuation, made it clear I meant what I said.

"Good. I know you've been doing well, but I also know Jones' birthday a few weeks ago..." He frowned.

"Yeah, it sucked. But I'm all right. Bec... she's not okay. Maybe ask Erin if she can check on her this weekend. She's probably traveling, but I get a feeling she's not in a good place." The familiar weight of dread settled in my gut at the mere thought of Bec.

Bec, Dillon Jones' twin, had taken his death stoically. When I came back and began my two-month bender, she'd stayed steady, never letting a tear fall. Over the next year as I trekked my way back to equilibrium through therapy, routines, and anti-depressants, Bec had disappeared.

She traveled with a wealthy aunt every weekend, or close. She was friends with Erin because they worked at the education center on post, but Erin had expressed a similar concern over the last few months especially. Bec's evasive tactics were becoming more extreme. I'd tried to talk to Erin about it, but she didn't feel she could share any details.

I'd tried to call Bec that day, tried to ask her if she

wanted to get together for lunch, but she'd shut me down. That false cheeriness in her voice had gotten under my skin—I hated there was nothing I could do to help her.

"I'll talk to Erin," Flint promised, and I knew he would. "Now go. And be the gentlemanly, entirely asexual being I know you to be when you're with my cousin."

He gave me a stern look, then turned on his heel and was gone.

I dumped all my stuff into my bag and tried to pull my thoughts up and out of myself. I'd been distracted most of the week, and today was ending in a shroud of irritability and anger. Not an unfamiliar emotional path, but it also signaled that the time had come for another visit to my therapist. I'd missed my appointment last week thanks to work nonsense and needed the stabilizing interaction of someone removed from all the swirling thoughts in my head.

Tuesday was my next appointment. I'd be fine—I wasn't hanging on by a thread. I just felt the crush of pressure, needed someone to talk to, and was feeling more and more caged by my job.

I rolled my head side to side to stretch my neck, rolled my shoulders out to loosen them up, and started the car. The radio came on, and of course, there was Whit.

Her voice drifted through the speakers, slow and smooth and rich like warm maple syrup on a Saturday morning.

My God, her voice.

I'd heard "Call Me Back," her song about being there for a friend, over and over again. It came from her first album—cute and a little jaunty, but the voice still hooked me. I switched the channel and let myself think about other things, fully aware that letting Whit's voice sink into my head while I was feeling raw and frustrated would only serve to frustrate me more.

The night passed as it often did, with Thatcher coming over to play video games and eat pizza. I went for a run Saturday morning, made sure my suit looked good, and drove to her place around four-thirty. It was odd being able to just go right up to the door and knock, and yet, her house wasn't a mansion. It was big, and nice, but not a gaudy palace occupying the space like so many houses in the nearby neighborhoods.

"She's just finishing up, and I'm heading out. Come on in," a woman with short blond hair and a black apron said. "I'm Amanda, Whit's make-up artist. You're Ben?" she asked as she walked.

I followed behind her into the kitchen.

"Yes. Ben Holder. Nice to meet you, Amanda." I would have shaken her hand, but she wasn't stopping. "Should I, uh... follow you?"

"Yes, come on. I'll show you to her room." She kept walking, her feet padding around the corner and out of sight before I could stop her.

"Um, are you sure she wants me in there?" I asked, feeling unaccountably awkward about going into Whit's bedroom.

"Yes. Don't worry. She's used to having a million people in there. Damon's finishing her hair." Amanda stopped at a doorway. "Leaving, honey. See you in a few weeks, yeah?" she hollered, then shooed me through the door as Whit's response bounced over.

"See ya, Mand."

I followed the sound of Whit's voice down a short hall-way, past one doorway which led to a huge bathroom based on the glimpse of a gigantic bathtub, and farther down the hall.

"Ben! We're in here!" This came from the room behind me.

I paced back and peeked into the bright white bathroom.

"Oh, hi. Sorry. Should I go?" I mumbled, seeing her sitting in a chair in front of a mirror while a stick-thin man with full tattooed sleeves fiddled with the hair on the side of her head.

"Are you done, Damon?" she asked, giving me a smile in the mirror.

"Almost... yes... *yes*. Let me spray you, and we're good." Damon sprayed her with hairspray, I assumed, and then stood back to admire. He walked in front of her and squinted, touched her hair in a few places, smoothing and tugging, and then gave her a pleased smile. "Perfect."

"Thank you. Have a good weekend."

"See you next week and hi Ben I'm Damon," he said, all in one breath as he grabbed a set of keys and gave me a finger-fluttering wave.

"Hi and bye, Damon," I said as he rushed past me. I shuffled out of the doorway so he could get by, then turned my attention to Whit.

And tried not to audibly express the torment building in me when I looked at her.

Good work, God, was all I could think.

"Sorry for the chaos," she said.

Or I thought she said, but my brain was busy cataloguing her standing there. Her long hair had been pulled over one shoulder, the other side pinned back behind her ear. Her face looked typically gorgeous, eyes dark with long lashes, perfect skin and lush, expertly glossed lips.

She tugged the tie on her short, silk baby pink robe tighter.

"I'm going to run put on my dress, and then we'll get going, okay?" she said, apparently totally unaware the sight of her was causing a severe case of heart-stop.

I grunted out an "uh-huh" and shifted my eyes away from her to the counter full of tiny pots and palettes of makeup.

Two minutes later, she emerged, clothed in a short red dress that fell halfway down her toned thighs. It had cap sleeves, a thing I knew about thanks to Bridgette's insistence on modeling her clothes when I was too young to protest. The dress fit close to her body—so close, I doubted she had much underneath.

I cleared my throat, pulling my eyes away from her, and turning to the doorway. "It's pretty cold out—you'll probably want a jacket."

"I've got one in the closet downstairs," she said from behind me.

"Do you have people do your hair and makeup for everything?" I followed through the hallway Amanda had brought me down, retracing my steps to the more familiar territory of the kitchen.

"No. I prefer not to, but when there's going to be lots of press, I do. And since the purpose of tonight is to draw attention to us being together, I figured I might as well look decent."

She pulled open a closet door in the entryway of the house and sifted through hangers until she pulled out a short black leather jacket.

"What's this event?" I asked, noticing the lines of the wood below my feet, the smooth curve of the arching doorway into the sitting room to the left of the entrance, the intricate weave of a pillow on the couch in that room I couldn't actually see—anything to keep from letting my eyes run over the dip and swell of her body wrapped so tightly in that dress.

"A fundraiser for a Veterans' organization. I'm not sure what."

My eyes jerked to hers.

"Oh, cool." Best to keep my voice level even though my heart accelerated.

"Something like Wounded Warrior project, but it's a local thing using music for rehabilitation of PTSD, I think. I'm sorry to say I've forgotten the name." She pulled on her jacket, then straightened to her full height—a whopping five-foot-five including her heels—and studied my face. "You okay with that?"

"Yep. I'm good." And then, to distract from my weirdly physical response to the fundraiser's focus, I said, "Am I acceptable?" while holding out my hands and turning side to side.

She made a face like she was closely evaluating me, tapping her chin with a finger, then nodded. "You'll do."

I chuckled. "Good."

"And me?" The sweet smile on her face did not betray the fact that she *had* to know she looked good.

I widened my stance and crossed my arms, mimicking her chin-tap thought process. "I'm going to tell you something I'm fairly certain no one has ever said to you."

Her face fell a bit. "Okay..."

"You are incredibly beautiful, Whit."

Her smile tugged to one side, and she clasped her hands in front of her. "Thank you, Ben."

"And if you're trying to make sure we get noticed, you

definitely chose the right dress," I added. Because I'm an idiot.

"Oh?" Her smile didn't waver for a second.

I nodded, finally having learned that if I opened my stupid trap, something dumb was going to fly out of it.

"Does it look like something someone you'd date would wear?"

"No," I said firmly.

"No?"

"It's better," I admitted.

CHAPTER ELEVEN

Whit

"Lieutenant Holder! Lieutenant Holder! What's it like dating a Country music star?"

"Whit, what's it like dating a hero?"

"How'd you two get together?"

"Is this the soldier you wrote your songs for?"

"Is this who you cheated on Jamie Morris with?"

"How'd you win your Purple Heart, Ben?"

At that, Ben whipped around to look at the gaggle of press crowding the walkway, held back only by a small rope that suggested they not get closer.

"Keep moving," a voice called out.

I held Ben's hand tighter, practically dragging him behind me. The press at the event was unusually aggressive and strangely well-informed about Ben. We'd been seen together last weekend, but I knew what this was, and my jaw tightened at the realization—Nikki must have sent out a press release, or at least a few well-placed tips.

"How long have you been dating?"

"Did you kill anybody in Afghanistan?"

"Did you bring him to this event to look good, Whit?"

I could feel Ben's stress, the rigidity in his arm pulsing with energy—frustration, rage, overwhelm, all of it. I'd have questions to answer, that was for sure.

"Just keep going," I said again, even though we were practically already in the car. Ru shut the door behind me, and I took a breath.

My gaze slid over to Ben. His eyes were closed, and he was holding his breath, then he let out a slow, controlled exhale.

"I'm so sorry." My voice came out shakier than I'd expected.

"How do they already know who I am? How do they have any idea that I was deployed or that I have a Purple Heart?" His voice stayed completely controlled, but everything in his body language said he wasn't feeling that way.

"I'm guessing Nikki leaked your name, and maybe even your service record. I had no idea she'd do that, and I am so, so sorry."

He faced the front again, staring at the road, or nothing, and not responding to me. I hadn't thought about this part, and now that it had happened, I felt like an idiot for failing to. Of course I'd considered that they'd find out he was a soldier—that was one thing that made him so attractive—but I hadn't thought about how vicious the press could be, how they'd ask things he didn't want to be asked, and that maybe, after having the experience he'd had, that even being *asked* could create a new kind of trauma.

His hands rested loosely at his sides. I reached out and put a hand on his arm. He startled slightly at my touch.

"Ben, I am truly sorry about this." My gaze searched his face for some kind of clue about how to console him, or make him better.

His brow furrowed, and he looked at me for a minute before he swallowed and spoke. "I knew they'd find out I was in the Army. I hadn't thought about the other stuff. I should have, I just didn't..."

"That's not your fault. I should have thought about it, too." We were quiet then, for a moment that stretched out as the buildings whizzed past our tinted windows. "What can I do?"

He shook his head.

"I think it's maybe what *I* should do. You need to understand something." He shifted so he now faced me. "I'm *not* a hero. I don't want to be called a hero—I didn't earn the title, and I won't wear it. If *that's* what you think, if that's why you asked me... then we're done."

The naked hurt and anger in his tone, on his face, made something clench in my chest. Again, he gave honesty and demanded it, and I wouldn't fail to return it.

"That's not it at all. I don't—I don't know what to say other than I'm not expecting you to act that way, or claim to be a hero, and I'm not putting that on you. You're Ben Holder, soldier, friend of my cousin, adorable guy, and we're friends. That's why you're here." I squeezed his wrist, then pulled my hand away.

Ru pulled into the driveway.

"Please come inside with me, Ben," I said, hoping he wouldn't leave while he felt so upset.

His chest rose and fell, then he nodded once and got out of the car. Ru opened my door and helped me out before

Ben could get to me, and I moved to the house and opened it for us.

"Thanks, Ru. Have a good night."

He gave me his usual smile and nod and disappeared back into the driveway while Ben followed me inside.

"Can I get you a drink?" I asked while settling my coat in the closet.

"No, thank you," he said, hands in his pockets.

I needed him to talk to me—to help me understand what I could do to make this better for him.

"Would you come into the kitchen with me?"

We both turned down the hall that led there.

I flipped on a few more lights and set my clutch down on the bar, then took a seat. He sat in the same place he had when he'd come to talk through our arrangement.

"Tell me what I can do to fix this." My hands stretched out to him on the countertop.

He shook his head. "I don't think there's anything. I'm sorry I reacted this way—I've had a crap week, and this caught me off guard."

He ran a hand over his head, and the hair just a touch longer on top now looked wild. Looking at him caused an ache in my chest—I didn't want him to be hurting—not because of me or anyone else. I didn't want him to feel anything but good.

"I'll talk to Nikki. I'll make it clear that as far as we're concerned, there will not be any questions asked about... your service."

He was inspecting the marble, smoothing a hand back and forth across a dark vein under his palm.

"Sure. But ultimately, I agreed to this, and I need to figure out a way to handle this kind of thing. I'll bring it up with my therapist next week," he said, so casually, no shame.

"You go to a therapist?" I tried not to sound disbelieving or even surprised, but it must've been there.

He gave me a strange smile. "I wouldn't be here if I didn't. In any sense of the word. I told you, I've been broken, and the process of putting myself back together has been a long one. It's ongoing, and it's not something I can just grit through."

"I know. I mean, I don't know, but I get it. I see someone on and off, too, and I get it. I'm glad you have someone who can help you sort through this." I hesitated, wanting to understand. "Can I ask you a question? If today's not the day, just say so."

"It's fine. What do you want to know?" he asked, only partly wary based on the look on his face.

"Which question bothered you most? Or was it all of them?"

"You might think it's the 'how many people have you killed,' and that would bother me, except I've been asked it so many times by people who don't seem to realize how incredibly inappropriate it is, I just ignore it now." He folded his hands together and looked down at his fingers, but said quietly, "It's the one about the Purple Heart."

That surprised me. "Really? Why?"

He made a placid smile, like it was all the same to him if he told me, though I could see from the tension in his shoulders he hated talking about this.

"People seem to associate that award with heroism, but that's a mistake. I did nothing to earn that—I got injured, and I was given an award. I got injured. My friend died, and *I* got a Purple Heart."

He kept his eyes from me, but I could see his lips

pressed together in pain, in anger, in frustration and so many unspoken thoughts. My heart rattled inside me, aching for him, breaking for him, and longing to somehow assure him that his survival wasn't a bad thing.

Before I thought of what to say, he spoke again.

"I used to have a hard time waking up every day and remembering that. So questions about the award, especially from people who don't understand... that's tough. I'm not a hero, and I never will be. I'm just a guy whose best option was the Army."

I stood up. I wanted to go to him. I wanted to wrap my arms around him and tell him he was amazing, and I was so glad he was here, and I was so glad he'd fought to stay here.

I moved to him slowly and stopped next to him at the bar. He swiveled to face me.

I stepped closer and asked in a voice with the barest volume, "Can I?"

He nodded once, his eyes not leaving mine, and I stepped between his legs and wrapped my arms around his broad shoulders.

My body pressed into his warmth, hoping to offer him something. My arms held him tight, my hands flat against his back. I leaned my head just to the left, my neck grazing the collars of his jacket and shirt. My throat felt clogged, so I held him a moment longer, then pulled back before he got too uncomfortable.

I wanted to tell him everything then—that I knew some of what he'd seen because *he* had told me about it. And all I'd wanted, in those moments when his eyes had burned with pain and fury at the loss he'd experienced, on behalf of his friend and his family, had been to make it better for him. I wanted to tell him that his vulnerability was astounding, and how much I admired him for it.

But my throat never did clear up, the words never able to get out. Instead, we were just there quietly for a few minutes, me standing near him where he sat on the chair at my kitchen counter, until he let out a slow breath and smiled sweetly before telling me goodnight.

CHAPTER TWELVE

Whit

It was an ugly thing to admit, but I could do it: I'd thought about Ben Holder more in the last few days than I'd thought about anyone else in my life.

Usually, my thoughts centered on me.

We all do this. We like to pretend we're concerned for others, but ultimately, we're mostly worried about how what other people are going through might influence us. And if we meet someone who's *not* that way—who is genuinely outwardly focused, it's a shock. It's confusing and convicting, and most of all, alluring.

Maybe thinking that way was a symptom of being in the industry I'm in.

This wasn't me—I wasn't alluring in that way. If anything, in the last few years, I'd allowed myself to sink further into self-centeredness as a way to block out some of those pesky things like my ugly non-relationship with my parents or the perpetual longing for something *more* that I couldn't seem to grasp no matter how many albums I sold.

I know. Again. How cliché.

But what *was* true was that Ben Holder had taken root in my brain and wouldn't leave. I'd thought about him often after that first conversation when writing the song, and sometimes while singing it, but really, this was a far more dangerous Ben.

No longer was he the nameless, sympathetic wounded soldier grappling with death and grief. No.

Now, he was Benjamin Michael Holder, brother of two. Now, he was an actual man with real depth, with a will to live his life without drowning in what had come before. He was a generous and easygoing person while still being *real* and not without problems.

All of it posed a danger to that idea I'd had of him—the untouchable, sweet, honorable man who was, if I was being honest, more than a little beautiful.

The fact that I'd see him again in a few hours didn't help things. Ben had been hanging around the edges of my consciousness from sun up until sundown all week. The meetings about the upcoming mini-tour had been shaded with him. The time I carved out to write—there he was.

We'd messaged only once during the week—both of us had busy days, and we'd made a plan to get together today. He would come to the house, and then we'd go out for cocktail hour—one last date before the holiday weekend.

I wasn't going to make it easy for anyone to notice we weren't together for Thanksgiving. In fact, I planned to lay low and make it impossible to find me. Reese had invited me up to his place near Fort Campbell and had promised Erin could make me some diet-friendly food. I'd told him I was still considering it.

But after the last week, I definitely needed something to distract me. Because the whole time Ben would be gone—to somewhere in Alabama, though it now dawned on me I wasn't entirely sure where his family hailed from—I would be thinking about him. And it would be annoying.

"Focus, Whit. You know you need a good burn right now. When you get on the road, you're going—"

"I know. I don't need a lecture."

Kendra was my trainer, a total beast, and she treated me like I was an adult who could make her own decisions about her health and who was capable of maintaining a healthy weight without being micromanaged within an inch of her life.

Oh, wait, no.

That was Kendra in my dreams. Kendra in real life was a warlord over my body—and I could admit it yielded amazing results, but not without a price.

I didn't eat freely. Every bite to grace my mouth was choreographed for months before a tour. Often frustrating and irritating, but it also created the image, let me wear the costumes, and created that *celebrity* look that didn't just happen by stumbling into it.

The dumbest thing about it? I paid her to do it.

Off-seasons—times when I wasn't about to go on tour—were gentler. But it proved hard switching out of it—I got nervous about how to handle eating or organizing my day *without* the rules. It was something I was working on, and Kendra had glared me into submitting to relaxing my eating a bit after this mini-tour over the holidays.

It would be good to do—for my body, my mind, every-thing. But I also knew myself. I was all or nothing, and I wouldn't be happy with nothing, hence the marked tendency to stay at *all*. And the burnout factor on that setting was high.

But for now, I could focus on *getting my burn* as Kendra liked to say. I followed her as she moved through our warm up yoga, then into a full Pilates workout. After that, she had me knocking out push-ups, a brutal ab routine, and finally a cool down walk on the treadmill.

"Whit? Ben's here," Nikki said, peeking into the workout room from the hallway.

"Oh, good. Send him in?" I hadn't planned to see him until after showering, but Kendra had pushed me for a longer workout since the holiday and then the tour were coming up, and I hated to refuse her.

I saw him before he saw me and wiped my face with a towel while Kendra made some notes. "Ben! In here!"

He entered the home gym where I'd just burned off a billion calories, and his gaze swept over me, then jumped to my face.

"Hey." His voice sounded a bit rough.

"Sorry—I'm a mess. This is Kendra, my trainer."

Kendra waved, and he greeted her with a nod and tight smile. I took the minute to appreciate him in front of me. He wore stylish, slim but not skinny jeans, and a nicely fitted button-down shirt. We were keeping it casual tonight, and he'd done well.

"How was your week?" I asked, running the towel down my neck. His gaze followed the movement, then snapped back to meet my eyes.

He cleared his throat, his brow furrowed. "Uh, good. Yeah. Week was good."

～

Ben

The thing about Whit Grantham? She knows she's gorgeous. That's as it should be—why should a beautiful woman have to *not* realize it? She might as well be confident.

I suspected she was fully aware of the effect she had on men. On *me*.

And seeing her there, cheeks flushed, hair a little wild, body bright from exertion...

That body.

Sorry. Call me a jerk, but was I not supposed to notice? I'd done my best to avoid really looking at her in person... at least, I hadn't done it how I'd wanted to. She wasn't mine in that way, even if we were pretending she was. But I was supposed to walk into her home gym and find her in yoga pants and a strappy sports bra and nothing else and *not* notice?

Yeah. Right.

But I was trying to be a good guy here. Hence my averting my eyes, only to find myself staring at her spectacular rear view in the mirror behind her. Or the intricate and not-all-that-substantial straps crisscrossing over her shoulder blades. Or the open expanse of her back and the smooth line of her spine running in the middle.

I was essentially surrounded, and she seemed oblivious to the fact that she was assaulting my senses in an undeniable way.

"I'm just finishing up here. Want to wait for me in the kitchen? I can be ready in... half hour?" She tossed the towel into a basket by the door. "See ya Monday, Kendra."

"Yep!" Kendra shouted from behind us. The trainer

looked like she'd been carved out of ebony stone—just absolutely what I imagined a celebrity trainer to look like.

"No problem. I'm sorry I'm in your space early," I said, though I was certain she'd said five.

She turned to me at the intersection of hallways—her room was to the right, the kitchen back to the left. "No, that's all my fault. I was running late all day. I'm sorry to say that, other than showtimes and hard deadlines, I'm often on the late side."

She bit her lip and gave me a look that was supposed to be apologetic—it probably did, except my focus still rested on absorbing her words and keeping my eyes on her face.

"Don't worry about it. I'm habitually punctual, but I grew up with a sister whose on time was fifteen minutes late."

Bridgette was a later person by nature. I used to get so mad at her, as did Bea, who was punctual to the point of being militant, but the fact that Bridgette was the oldest and the only one with a car for much of Bea's high school years forced her to cooperate with Bridgette's bad habit of running late.

See? There. Thoughts of sisters, and I'd re-entered a world with the laws of gravity.

Whit put a warm hand on my arm and squeezed. "Well, make yourself at home in the kitchen. I'll be fast getting ready—no hair or makeup, so lower your expectations, but it means I'll be fast."

She flashed me a bright smile, then hustled down the hall, which I definitely did not watch.

A smile touched my lips, because I had absolutely no response to the comment about expectations. All my expectations for her had been blown out of the water when she'd hugged me last week, and I'd been reeling ever since.

Something about her compassion in those moments shook me. It was far more... *feeling* than I thought she was. I was attracted to her physically, sure—I had a heartbeat, didn't I? But the main reason I'd agreed to help her was because she was Reese's cousin and I wasn't dating anyone else anyway. I couldn't deny that spending time in her world sounded intriguing, but she struck me as sort of self-absorbed and simple. Not *simple* simple, but just kind of... basic. The kind of person who was nice, but not going to invest in other people because their head was down, working toward their own goals.

Exhibit A: asking me to fake-date her so her reputation would improve and she could manipulate John Smith Johnson into working with her.

My impressions weren't based on anything real prior to meeting her, but I could admit I'd judged her and not allowed the other evidence to match up with what I'd seen. Her songs were alternately happy and effortless, but also deep and affecting. It'd been easy enough to see her as an artist who was brilliant, but only looking out for herself.

Her concern for me, for my reaction and frustratingly visible upset after the press' questions last weekend, and then her gentleness with me... it got to me. It snuck up on me. And now, I stood on shaky ground, not sure how to take her.

I liked it better when I knew what to expect, and the fact that now I wasn't so sure what I'd get from her—maybe self-interest, but maybe genuine interest in *me*, well... It made me more nervous about tonight than I'd been for any of our other dates.

Sure enough, half an hour later—twenty-eight minutes, if someone had counted, which I most definitely had not—

Whit breezed into the kitchen looking clean, relaxed, and beautiful in a way that hit me between my ribs.

Nikki walked in behind her, startling me from the daze I must have fallen into watching Whit as she moved around the kitchen putting things from her drying rack away, tucking an empty glass into the dishwasher.

"Where are you two going?" Nikki asked, addressing me, which was nice.

I often felt like an accessory in the room, which I basically was, but it didn't make me like Nikki very much.

"I was thinking Robbie's Kitchen. Is that okay?" Whit asked, turning to face me.

"Robbie's is great. That sounds good." My stomach rumbled, though it was mercifully quiet, so hopefully, they hadn't noticed. Robbie's was so good, and I hadn't been in a while.

"Great. Ready?" Whit grabbed a large purse and slung it over her shoulder. "You good to drive? I gave Ru the day off."

"Oh, sure. Yeah." I pulled my keys out of my pocket and gestured for her to lead the way.

"Ben. A word?"

Nikki's voice stopped me and Whit.

"What's up, Nikki?" Whit asked.

"We need *more* here. You two are adorable, but you might as well be cousins." She pursed her lips and fluttered a pen between her fingers.

"It's fine," Whit said.

When I glanced at her, her cheeks were pink.

Was she embarrassed by Nikki's suggestion, or embarrassed by the fact that we apparently had no outward chemistry? That wasn't a shock since we weren't very physical, but the chemistry between us felt like it was developing pretty rapidly to me.

"That's easy enough to fix," I said, not sure exactly what I had in mind even as I said it. "As long as you don't mind..."

Whit's eyes fluttered, and then she smiled brightly—maybe a little too bright. "Of course not."

CHAPTER THIRTEEN

Ben

The car ride was strangely tense. I wasn't sure why, other than maybe Nikki's suggestion had upset Whit.

"Hey, should we talk about what Nikki said?" I kept my eyes on the road ahead.

"Sure. What, exactly?"

She sounded casual, but she wasn't feeling it. Nothing about her posture relayed the calm she sometimes had. Nothing had felt easy between us since Nikki'd spoken.

"Maybe we should discuss what you're comfortable with. I don't want you to be worried."

I opened and closed my hands around the steering wheel, wishing I'd waited to talk about this when we were sitting down and I could pay close attention to her body language, her face. But then, we wouldn't have privacy, so it was now or never.

She remained quiet—so quiet, it made me nervous, except I had nothing to be nervous about. This was her show.

I pulled into a spot a few blocks from Robbie's Kitchen. The November day was chilly but nice, the sun still working its way down so the sky was light. I kept the car running so we'd have the heat, but put the truck in park, unbuckled my seatbelt, and turned to her.

She did the same, though she bit her lip as if worried about something.

"I saw Jamie last week. Unexpectedly, but I'm sure there are photos. I think Nikki wants us to compensate for that, despite the fact that I was surrounded by about six other people during the encounter."

Ah. Okay. I could handle this.

"So, we'll compensate. We were always going to need to appear together—that's why we've made a point to hold hands. We'll just up our game. If people are going to make something out of every time you're seen with a man, it's going to be a long road, I'm guessing. So let's firmly establish you and me as a thing, and make sure everyone knows we're both really happy about it, and then people can shut up about you and Jamie, or anyone else."

Her eyebrows rose, and she chuckled. "Oh, that's all I need to do? Sounds easy."

She was mocking me, but I'd just made a complex situation seem simplistic, so I supposed I deserved it.

"I just mean, don't stress it. We talked about this from the beginning. Plus it's not like it's a hardship to touch you, Whit. It's felt pretty natural thus far, at least for me..."

"Me too," she added quietly.

Something in my chest swirled, expanded, warmed. "Good. Let's go eat."

~

Whit

Ben pulled me close so I was tucked into his side, his hand on my upper arm as we walked the few blocks to the restaurant. It wasn't quite winter yet, but late November in Nashville could be surprisingly chilly. I almost never wore enough clothing to stay warm outside, and tonight was no exception. My faux-suede jacket was warm and comfortable, but the chilly breeze cut right through it. Being held against Ben's big body helped immensely.

But I couldn't shake the worry. Ben's closeness registered in a new way—in a very aware, uncomfortable way.

Uncomfortable in that I liked it. I liked it a lot, wanted more of it, more of him, and more time for us to be together. When Nikki suggested he be more demonstrative, or both of us, a thrill of excitement had gone through me, and then the reflex against that.

I didn't want to have this kind of relationship. I wanted something clean cut and contractual—not messy with *feelings*, or swirling with heat and chemistry. That was all fine, but I didn't have time or energy for it.

I didn't want it.

But as the wind stung my cheeks and I tucked my head down and toward his chest, my heart was beating harder than it should have been considering our pace. It churned because of *him*.

They seated us right away at a two-person booth. It would have been ideal to be seated at one of the long communal tables in the middle, but I couldn't summon regret, or the words to request we be moved. It wouldn't make sense, anyway. If we were really dating, we'd want some privacy.

We ordered—him brisket with three sides that would no doubt be mind-blowing, and me, grilled chicken over a salad, hold the candied pecans, dressing on the side.

Ben was eyeing me when I closed my menu and set it down.

"Do you like barbecue?"

"I love it." No question.

"But you ordered grilled chicken on a salad." A frown created brackets around his mouth. He seemed sad for me, regretful.

I reached across the table for his hand that rested there and hid my amusement at his expression. I laced our fingers together and shoved away the flutter in my belly at the contact. "Ben, honey, you've seen my body, right?"

His brows popped, and he looked side to side. "Uh... I'm not sure how I'm supposed to answer that."

His cheeks pinked, and I had to bite my lip not to laugh.

"What I mean is, I can't look like this and eat barbecue on a regular basis. I can't look like this and eat much of anything but lean meat and vegetables." I tightened my grip on his hand, then pulled my hand back.

He stared at his hand a moment, digesting my words. When he looked up, his brow was furrowed. "Does that make you happy?"

"Does eating salad make me happy?"

"No, does looking that way make you happy? I assume the eating is a means to the physical appearance as an end."

His voice held an edge to it, but I couldn't tell what it was. A surge of annoyance that he was questioning my food choices, like he had any idea of the pressure I faced, stole my focus.

"Happy? That has nothing to do with it. It gets me publicity, helps me feel confident... plus you have no idea what it's like to be anything less than super fit in this world." I sat straight and watched him.

The waiter came and delivered our food—Ben's looked predictably amazing, and mine looked like a salad with grilled chicken and exactly zero adornments.

We both dug into our meals, him sawing a piece of brisket with the side of his fork, then wolfing down half the meat, homemade mac n' cheese, coleslaw, and cornbread before he looked back at me.

"I'm not judging you. Or, I'm not trying to. It just seems silly to me. You are obviously extremely fit, but if you have to be so regimented to look that way, I'm not convinced it's worth it unless you're one of those eat-to-live people. Are you?"

He was concerned. In an alternate universe where this wasn't my life, it would be sweet. But his calling into question my food—really, my way of life, and his pressing on this subject I'd made peace with and accepted because I'd had to—was wearing thin.

I chewed a bite of my food and swallowed before responding. "No. I'm definitely a live-to-eat person. So it's not easy for me, but now that I've been doing this a few years, I feel all right about it. I've gotten used to it."

He watched me as I took another bite, not refilling his fork for himself. "You know you're beautiful, right?"

Where did that come from?

"Yes..."

"And you know that your body looking like it does, while it's... great... doesn't make you any more or less beautiful?" His voice was gentle, but his words were harsh.

Of course I knew that, but hearing Ben Holder say it

like it was something I needed to hear—like maybe I'd lost sight of the reality that beauty was more than physical—made my pulse throb at my temple. He had no idea what it was like to be me.

I must have physically blanched. "I'm sorry to tell you, but that's just not true."

The look he gave me was a confusing mix of pity and determination.

"It's true. I know you live in a world that suggests that for you to be considered pretty and successful, you've got to wear certain clothes and have a certain body fat percentage or whatever, but I can tell you that you will be beautiful no matter what you do. Your songs, your talent, your kindness —though you couch it in self-motivation—those things are your beauty. The outside is magnificent, but it's all of you that creates the beauty."

No one spoke to me that way. No one was that earnest and sweet and humiliating. Cheeks flaming, the brutal mix of embarrassment, anger, and pleasure swirled in my belly.

"I'm not trying to sound like I know what I'm talking about—I've probably just mansplained this and infuriated you, and rightfully so. I'm messing it up. I guess I just want it noted in the official records that if you started eating barbecue and happened to also pack on a few pounds, I'd still think you were inordinately gorgeous."

His blue eyes pinned me in place, his left cheek curved with the half-smile on his face.

Oh my.

I took a drink of water, then forced an easy smile. "So noted."

We turned our attention to our meals. I thought we might go on like that indefinitely until his hand slid into my view next to my plate. His long legs bracketed mine under the small table, but I'd put that out of my head until now, when I felt his knees leaning inward against my legs.

I looked up to find him with an indecipherable expression on his face.

"We're getting some attention—take my hand."

I set my hand in his immediately, and his fingers curled around and stroked my wrist.

"Do you want a bite of macaroni and cheese? It's basically the best thing you can put in your mouth."

I let out a laugh and acquiesced with a nod. He speared a small cheesy noodle with the fork in his other hand and held it out to me. I leaned up off the booth and took it in my mouth, the creamy, rich flavor immediately flooding every taste bud as I slumped back in my seat.

I closed my eyes and refused myself the audible moan that threatened to escape. When my eyes blinked open, Ben was watching with a grin.

"Good?"

"So, so good. I don't remember the last time I had pasta. Or cheese. Let alone mac and cheese."

"Woman. That's no way to live," he said lightly, but I could see he was still concerned for me. "I guess it's safe to say you don't want dessert?"

"Not tonight, thanks."

He signaled the waiter, who brought the check quickly. Ben paid, despite my insistence that I should.

"The deal was, I pay."

"That's sweet. But it's not going to happen every time. Let me have this one."

He leaned forward and tucked his wallet into his back pocket, then stood and offered me a hand. I took it and held on as he led the way through the restaurant, feeling eyes on us as we moved past the three large communal tables and out the door.

He walked to the next building and pulled me to the side, then nudged me so I turned and backed up a step until he had me leaning against the brick wall. The large windows that made up the front of Robbie's Kitchen were inches from us, and plenty of people sitting in the frontmost bistro tables would be able to see me if they were looking.

"What're you doing?" I said quietly so none of the crowd standing in line outside the über-popular restaurant could hear.

Something flashed in his eyes. He stepped close, put one hand on my waist, and the other rested lightly on my opposite shoulder. He leaned in so his lips just barely grazed my ear. Despite the street noise of cars, the loud chatter of the crowd waiting to get inside, all I heard was Ben's voice.

"I'm making sure it's clear we're not cousins. Because if we'd been on a date and I'd been staring at you for an hour, I wouldn't be able to stop myself from kissing you. But I also wouldn't want our first kiss to be on a street corner in front of a crowd, so I'm going to kiss your cheek, and then we'll walk back to the truck. Okay?"

He pulled back and surveyed my face.

I nodded, barely able to breathe. Other than the hug, this was the closest we'd been. This was absolutely the first time I'd gotten a real sense of how sensual he could be, and it sent my pulse racing. He kept his eyes on mine, brought his hands to either side of my head and held me there, his hands wrapping around the back of my head and sifting into my hair, his thumbs at the sides of my face.

He moved slowly then, just like my heart and mind,

because they'd slowed down to a hollow, distant drum beat as his warm lips pressed into the space just at the corner of my mouth, lingered there, and pulled back.

A flash went off, and then he pulled back completely, grabbed my hand, and we walked back to his truck.

CHAPTER FOURTEEN

Ben

Damn. *Damn. Damn.*

I had been so close to kissing her. *Soclose.*

I wouldn't pretend to understand the pressure of her level of fame. It was insane. Everyone was *always* looking. I bet someone had been taking her picture every five minutes through dinner. For all I knew, someone had been recording the whole dinner, hoping they could sell it to TMZ or some other celebrity-mad show.

But watching everyone watch her, knowing she wanted us to be seen in situations that were clearly romantic, I'd gone for it.

But right as I would have kissed her, I had stopped myself. Because part of me did want that first kiss—badly—but I didn't want it to fall under the auspices of duping her adoring public and convincing Johnson she wasn't a problem.

I wanted it to be because she *wanted* me to do it, and I wanted it to be where no one else could see.

Dangerous thinking, obviously enough.

I pulled up in front of her house—we'd hardly talked on the fifteen-minute ride back.

"So I'll see you the first week of December, right?" she asked, unbuckling.

"Yes. I'll be around, just working, except when I head home Wednesday through Sunday this week. Are you doing anything with family?"

It was dark, so I could only see the shape of her next to me.

"I'll probably drive up for dinner with Reese and Erin."

The mild dread in her voice made me chuckle. "Hopefully, they won't be too over the top. They're nearly insufferable now, aren't they?"

"I haven't seen them since the concert, and even then, it was tough. I'm sure you've gathered I'm not huge on PDA..."

"Unless it benefits your image." Then I realized how that sounded. "I don't mean—"

"No, you're right. I'm a pretty private person, so it doesn't come naturally to me. And I guess I should say thank you—I'm sure they got some good shots. It probably even looked like we were actually kissing if they shot from behind you."

"That was the idea." My pulse picked up at even the mention of the near-kiss. Well, it had been a kiss, but on the cheek.

"Thanks. You should brace yourself—that'll likely hit tabloids, so your friends and family may hear about it. Since you've been at a few events, they'll have your name and splash it around. Hopefully nothing too personal about the Army."

Her voice thrummed low and smooth. It made me want to get closer to her.

"It'll be fine. My sisters both tend to be in their own worlds, and my mom isn't tuned into celebrity stuff."

"Well, I hope you have a good Thanksgiving. I feel like we're about to go into a real intense time in our arrangement in terms of the tour. We have some time booked out on that Saturday before to talk about what you can expect, right?"

She pulled her purse over her shoulder, and I could see the shadow of her hand reach for the handle on the door and rest there.

"Yep, we're good. It's low key for me until the new year, so if anything else comes up, let me know. And don't be shy —if you need anything, let me know."

Okay, okay, man. She gets it.

"Thanks, Ben. See you soon."

She climbed out of the truck, and it was only then it occurred to me I should have gotten the door for her, escorted her in, but I was parked just feet from her front door. She had a cobblestone circular driveway, and even though my job was boyfriend, my reality was friend. Walking her to the door would create unnecessary awkwardness.

The days before Thanksgiving were busy. And frustrating. For some reason, there was a constant need to scramble and look busy. To "get after it," as they often said. The new battalion commander who'd replaced LTC Wilson was LTC Baker. Because he was just starting out and the battalion wasn't slated to deploy again until next summer, his restlessness was palpable.

Since LTC Wilson had been a great commander—yes, in my limited opinion, but also according to many people who'd been around to know the difference—so when Baker arrived, there wasn't a huge need to change things. People knew their jobs, knew their roles, and the companies were functioning well. The battalion had been through a rough couple of years between the difficult deployment with multiple casualties, and then the loss of Specialist Smith last spring.

Through it all, LTC Wilson had kept it together, and even for me, who'd fallen apart, he'd been a stalwart supporter of my seeking help and recovering. One thing he did well was make people go home—make them stop working needlessly and take their long weekend when it was given.

As I drove away from Nashville heading South, I wondered just how much of LTC Wilson's ability to do that was thanks to Major Flint's overnights and weekends working on his behalf the last year before Flint decided to have a life. I couldn't be sure. But it was good Flint had figured out how to create some boundaries before his new boss showed up. And lucky for him, he would be moving on after he promoted to LTC in the spring, most likely.

Me? I was stuck there in the musty old building I alternately hated and tried not to hate. I liked many of the people, but had grown tired of stressing out about filling in information on tracking spreadsheets, aka my life. I was tired, after only two weeks of Baker in charge, of being made to feel like leaving at five was ducking out early and shirking my duties.

The Army would take. It would take, take, take, and

take some more. And the longer I stayed there, the more I felt like I didn't have any more to give it. I wondered if I'd given it everything I had when I lost Jones. When I lost myself. Now that I'd effectively found myself again, I wasn't ready to give any more.

But the thought of stepping away from this life—the one I'd planned for during high school, then college, and the only adult life I'd known—that was a tasking that felt too big. I kept pushing it out of my mind, knowing that the time for me to decide whether I was going to get out, or promote and move on to the next job, at which point I'd then owe the Army time, was coming.

By the time I pulled into my mom's house in Alabama after the five hours it took to get there by car, I was exhausted. I should have known that expecting peace and quiet was a fool's errand.

"You have some explaining to do, Benjamin Michael."

This was Bridgette the minute the screen door swung shut and I walked into the living room. She loved talking to me like she was in charge of me. I suspected it was because her toddler was still too young to control.

"About?" I asked, wandering down the hallway, still carpeted with the same copper brown medium shag it had been all my life.

"*About you dating Whit Grantham!*" she shrieked.

I couldn't help but laugh. "Oh, that."

I tossed my bag on my bed, the same single bed I'd grown out of my sophomore year of high school when my growth spurt had hit.

"Yeah, *that.*"

I looked over at her with her hands on her hips, her loose dress bowing out over her belly. *Wait.*

"I'm evidently not the only one with some explaining to

do, Bridgette Michelle," I said, and stood, placing my hands on my hips and swiveling my neck in an exaggerated move.

Her face reddened. "Don't you dare suggest that me being pregnant is the same as you dating an A-list celebrity."

Her blue eyes were wide, lashes darkened with mascara to make them even more noticeable, her blond hair typically wavy and beautiful. Both she and Bea could have been beauty queens if they'd ever wanted to be.

"Right. Because a new life is *far* less interesting than my dating life," I said, shaking my head in mock scorn.

"Oh, come on. You know I want like six kids, and Bat said he's along for the ride."

Yes. My sister called her husband *Bat* as in *Batman* because she said he looked exactly like Christian Bale playing Bruce Wayne.

He doesn't.

But Bat, or Walt Miriam as his parents had named him, was happy enough with whatever Bridgette called him because he was completely gone on my oldest sister. He'd literally said as much to me the day of their wedding three years ago. He'd said, "Ben, how'm I going to survive a lifetime with her? She bends me out of shape so bad, I'll be twisted in knots the rest of my life."

I'd had no response, not sure whether that was a good thing or not, but when I saw his face as she appeared at the end of the aisle and heard him whisper "oh, thank God," I'd known he thought the knots were a good thing.

"Well, good for you and Walt, Bridge."

I sat on the edge of the small bed and pulled off my shoes, then slid my feet into the house shoes I always wore when at home. My mother was laid back—just like my dad —but one thing she had no tolerance for was dirty shoes *tromping around her floors.* It was the only time I ever heard anyone use the word *tromping*.

"Tell me."

She crossed her arms over her belly, not yet big enough to act as a shelf like it had at the end of her first pregnancy, and she pursed her lips. She gave me the look I knew too well—the exasperated, my little brother is annoying me, but I'm going to get my way, look.

"Yes, I am dating Whit Grantham."

Her nostrils flared slightly, her lips flattened as her eyes fluttered, and then, it started.

"What! How? When? Where? How did this happen? *Why?* What is she like? Is she as pretty in person? Is she stuck up? Are you *sleeping with her?*"

Just then Bea poked her head in, her equally long blond hair pulled back into a ponytail, the same way she'd worn it since I could remember. She quirked an eyebrow in question.

"I just told Bridge—"

"He's dating Whit Grantham! Can you believe this?"

Bea gave me a puzzled, amused look, and shook her head. "What?"

I stood and pulled Bea in for a hug. My sisters were sturdy girls, medium height, nothing you'd call waifish, but Bea had always seemed *slight* in some way. I hugged her to me. And she squeezed me back, then released.

"Good to see you," I said, genuinely feeling it, followed by the chaser of relief that I really did mean it.

It wasn't so long ago I'd hardly meant anything I said, especially to those closest to me.

"I am going to pull your leg hair out one by one if you do not sit your narrow butt down and tell me what is going on." Bridgette was fast reaching her breaking point.

I ducked my head, remembering her slew of questions. "I met her a couple months ago—she did a concert at the base, and I gave her a tour. She also happens to be related to a friend of mine. We went to a charity event a few weeks later, then another one, and since then, we see each other regularly. She is prettier in person, she isn't stuck up, and that's none of your business."

"I can't believe my brother is dating Whit Grantham. Do we get to meet her? Also, why did Bea get a hug and I didn't?"

I laughed at her, enjoying the familiar barrage that was being in a room with Bridgette Holder-Miriam. I pulled her to me and squeezed, then released.

"Oh, I don't know. Maybe it was due to the interrogation the minute I stepped into the house?"

"What did you expect?" she said, pushing me away from her.

"Maybe something like, 'oh, hi, Ben. Great to see you. How was your drive?'" I said in the mocking voice I always used when making fun of her.

She pulled her phone from somewhere (did her dress have pockets?) and shoved it toward me. "I'm supposed to see *that* and not demand the full story?"

I looked down at the screen and read the headline that accompanied a photo of Whit looking dazed past the camera, our bodies pressed together, my head ducked down—probably from when I had been whispering in her ear. My hand was on her shoulder. Her expression... *whoa*.

Country's Queen Whit Grantham hits the streets with new man, Lieutenant Ben Holder, US Army. More on this 'Stolen Moment' below.

CHAPTER FIFTEEN

Whit

Six nominations.

Six.

More than I'd anticipated, for sure.

Best Country Solo Performance. Best Country Song. Best Country Album. Best Album. And there they were—Best Pop Duo/Group Performance, and Best Record for the song I did with Jamie. I swallowed, chuckled a little bit, and clutched the phone.

A weird, giggling laugh broke out as tears leaked from my eyes. "I can't believe this."

Nikki shook her head, allowing herself a full smile, for once. "I can. You've worked yourself nonstop since you won that contest, and it shows. Your work is paying off. This is going to go a long way toward working with Johnson."

At the moment, I didn't care about Johnson—I wanted to scream and jump on the bed and drink a bottle of champagne alternating with homemade ice cream. And the strangest thought that I wanted to toast with Ben.

Hmm.

I hadn't seen him in two and a half weeks—between Thanksgiving, my schedule, and his, especially since he was about to take two weeks off to join me on tour, we hadn't planned any dates.

But I'd missed seeing him. We'd swapped *Happy Thanksgivings* and otherwise hadn't interacted. But then, as though I'd summoned him with my thoughts...

@TheRealBenHolder: *Congratulations! Just saw the very impressive list.*

I smiled to myself, a simmering pleasure growing in my chest as I thought of him checking for my name on the list of nominees.

@WhitGranthamOfficial: *Thank you! I'm blown away.*

@TheRealBenHolder: *We should celebrate. You can't be this fancy and not get taken out by your boyfriend, can you?*

That feeling in my chest warmed, expanded, took over, but then, I realized I was booked solid tomorrow and Friday. I didn't have time for him again until Saturday for our next date.

@WhitGranthamOfficial: *I'm sad to say I don't think I have time until Saturday.*

@TheRealBenHolder: *What about tonight? It should be a rule that you don't wait more than a few hours to celebrate six Grammy nominations.*

Well, that was adorable. And appealing. I checked my watch—four o'clock. I was pretty much done for the day.

@WhitGranthamOfficial: *I could actually do something tonight.*

@TheRealBenHolder: *Done. I'll be there at six—six thirty at the latest.*

@WhitGranthamOfficial: *See you then.*

I wandered around the house after Nikki left, chilled a bottle of champagne, put things in my Amazon cart and then didn't check out. Finally at six-fifteen, the doorbell rang. Knowing he was right outside had me jogging to the door.

I hauled it open (it was a huge, heavy door), and there he stood, looking more handsome than I remembered him looking. Had he gotten taller? Maybe that's because I was barefoot.

He stepped through the door and kept coming until he'd hooked his arms under mine and around my back, then lifted me up, hugging me and circling around.

Exactly the right kind of hug.

"Congratulations," he said as he did it.

I chuckled and hugged him back as he turned and set me down.

"Thank you." My eyes were surely twinkling and my face beaming.

"Where do you want to go?" he asked, his face full of a genuine happiness.

His gaze flickered down over me, taking in my sweats, bare feet, and the super soft unicorn T-shirt. His smile changed to a look of confusion.

"Would you mind if we stayed in?"

It would be insanity if we went out. I didn't want to make statements, do the whole adorably overwhelmed thing. I wanted to relax and catch up with Ben and celebrate without a million eyes on my every move.

"No, of course not. It's just... I assumed you'd want to go somewhere and toast to your success?"

I grabbed his hand and pulled him along behind me into the kitchen. "I do want to toast. I have champagne."

I dropped his hand as we entered the bright white room and found the bottle on the fridge door. I pulled down two fancy champagne flutes and grabbed a kitchen towel. "Okay if we go to the living room?"

"Whatever you want," he said, typically easygoing.

He followed and pulled off his coat. A huge sectional sofa with a big ottoman took up the middle of the space. On it was a large tray that allowed the ottoman to act as a table. I set the flutes, bottle, and towel there. A roaring fire lit the fireplace—one reason why this was my favorite room, especially this time of year. I hadn't put up a tree or any decorations because I knew I'd be gone for the holiday itself, and then when I got back, it'd be January, and there was nothing worse than lingering Christmas décor when you just wanted to get on with it.

"Just toss that on the back of the couch, or wherever. Sorry I didn't grab it from you," I said as I saw him looking for a place to drop his jacket.

I settled into the corner of the couch and pulled the tray so I could reach. Ben sat on the cushion next to me, though not all that close, and watched as I removed the cage and covered the bottle, cork intact, with the towel. Then, very slowly, I eased the cork out, no sound but a small hiss, like the bottle took a breath, before it was out completely.

"That was ninja-level champagne popping. Or, not popping," Ben said, wonder in his voice.

"Ah, yes. A kind of reverse party trick in that it's completely unimpressive and not at all showy, but I learned at an early age that letting the cork pop, at least according to my father, bruises the champagne. It's probably the most valuable thing he taught me." I poured us both some of the golden, bubbling drink, and handed him his flute.

His smile looked warm and sweet. "To the hard work and sacrifice you've made to get here, to the Grammys recognizing that, and to whatever is in store next. Congratulations, Whit."

I couldn't speak, feeling choked up at his genuine joy for me, the real congratulations, and the realization that this was the first time I'd celebrated anything like this with someone I wasn't paying. Technically, he was contractually obligated to me, but in the end, I knew in my gut he was here just for *me*.

I nodded in thanks and touched my glass to his, the light *ting* sounding loud in the room. We each sipped the fizzing liquid, and I grabbed a remote to turn on some music so the fire wouldn't be our only accompaniment.

"Do you feel like you're floating?" he asked, watching me take another drink and curl into the corner of the couch, my knees pulled up next to me.

"Sort of. It's surreal."

"But you won a Grammy for your first album, right? Or, more than one?"

I nodded.

"So were you expecting this? Tell the truth—did you expect it, or was it a surprise?" He eyed me, waiting for my response.

"I expected one, maybe two nominations. I didn't expect *six*. I thought maybe best Country performance and maybe one for the song with Jamie since there'd been some Oscar buzz about the movie, and people had said the song had a chance, too. But not six. It's an embarrassment of riches, whether I win a single one or not."

He gave me a look. "Really."

It wasn't a question.

"Of course I want to win. I'm not one of those people who will pretend to demur and say winning doesn't matter. It does. I want to. I want all six of them, now that I know it's possible. It really is an honor to be nominated. But I won't pretend I don't want them."

The smile he gave me was its own kind of fire, brilliant and hot.

"That's one reason I like you, Whit. You're not afraid to be *you*. You're not afraid to go after what you want and work hard and admit that you work hard. I admire that."

"Thanks. I'm not sure everyone agrees with you, but I appreciate the thought."

I tipped back my glass and finished it, then poured a bit more. Ben hadn't had more than a sip or two.

"I think six nominations can officially serve as your notification that, whether people say they like your ferocious work ethic and your talent, they like what comes from it and want more." He quirked an eyebrow at me.

"Fair enough," I said, and took a drink, then let my head rest against the back of the couch and watched the fire crackle and pop, tendrils of smoke swirling up into the chimney. "I wish it'd snow."

"Yeah, that'd be nice," he said, and settled back into the cushion, his head a foot or so from mine.

"I bet we'll run into snow on the tour. We'll be in New York, Chicago, all kinds of places between. There's a good chance." I let my eyes close and breathed deep.

When was the last time I'd just sat with someone, music in the background with a fire in my fireplace?

Had I ever done that?

"What's wrong?"

His voice cut in, and I rolled my head to look at him.

"I just had this thought that I'm not sure I've ever done this—just sat on my couch with someone and listened to the fire and music. I don't slow down well, and I'm rarely with people I don't employ." The heat then stung my cheeks. "I guess I sort of employ you, don't I?"

He put his big, warm hand on one of mine. "You aren't paying me, so no. I'd like to think we were becoming friends anyway, but now we definitely are."

The smile crept over my face as I looked back into his blue eyes. *Friends. I like that.* "Good."

"So you and Jamie never just... hung out? Or other friends?" He set his glass on the tray and settled back in.

"Jamie and I were never just relaxing together," I started, then saw his eyebrows raise and quickly added, "not like *that*. No, we liked each other, but we were hardly ever together. Neither one of us was very good at taking down time. I think Jamie and I are actually a little too alike in terms of our intensity with work."

"I can see how that would make it difficult to just *be* together. But that resting is particularly important when you're worked to the bone. Isn't it?" He held my hand palm-up in his, and with the opposite index finger, traced slow shapes into my wrist.

It was an unexpected kind of contact. It felt intimate, sweet, a little seductive. But it felt simple and comforting, too.

"I'm sure it is. Kendra tries to help build in mandated rest. But it's usually pretty solitary, or I end up doing it with employees who've become friends. I love Amanda and Damon. Nikki and I get along well for the most part, and Ru and Kendra are great. I have a few other people you'll meet on tour—all great. So I know I'm blessed in that way. The people who work for me are amazing."

He waited, evidently hearing the words I hadn't said. "But they work for you."

"Yep."

"Sounds lonely."

He looked down at the finger that traced unknown messages into my skin. Watching his finger sliding along that parchment-thin part of me, feeling the warmth of his hand cradling mine gently, a pang of longing hit me so hard that my chest ached.

"It is."

CHAPTER SIXTEEN

Ben

I'd just gotten reamed by LTC Baker, and it would likely be the last time for the year. *Thank God.* In just a few short weeks, Baker had made his presence known, and not in a good way. He wasn't the kind of commander you looked forward to sitting down and talking with.

And now, he would likely do everything he could to make my future in the Army less than ideal. Because I was an idiot and talked back when he asked rhetorical questions while he soap-boxed me into oblivion.

I knew I'd pissed him off as the red wave of anger washed over him from his shining bald head to where his neck met the olive-green collar of his uniform. *Perfect.*

Just another thing to make me question what the hell I was doing here anymore. And that was the question: why was I even considering staying in? I never felt excited to go to work. I never felt like what I was doing made any difference at all. On the worst days, the heaviness of future deployments, future loss, future injury loomed over me.

Everyone didn't feel this way. Major Flint didn't, and we'd been through the same deployment—he'd held my hand while we waited for a MEDEVAC for Jones as he died in my arms.

Shit. I didn't want to be thinking about that.

But as I packed up my water bottle and coffee mug and signed out of my computer, I knew the truth of the situation wasn't that simple. I didn't want to continue doing the work of the Army, but I had no idea how to do anything *but* the work of the Army. I had no skills, no degree that had a clear non-Army job attached like teaching or engineering or accounting.

And maybe the worst part? I'd always planned on this. I'd planned on the Army. It'd been my plan since graduating high school. I'd envisioned retiring after twenty years, maybe more. I'd seen myself as a soldier for life.

But I was faced with the larger reality that I didn't want to be a soldier anymore and had no idea how to get out, how to figure out what came next.

A year ago, these kinds of thoughts would have sent me into a tailspin that very few things could pull me out of. I took a deep breath and looked out at the horizon while driving. What a relief to feel the walls hold—the edges of my mind weren't collapsing in on me at the thought.

I was discouraged and angry with myself for assuming I'd love the Army and not having any Plan B, but I'd figure out something. Either I'd move forward in my Army career, promote to captain, and move to go to the captain's schooling that would take place before my next longer assignment, or I wouldn't.

I'd be forced into figuring that out in spring. For now, I'd just... see. I'd see if Flint and Thatcher and the other people I liked working with could make me want to stay enough to actually do it. And I'd try to figure out what the hell I'd do if I got out.

Saturday morning, I worked out long and hard, then cleaned up and sat around mentally preparing for whatever was in store for me at Whit's. Today was our big pre-tour meeting. As I grabbed my keys, my sister sent me a message —it contained a link.

I clicked on it to find a photo of Whit with her hand on Jamie Morris' arm. They were both smiling, both angled toward each other, evidently having lunch together or doing something that necessitated sitting near each other.

Super.

I messaged her back. *"Don't worry about it. They're collaborating."*

Her response wasn't a kind one, and despite what I'd told her at Thanksgiving—that I knew Whit hadn't cheated on him, nor him on her, for that matter, and that I trusted Whit, she was skeptical. Bridgette would always fight like an angry badger to protect her family, and I suspected, especially her little brother. There was no point arguing with her or trying to talk her into trusting Whit until she met her.

Which she probably would never do.

I knocked on Whit's door right on time, and Nikki opened it for me.

"We're meeting in the dining room—she's just finishing up reviewing the rider and a few details with Jeremy, the tour manager. Then, we'll talk through some of the logistics with you. Jot down any questions you have as we go— Jeremy is incredibly tightly wound about timeliness and won't answer questions until he's done with his presentation."

I followed her to the dining room, a room I had never seen but which turned out as anticipated—expertly decorated, airy with a touch of down home, and absolutely gorgeous, since Whit sat inside it at the far end of the table. A man who looked like he was probably only an inch or two taller than her with jet black, slicked-back hair and pale skin sat to her left, and they were both silently reading the screen of a laptop angled between them.

"Yes, that's all good," Whit said.

And just those few words, totally unrelated to me, made my stomach turn over.

"Okay. Then that's it. Is this guy going to make it—" Jeremy started, then stopped as he saw Nikki sit down to the right of Whit and gesture for me to sit next to him.

Some juvenile part of me had a mini tantrum that I wasn't getting to sit by Whit, but I told that baby Ben to shut it.

"Ben Holder, nice to meet you."

"Jeremy Lantz, nice to meet you. Here's your schedule, your print of procedures—things like loading and unloading, call times, packing suggestions, and a bunch of other stuff. We've got a few legal docs to sign, and then Whit should fill you in on anything else, but you can always contact me."

He shoved a pile of papers in front of me on the table. It looked like it was about twenty pages deep.

"Thank you," I said, looking down at the stack.

"And by you 'can always contact me,' he means never contact him under any circumstance unless you want your head ripped off," Whit explained.

I looked up to find her smiling back at me. Jeremy

grumped out something unintelligible, and she added, "What? You know that's true. Ben won't cause any trouble. Isn't that right?"

"Yes, ma'am."

After another twenty minutes of lists and rules and schedules, none of which I fully absorbed because the insanity of what I was about to do dawned on me, Jeremy and Nikki both left. Whit showed them out—clearly more for Jeremy's sake than Nikki's, and once the door closed, she sank back against it and gave me a wan smile.

"He's great, but I end up with the biggest headache after I meet with him." She then pushed off the door and walked straight over to me. The smile grew on her face as she got closer. "Hi."

I looked down at her now since she stood so close. Rather than resisting the urge, I held out my arms, and she kept walking until she was pressed up against me.

"Hi," I said back, hugging her tight before letting go, and experiencing the very real sensation that I wanted to keep my arm around her, keep touching her.

"Sorry about the information overload. Do you have questions?" She smiled, her eyes full of concern and care.

The only question now was how I'd keep on resisting her.

CHAPTER SEVENTEEN

Ben

"Thank you, everyone! See you again soon, Boston!"

Whit yelled, then came barreling off the stage, a ball of energy so bright, she was impossible to miss in the dark backstage. The stage techs pulled her guitar from her shoulders and handed her a towel. They ushered her past me, and I was pretty sure she had no idea I stood there, but then she turned to look around.

The crowd was still raging, and I couldn't get to her—people were packed around her, fixing her costume, wiping her face, Amanda swiping on more gloss, and about a hundred other things I couldn't see. The crowd roared at a deafening volume out in the stadium, and the lights stayed low.

Ah, of course. The encore.

Another burst of activity, and then she stood right at the side of the stage until the music changed, then strolled back on, and the crowd, though I wouldn't have thought possible, got louder.

One of the stage-hands pulled me up closer to the side so I had a perfect view of her profile. She smiled widely, a burning flame on stage, and wow, she'd changed clothes in those hurried moments backstage. Now she wore a startlingly short white dress covered with something that reflected off her like little mirrors. Her boots were black this time, her hair down and wavy under the white cowboy hat on her head. She strummed her black guitar, the beginning notes of one of her most famous songs from her first album, the one that had won her first Grammy, filling the venue.

I'd been glued to her the entire concert. She'd played months ago at Fort Campbell, but I hadn't *known* her then. I was still piecing together who Whit Grantham actually was, but knowing even the barest details about her made me like her even more. Being close to her in any kind of way was like a punch to the gut leaving me breathless and a little achy.

Being physically close to her during these moments where she literally pulled in energy and excitement like they were owed to her—not in a self-righteous way, but simply because she was so damned luminous and charismatic on stage and people *loved* her—threw her brilliance and stardom into a new and unignorable light.

And she was good. *My God*, was she good at this.

Her stage presence, yes. But her voice—her talent eclipsed anything I'd seen in real life. She sounded as good as, if not somehow better than, her recorded music. She proved gut-wrenching in the slow songs.

She ended the encore, and the now-familiar tingling sensation gathered in my spine, the sweet anticipation of seeing her up close and talking to her racing through me. She was greeted by the same flurry of helpers pulling and guiding, and before I realized it, she'd been ushered off stage right and somewhere else.

Someone grabbed my wrist and pointed the way to go. This Boston concert was the third show of the mini-tour and my first, so I hadn't learned what to do or where to go.

Whit had gotten extremely sick and had missed eleven tour dates on her summer tour. They'd rescheduled the concerts for these few weeks over the holidays and into the beginning of the new year.

I hurried after the crowd following her and watched as she was dusted with powder, patted, and her chest rose and fell in that dress. I caught her eye from where she sat and shook my head lightly, the gesture the only way I could think to wordlessly show her how amazing she was.

She winked at me, the first time we'd made eye contact, and just that action made my stomach drop. But too soon, she gave her attention to someone else right in front of her, chatting away. Once they'd finished the madness, she was ushered into the next room where a small crowd of people waited.

A few members of the press peppered her with quick questions, one after another, while others asked for radio sound bites. She'd be visiting a few TV and radio outlets tomorrow in person, and they'd get what they wanted from her one on one then, but for those who didn't rate a visit, they apparently got post-concert access for a few minutes.

She was handed item after item from people asking for her autograph, and these weren't even technically fans.

After fifteen minutes, she was hustled out the door, out the long route through the back doors, and dumped into a car that drove off immediately.

I came to the doorway and stopped, watching Ru speed away like he was driving the president.

"We'll take the next one," Amanda said. "She'll probably be pissed they didn't have you in there with her."

"I don't mind. I'm just along for the ride." And I meant it.

"Well... that's adorable. And probably one more reason she'll be pissed you weren't with her in the first place."

Just shy of an hour later, Amanda, Damon, and I arrived at The Four Seasons Boston Hotel, and Amanda led the way into Reception—she'd told me she'd take care of check in. That was a relief since I hadn't been given any information about my room or how to check in. Would the room be under my name? Somehow, we hadn't covered that, nor had the twenty-page packet from the tour manager.

I took in the lobby, feeling shabby in the upscale entrance of this no doubt extremely expensive hotel. My reflection bounced off the large black and gold squares on the floor and from just about every other surface—marble counter tops at check in and concierge, pristine windows and doors, mirrored table tops without a smudge.

I'd flown in from Nashville this morning, not able to get off work to leave earlier in the week and travel up with her— the Army was good about giving leave during block leave periods, but rarely could you finagle an earlier departure, not that I'd had enough leave built up for that, anyway.

I hadn't gotten to talk to Whit—it had been from the airport into a car (admittedly, I'd felt more than a little swank having someone hold a sign with my last name on it —that was a first), then to the venue. Some hulking bodyguard had shown me to the greenroom area, but Whit hadn't been there. A while later, she'd shuffled past in a small group, and then the lights in place must have gone down because the crowd's screams had been making the backstage area vibrate. Unreal didn't cover it.

By the time I was escorted to her room by Amanda, who insisted I should go there first, my heart was about to pound out of my body. The build-up of the journey, of the concert, and of having no time to even say hi, had me ready to crawl out of my skin from the anticipation of being with her.

So, yeah. I was *there*. Things for me had escalated.

A bodyguard stood posted outside her door. My first thought was that he looked terrifying, maybe only two inches taller than me, but he outweighed me by fifty pounds or more and had a case of disappearing neck. My second thought? *Good.* I wanted anyone approaching that door to be terrified unless they had official business with Whit.

He nodded to Amanda and opened the door, then pushed it wider, and she charged through. My heartrate ticked up—her scent tickled my nose, the faintly floral and citrus essence that was purely her.

Whit stood at the far end of a large, modern living room, looking out at the city's lights and the newly snow-covered Boston Common that stretched out below her feet. Her hair was still wavy and flowing, her dress still nearly indecently short, and her toned legs looked like they might be glowing, but her feet were bare, and she'd lost the cowboy hat backstage, I assumed. And she was yelling into the phone.

"Where is he? I've been here an hour. He should have

been with me. I shouldn't have to call you directly to find out where my—"

She stopped abruptly, and Amanda elbowed me and raised her eyes to say *told you so*.

Amanda tossed her stuff on the dark gray couch, and I propped up my suitcase and dropped my backpack next to it on the gray and white patterned carpet.

"If he left half an hour ago, how is he not here?" she asked whoever was on the other end of the call with one hand propped on her hip, still evidently oblivious to our arrival.

I walked to stand behind her and leaned down to say in her ear, "I'm here."

She startled, then swirled around and threw her arms around my neck and tossed her phone onto a nearby plush chair. I wrapped my arms around her and pulled her to me, the unmitigated thrill of having her close pulsing through my whole system.

She held me close, tight, and long. Then, when she pulled back, she held me away from her by the forearms and surveyed my face, letting her gaze dip down to run over my jacket, the little water droplets no doubt catching her eye.

"Hi."

I smiled back at her like a doofus. I was such a sucker for this woman, and she had no idea. "Hi there, Ms. Grantham."

"I was just yelling at Nikki because she didn't get you to me to ride with me. They were supposed to bring you straight to me before the concert!"

She pulled me back in and hugged me around the waist, my arms pinned to my sides by her surprisingly strong ones.

"I'm sorry. I just did what I was told, tried to stay out of the way. I didn't want to bother you or mess up your pre-show routine."

I had wanted to see her, almost desperately, which was pathetic in itself, but knowing she wanted to see me, too, that it hadn't been *her* plan to let me get shown around by unknown people and then corralled by bodyguards, made me feel good.

Real good.

"I wish I'd known when you got there. I thought maybe you were late and had just arrived when I saw you after—no one would update me. Did you see the show?" She pulled back, her beautiful teal eyes glittering at me.

"I did. I was right off stage. You were awesome." Those words were impressively inadequate.

"I didn't see you. I'm so sorry," she said, squeezing my arms where she still held me.

If only I wasn't wearing a jacket or sleeves so her hands would be on the skin of my arms. I wanted her touch with a suddenness that shook me.

I swallowed that desire down. "Don't apologize. You were in the zone. I loved seeing you perform again. I don't think I'll ever get tired of that."

Suddenly, the droplets on my jacket seemed fascinating, everything to focus on to avoid seeing her response.

"That's... I'm glad. I'm going to get cleaned up, and you can get settled, and then we'll hang out a while? I'm always wired for a while after a concert." She dropped her hands and moved over, giving a wordless hug to Amanda who'd set a few things in Whit's room.

"Sure. Do you know what I do about getting my room?" I asked, searching back and forth between them to indicate I wasn't sure who might know.

Amanda's brow furrowed for a minute, and then she

pressed her lips together while Whit said, "Oh! Of course. I'm sorry, we should have talked about all that. Your room's there."

She pointed to the doorway to the left, then wandered in the opposite direction, into the other bedroom.

Oh.

CHAPTER EIGHTEEN

Whit

Ben Holder was adorable.

No. Not only *adorable.*

His surprise at the room he'd have, the fact that he'd be sharing a hotel suite with me? Not something I saw, having walked away just after pointing to his room. But I could *feel* it, hear his shifting as his jacket moved with his body. Thank goodness he couldn't see my face because lots of things were happening in me at the moment, and his disarming warmth had me wanting to share them all. With him.

He was just so darn *sweet*. And open, too—not afraid to share his thoughts. I mean, really, who just comes out and says things like he did, but with nothing to gain?

It also embarrassed me a little that he was forced to share the suite with me and would have to any time we were in hotels, because people loved to sell stories, make a few bucks, and we'd need to make sure no one was selling the story that my devoted boyfriend and I weren't spending nights together. We'd tip housekeeping handily to keep their end of things quiet, and since I often had a two-bedroom suite even when single, that wouldn't automatically wave the red flag for nosey guests or employees. Add to that our careful choice of establishments based on their discretion, and we could be reasonably confident in the staff not being the cause of a leak to the press.

Whatever your perspective on all that, in the press, it meant certain doom. So Ben would be stuck with me—on the bus, backstage (especially now that I'd made sure Nikki knew I wanted him with me even when there wasn't a photographer to catch the moment), and in the hotels.

I hopped into the shower after removing the quarter inch of goop that made up my stage makeup and felt like a new woman upon emerging. Sometimes, I liked going out after a show, but tonight, I just wanted to huddle up with Ben and talk and look at his pretty face and maybe let him trace words into my wrist if he wanted.

Do you hear yourself?

I braided my damp hair—Damon would fix it tomorrow, so I didn't have to worry about blow-drying—and pulled on soft sweatpants and a slouchy top, then went to find Ben.

He'd left the bedroom door open with the light on, so I peeked in. "Ben?"

"Hey! One sec," he said from the bathroom.

I heard a few things clinking around on the counter top, and then, out he came. My heart took a moment, stuttering and stopping before it remembered its *one* job and started beating again.

But really, I couldn't blame it.

Because there stood sweet, all-American Ben, fingers

pulling down the last few inches of his thin T-shirt, belt hanging loose and unsecured around the waist of his jeans until he grabbed it and threaded it together as he spoke.

"Sorry. I showered too—didn't want to keep smelling the airplane on my clothes."

He finished looping the belt together, and I swallowed, blinked away now that the blush had undoubtedly crept into my cheeks. He must've noticed.

"Everything okay?"

"Absolutely." My attention remained resolutely on the rest of the room.

Not quite as spacious as mine, but otherwise exactly the same. Huge bed with pristine white linens. Dark, polished wood dresser with a large flat screen, small espresso machine, water bottles. At the far end next to the windows sat a small sitting area with bright yellow chairs and a tiny table.

"I just wanted to see if you were up for hanging out a bit, or if you're tired."

He ran a hand over his hair, which looked a little longer than it sometimes did on top but still close-cropped and soldierly on the sides, and then let that hand slide back again, smoothing over the hair and letting his arm drop.

If I'd ever wanted to touch something as bad as I wanted to touch his wet hair, to smooth it down and maybe wipe away the tiny drops that had fluttered onto his forehead and temples, I couldn't think of what it was. I clasped my hands behind my back to avoid doing something crazy like reaching out and fixing it. With it smashed down to his head in the front, he looked young.

"I'm beat, but I do want to hear how things are going. Living room?" he asked, and we both turned to find spots on the couch one room over.

The suite was unnecessarily big, like they all were, but I couldn't deny it brought a welcome change from the cramped quarters of the bus. This tour had far more hotel time and far less bus time because it was East Coast only, and things were closer together. We'd also tacked on several of the missed locations to the end of the tour and smashed one or two in at other times so I wasn't having to move at the pace I normally did, a concert every two days—sometimes it was only a day between, but there were a few where I had more time.

I was thankful for that. This last tour had taken its toll on me by the end, and even though I loved performing, I had been ready for a break. The fall had been nice, but it had taken me all that time just to recover. I hadn't written much at all until late in the year, and I should have been writing from the minute I'd stepped off the bus in August.

"So, how's it going?" he asked, stretching his long legs out in front of him so his feet rested on a low ottoman.

"Really well. It's short tour, so I shouldn't hit burnout, and that helps me mentally at this point. I always have energy and excitement, and I love every show, but there are times when knowing how many more I have just takes it out of me, and it's hard to imagine just going and going. But this three weeks or whatever it is, it's a good length." I sat on the cushion next to him and stretched my legs out, too.

"It's hard to imagine you giving that much on stage at every show. Is it always that way for you?" His head was resting back against the couch, and he'd snuggled as much as he could into the back—not the most comfortable couch, but he had a way of making things look appealing.

I let myself lay back and scooted just a little closer to him, about eight inches apart. After wanting to have him there for so long, I yearned to be close.

"It is. Not quite as much if I'm sick, and of course, there are some shows where the vibe or energy feels different. If I'm in a bad mood, or low energy, or distracted. But ultimately, those people paid a lot of money for me to get up there and do my best and deliver *that* to them, so whether I feel like it or not, I do it and try to give it all I've got while I'm on stage." My hands dropped to either side of my body, my bones getting heavy.

"You're relentless."

He picked up my hand and pulled it across his chest—he'd stretched out so much, he was essentially lying down. He held my hand with one of his, and much to my fluttery heart's delight, started tracing the veins in my wrist, the lines in my palm, the length of my fingers.

"It's the job," I said.

"I'm not like that with my job. I never feel that way—like I want to give everything to it, like it's an offering I'm giving."

I tilted my head to study him and watched as he kept his eyes focused on his fingers sliding along my skin.

I thought about that, about why that might be and what it meant. "Do you think that's because your job asks so much of you?"

His fingers stopped for a moment, then continued. "Maybe. I usually feel like I've given it all I ever want to."

"Tell me what you mean." My voice came out soft so he'd know he didn't have to if it was asking too much.

I felt his gaze on me and looked up—his blue eyes were remarkably sad, and in that moment, the drum beat of my heart urging me to kiss away the pain there resonated loudly in my whole being.

"I lost a friend. It was the hardest thing I've ever been through, or I thought it would be, until I got back and couldn't figure out how to function again. And the last year and a half since then has been the biggest thing I've ever done."

"What's that?"

"Figure out how to want to wake up every day, and do it."

He stopped moving his touch over my skin, instead letting his fingers encircle my wrist and hold it gently, like he was bracing himself with my arm, steadying himself.

I searched his face, looking for the shadows and misery I'd seen when I'd spoken to him at a moment that had to be the beginning of his lowest days on Earth if I'd pieced together the timing correctly. It'd likely been within a few weeks of his return from Afghanistan.

"I'm so glad you did," I said, letting my free hand come to rest on his.

He smiled just barely, though not regretfully. "I am, too. But I think that's why I don't want to give any more to the Army. I haven't got it in me."

"I can see why. So what will you do?"

He laughed, something amused and a pinch despairing. "I have no idea. I majored in history, minored in military science, and the only job I've ever had is the Army. I have no idea what I want to do, much less what I *can* do."

I pulled my hand away, regretting it instantly because I loved being connected to him, I was finding. As soon as I did, he gently set my arm back at my side and folded his hands over his chest.

"You'll find something. You don't have to stay in just because you don't know what you'd do if you got out."

A little more back and forth, and soon, nothing but his slow, quiet breathing remained in the room—he'd passed out. I wasn't sure what time he'd started traveling, but instead of feeling irritated, I let my eyes close, too.

Hours later, I startled awake and found him in the same position he'd been in. I checked my phone—three hours had passed. His arms were crossed, hands tucked under his arms, face peaceful. I admired the stubble dusting up his neck and onto his jaw and cheeks. My hand ached to smooth its touch over that face, explore it with my fingers and then my lips.

Instead, I settled for a hand on the warm curve of his bicep. "Ben, wake up."

His eyes shot straight open, and he sat up.

"Sorry. I'm so sorry I fell asleep," he said, his voice delectably rocky and low.

"Don't worry. Let's go to bed." After standing up, I grabbed my phone and moved around the ottoman one way so he could go the other.

He stood there looking completely disoriented, his eyes searching the couch, the floor, the coffee table.

"Are you okay?"

"I don't know what I'm doing," he said, looking at me with tired eyes.

I hid the smile, but reached for his hand and guided him past the ottoman and toward the door to his room.

He followed obediently, shuffling along as if still asleep. He must have been just partly awake, because he appeared confused. "This is your room, too?"

"No, honey. This is your room. I'm helping you get to bed so you don't get lost," I said, letting out the small chuckle I couldn't hold back.

"That's nice. You're so nice." He slumped onto the bed then inched up to set his head on the pillow, his eyes closed the whole time. He tucked one arm under the pillow. The other, he pulled in to his chest.

"Do you want to put on pajamas?" I asked, no longer able to stifle my laughing at his delirious state.

He cracked one eye open, then the other. He blinked like he was trying to clear his vision, or to see me better. I sat down next to him on the edge of the bed.

"You okay?" I asked quietly, the late hour making everything feel slow and silent.

He reached out a hand and touched my ear, ran his fingertips over my shoulder and down my arm.

"*Mercy*, you're beautiful."

His arm fell still, his eyes closing before I could respond, and his chest rose and fell with the deep breathing of sleep.

I gritted my teeth against the regret that this was all becoming too much, the longing for it to be more, and a thin tendril of hope that it could be what my heart seemed to know it wanted swirled in my mind as I got up from the bed. But no way could I not to return the sentiment, even if he was already asleep.

"You are, too."

CHAPTER NINETEEN

Ben

I spent the day alone.

For the record, I spent the night alone, too, even though it surprised me how my sleep-state honesty serum hadn't driven me to beg Whit to curl up next to me, stay with me, to let me pull her close and bury my face in her hair.

I was weak for her. Looking at her from across a room threw me off-balance, literally. Being within ten feet scrambled my brain so much, I could hardly hold a conversation lately. Sometime in the last few weeks, my relationship with her had become less casual, more friendly, attracted-but-not-acting-on-it and more wretched without her, *attached*.

It wasn't out of sight, out of mind. She wasn't ever out of my thoughts. It felt like, whether I liked it or not, she carried around a piece of me that was constantly aware of or thinking about what she was doing.

So a day alone? Bring it.

I slept like the dead and woke to find a message from Whit on my phone that said she'd be out until the late afternoon, that we had a cocktail hour event that evening, and that I should call her with questions.

Part of me wanted to call just to hear that voice, the rich, melodic sound that made my blood race through my veins. But I didn't. A day away from her, even though I'd spent weeks away from her at this point, would be good.

It wasn't like she'd never heard she was beautiful. I'd made my thoughts on that clear ever since the beginning, but it was that *you are, too* that came after, the one I wasn't completely sure I hadn't hallucinated, that undid me.

And okay, I'd also concede that the dreams that followed had been incredibly sweet.

But it was more than just that moment. When she'd turned around and wrapped her arms around me, I could have sworn she'd missed me like I had her. I would have placed a bet on the fact that she'd felt that same swirling mix of joy, desire, and relief as we'd hugged each other tight.

And when I'd admitted that I had no idea what to do with myself, my life, my future, she hadn't pitied me. She hadn't seemed to need to prescribe a fix for me like Bridge had when I'd mentioned it at Thanksgiving—she just had faith in me.

It was kind of staggering, coming from her, this super power of determination and achievement.

I wandered around the chilly Boston Common, padded along the Freedom Trail for hours, investigated Bunker Hill like the good soldier I was, wandered through book stores and an instrument shop, and sipped a seven-dollar cappuccino at a café by myself.

Sipping that cappuccino—which tasted admittedly

verging on miraculous since, at three in the afternoon, my energy and will to go on were flagging—I let what'd been sitting on my shoulders all day down to inspect it: I wanted Whit.

In all the ways, I wanted her, and it made no sense for my life. I had no idea of my direction. I would disappear into the madness of her life, get lost in the ruffles of fame and sequins before I could find my way. It was stupid to even let myself think it, but there it was, glaring back at me in the swirling foam of my drink.

It wasn't all fun and games anymore—not that it ever really had been. It wasn't simply me fulfilling my side of the deal, a deal supposedly motivated by me getting access to travel and maybe sporting events and award shows.

Right.

And a year ago, that would have made me feel inconsolable. A year ago, that might have kicked off a long weekend with whiskey as my only friend, eventually texting Thatcher or Flint back after ignoring them, allaying their concerns that I'd done anything irreparable.

Now, it gave me something like determination. Or at least, it didn't feel as dead-end as my logical brain thought. That *you are, too* rang in my head as I slugged back the last of the liquid before it cooled completely, and then wrapped up in my scarf, hat, gloves before launching myself back out into the Boston winter to find her.

I came in the hotel suite to the tune of Whit's voice arguing with Nikki, yet again.

"I'm going to be working with him a lot if we get the Oscar nod, too. What'll we do then, have Ben propose to me on stage?"

Whit was pacing around the living room in sweats and a

T-shirt while Nikki sat stiff on a chair in front of the windows, her clothing black and business-like as always.

Nikki's voice sounded casual. "Of course not! If we do an engagement, we need it to be more of a surprise, but make sure someone's snagging photos—"

"You are not serious." Whit's voice, on the other hand, sounded deadly.

Nikki must have let the door opening and closing register, because she shifted her focus to me. "Ben, you need to kiss Whit tonight at the event. Make sure it's public, make sure it's *good*."

My heart picked up and ran with the idea, though fortunately, my brain didn't start imagining that scenario just yet. With incredible genius, I said, "Uh..."

Whit scampered to me on her tiptoes, practically running. "Ignore her. No."

I looked from her face to Nikki who had now stood, collecting her bags.

"Don't ignore me. The whole point of you being here is to help the image. If that's what you agreed to, which I happen to know it is since you signed a contract to that effect, then you'll kiss Whit like you're gaga over her and make the press and everyone else forget about the fact that she's repeatedly been seen with Jamie Morris, a man whom she supposedly cheated on."

Whit's face appeared thunderous. I'd never seen her look angry—nothing close, if this was it. She took a long, slow breath, then said in a deceptively calm voice, "Nikki. I'll see you in DC."

Nikki's dark eyebrows lifted. She blinked slow, then padded soundlessly to the front door. When she opened it, she looked directly at me. "Remember why you're here."

Then she was gone.

I turned to Whit who seemed to be having a rather animated conversation with herself and touched her lightly on the elbow. "Talk to me."

She took another slow breath. "You don't have to do this."

She wouldn't meet my eye.

I waited for her to turn to me, but she kept herself tilted away, not allowing herself to turn.

"Whit, look at me." She moved slowly and brought her eyes to look into mine. "I'd be honored to kiss you."

Nothing about her face changed except the color of her cheeks, then the visible rise and fall of her chest. "You don't have to. I'm sick of the press."

I stepped closer, putting my hand on her shoulder. "It wouldn't be a burden, I can tell you that."

If I was breathing a little heavily, could you blame me? We were plotting out the very thing I'd been trying to figure out how to accomplish the entire half hour walk back to the hotel.

She chuckled despite her serious face. "You're too sweet. This is too much."

Next, she studied her hands.

"I'm pretty sure kissing is a normal part of any relationship." I inched a little closer, watching her, waiting.

One of her dark brown brows raised, then lowered as she looked up at me again. "I don't want you to feel pressured about this. I'm ready to—"

"I'm fine. I promise you I'll tell you if something happens I'm not okay with. But I have a stipulation."

I searched her face, the tension in it obvious. Her mouth was pressed into a thin line, hiding her plush lips. Her jaw seemed hard, making that line I'd like to study up close more vivid.

She cleared her throat. "What's that?"

Where I got the boldness, I'd never know, though I was glad for it.

"I don't want our first real kiss to be in front of a bunch of strangers and cameras."

Her eyes fluttered, and adrenaline shot through me as though it hadn't been cranking already.

"It'll look forced, maybe even *look* like a first kiss. It shouldn't look that way... it should look practiced, and—"

"I see what you're saying. I do. Okay, so let's... I guess we should practice."

That voice. It wrapped around me like a silk robe, not something I'd ever thought about wearing or touching or being wrapped around me, but that was her voice.

All I could do was nod. No way I'd kiss her now, even though she stood right there, looking up at me, the neck of her T-shirt sliding off one shoulder.

She cleared her throat again—wait, was that a nervous tick?

"Okay, well, we probably better get dressed. The cocktail thing is at five."

"Okay. I'll be ready."

CHAPTER TWENTY

Whit

I'd be honored to kiss you.

It wouldn't be a burden, I can tell you that.

Oh, honey, did I know what he was talking about.

I would have kissed Ben Holder the night I met him if he hadn't been such a wreck. I say that with all the possible compassion my heart can summon, because more than anything, that night, he'd needed a hug. I hadn't given him that, either.

And now, every time I saw him, it was like he was a giant magnet and I was steel, feeling drawn and pulled and urged toward him regardless of what lay between us.

Let's be honest about that—a lot lay between us.

First, I was one of the most famous people in the US, maybe the world.

Second, I wasn't great at focusing on anything other than my career. And by _wasn't great_, I meant I never had done much of anything but think about me and my career—not since I was a teen, and even then, my focus had been on music. I'd certainly never factored in another person.

Third, he had no idea what he wanted—Army, or not?

My heart of hearts told me he'd end up staying—patently incompatible with my lifestyle.

And we couldn't forget the whole *contracted to be my fake boyfriend* thing, though a not-small part of me whispered several hundred times a day, "What if he was your *actual* boyfriend?"

That part of me was what had me telling Amanda to hold off on the lip. "Just wait. I need to go talk to Ben. Can you do it last, right before we leave?"

She eyed me, a knowing look passing between us. I had very few secrets from Amanda, and this wasn't one. She'd figured out I had more than a casual, business interest in Ben, and she'd declared in no uncertain terms that she was all for it. No way could I have avoided her knowing about the contract, both because she was practically the person I was closest with in this life, and also because she was incredibly observant. "It'll make you human," she'd said.

"Sure, no problem. Are you dressing first?" she said, her side-eye at my sweat pants speaking for her.

"Of course."

I left the bathroom and moved to the bedroom where I pulled on the dress, the satin lining cool against my skin. Damon had swung by an hour ago and done my hair in long, romantic waves, my typical style for events and anything other than a casual concert.

"Good?" I asked, back in the bathroom where Amanda was organizing her supplies.

Her expression told me everything. "He's a goner."

With that, I made my way to Ben's door. It was cracked, so I spoke softly. "Ben?"

"I'm just shaving. Almost ready—come in," came his voice from the bathroom.

I smoothed down the dark green velvet of my dress. The sweetheart neck with off-shoulder cap sleeves was more than a little flattering, and the dress showed off every curve and dip of this body I worked so hard for. It was going on my list of favorites, for sure.

I pushed through the door and took a minute to appreciate how tidy Ben's room was. He hadn't spread out everywhere, maybe out of habit, maybe just because he knew we were leaving in the morning. He had a book on his nightstand, a charging cord, and his bag sat with the lid resting open against the wall on a bag stand.

I walked into the bright lights of the bathroom, prepared to tell him I was ready to get the kiss over with so we could appease the press and move on from this idiocy, and then, I saw him.

More like, I was stunned by the visual brilliance of him in front of me.

He leaned over the counter toward the mirror, his head canted to one side, slowly pulling a razor down the angle of his jaw.

"Hey," he said without moving his lips, though his eyes flitted to me, then quickly back to finish the job.

The thing was, he was so casual. He was so comfortable with me there in his bathroom while he shaved his face, but I was literally vibrating out of my high heels feeling like I'd walked into a steam room, because this guy was standing there in his slacks, belt undone *again* like it was usually the last thing he did up, and shirtless.

Yep. Just topless.

Just miles of golden skin my fingers ached to touch more than I'd ever wanted to strum a guitar. More than I'd wanted to press my fingers against the strings and frets of the Gibson I'd seen in a store in downtown Nashville when, at just sixteen, I *knew* my mother wouldn't allow it.

He flipped on the tap and rinsed the razor, wiped his face on a towel, then his hands. I worked on keeping myself in place, clenching my toes in the base of my heels instead of letting the magnetic pull of him draw me in and attach me to his back. My cheek itched to rest on the expanse between his shoulder blades, my hands begging to run along his sides and wrap around front.

He turned to me.

"You're stunning," he said.

Cue the mildly hysterical giggle that escaped.

"Likewise," I returned, my eyes mapping the chest in front of me.

It was art. *Art,* I tell you. Sculpted in a way that seemed like a joke, the muscles stacked like piles of stone under a liquid-smooth sheet, with everything defined in a way I hadn't expected from someone whose life didn't depend on other people's opinions.

His answering smile seemed pleased. He moved in my direction, his cut chest coming within inches of me. My hands balled into fists.

"You seem... agitated."

"Me?" My voice came out a little high, a little short.

"Yes." His voice thrummed low and smooth, and when I glanced at his face, he seemed more than a little happy at my discombobulation.

"When will you be ready?" I asked, not entirely sure what words were coming out, what to do with myself.

He stepped closer, placing his body mere inches from

mine, and the fresh, clean scent of him filled my senses, along with the warmth emanating from that body.

Oh. Hi.

"In a minute. But I was thinking we should practice before we go."

He took a big breath, then gently put a hand on my waist. He searched my face, and before I could think twice, or wuss out, or let my head explode, I nodded.

The descent of his head seemed achingly slow—literally like my lips were aching to connect with his, but he was moving in a way that gave me every opportunity to stop, to move, to tell him this wasn't what I wanted.

His other hand came to my cheek, and then, we were kissing. My hands found his waist, then slid around and up his back as I stepped fully into his space. His lips were soft, his taste minty and warm, his hold on me gentle. He broke the kiss and pulled back just enough to look at me, but I urged him back down, one of my hands pulling that smooth jaw to me.

He kissed a little like I thought he would, a lot like a surprise. Something dominant and certain that I'd seen in the way he carried himself, in the way he interacted with others, but I'd never felt *with me.*

Or had I?

Every time he spoke to me, talked with me, he was straightforward. This kiss, the press of his body against mine, the pull of his hands on my back, in my hair, was nothing short of honest.

I let my hands glide against the skin of his back, sliding down along his spine and around to the taut muscles of his belly, if that's even what it was called when formed like this. He stepped closer, practically overtaking me, holding me to him with a strength that surprised me.

I pulled back, wobbled a bit, but he steadied me with one hand still at the back of my head and the other locked around my lower back. We breathed together, looking back at each other. He was absolutely breathtaking with kiss-swollen lips and flushed cheeks, his eyes glittering back at me.

I cleared my throat, my nerves returning, if they'd ever left. "So... that's done."

He pressed his lips together like he was trying to resist, but then released me before he started laughing. His smile was practically paralyzing, so vibrant and beautiful.

"All right. Done." He raised an eyebrow at me, as if trying to decipher my mood.

I was still too addled from the kiss, my heart galloping, my skin flushed.

Stepping back out of his grip, I let my eyes skate over his gorgeous torso one more time, and I tripped over a towel on the floor. He grabbed my arm before I hit the wall, and I got my feet under me. Then, he ducked down and forced me to look him in the eye, where I found pure amusement in the twist of his lips.

"So, I'll be in the living room when you're ready." My voice had that husky quality to it, one more piece of evidence for him that his kiss had literally and metaphorically knocked me off balance.

"I'll just be a minute."

I left the bathroom, moved out of his bedroom without a backward glance, and sat lightly on the edge of the dark gray couch of the living room.

That was...

That was...

My mind was a loop. His lips, his hands, his scent, his taste. Again.

His lips, his hands, his scent, his taste.

Again.

I had to knock this off before he came out and saw me, still downright unearthed by the cataclysmic event that had been Ben Holder kissing me. Particularly since, if he followed Nikki's orders, we'd revisit that delicious happening in the next few hours. He'd be fully clothed, which felt like a loss on a couple of levels, but was for the best.

No one else gets to see that Ben is my own personal Abercrombie and Fitch model. Because *yeah*, he had the whole thing going on.

But it wasn't just the physical. He was working his way in, right past the arm's-length approach I took with pretty much everyone. He'd been compelling to me the first time we met. Now, he was unavoidable.

I stood and smoothed the tangles out of my hair, refusing to savor the fact that his hands had put them there. I took a deep breath, slowly let it out, and went to find Amanda so she could do my lips.

CHAPTER TWENTY-ONE

Ben

My hand rested on her lower back, the smooth velvet of her dress the best thing I'd ever touched. She was smiling, stopping every once in a while to chat with someone who flagged her attention. She'd introduce me, I'd shake hands or nod, but I never moved that left hand.

She'd seemed thrown after the kiss, more discombobulated than put together, and for Whit Grantham, that was rare. In fact, I'd never seen her anything but on her game. So it gave me no small thrill to see her flustered, especially since it felt like my blood had turned to lava.

But when I came out and met her in the living room, fully dressed in my black suit, dark gray shirt, and black tie, she'd met me with a warm-ish smile that hadn't quite reached her eyes. It was then I'd started questioning the memory on repeat in my mind since the moment she'd walked out of the bathroom.

No. It had been her hands running over my skin, her tongue responding to mine, her lips moving against mine, her body pressing closer, her cheeks flushed, her balance off-kilter. I hadn't imagined it.

But every polite smile she gave to someone else, every small laugh she gifted out, every simple nod or handshake, felt like a test. It wasn't, of course, but ultimately, it still felt like it. All I wanted to do was pull her into a corner and take up where we'd left off. And the brutal part was, Nikki had tasked me with doing just that.

But when? Where, exactly? And how to get back the Whit I'd had earlier today and not this polite, accommodating one now?

After probably the twentieth mini-conversation, schmoozing like she'd taught a master's class in it, she excused herself to the bathroom. I was left to sip a cocktail—something over the top and too sweet for my taste, so I was barely sipping—and talk to a nice couple who'd paid whatever it was people had paid to come here.

Then up sidled two younger couples who surrounded me.

"So you're with Whit Grantham?" one of the men, decent-looking and slugging away at a martini, asked.

"I am." I'd learned quickly that keeping my responses minimal was the key to not getting too wrapped up with any given conversation too long—a tip Whit had given me the first time we went out, and I'd stuck to it with great success.

"I can see why," the man's date, a glamorous-looking woman said as her eyes took me in from head to toe, then she tipped her drink to me and drank some down.

The other couple both chuckled gamely, but the other

woman said, "And how do you feel about her being with Jamie Morris whenever you're not around?"

I wouldn't have been surprised to see a microphone shoved into my face, but so far, no sign of one. I took a sip of my too-sweet drink to buy time.

"He must be fine with it," the other guys said. "I'll admit I'd take what I could get from Whit Grantham if she wanted to give me some."

He raised his eyebrows at the other guy, and they laughed like old friends.

"Hey, I would too. The woman is—"

"I'm honored to be with Whit," I cut in, not interested in what descriptors these two would use. My neck was getting hot, my jaw tightening.

"You sound thrilled, yeah. So what's she like?" one of them asked.

"Yeah, does she use that voice in bed? My God, that'd be enough to—"

"Excuse me, folks. I've got a call." I waved my phone and hoped I could make it across the room and away from these idiots before my temper exploded. My heart racing, my jaw clenched, I went to find Whit and see how much longer we'd have to stay.

I didn't want to be a creeper, but I wanted to make sure she was okay while I also made sure I was okay. I didn't want to stage the kiss if she was upset, or concerned, or... anything other than ready for it. But if those jerks were questioning me about Morris, then obviously, we had work to do. I took a slow breath in through my nose, held it, let it out.

The restroom doors were tucked away in a dimly lit alcove. Just as I turned the corner, Whit came out of the bathroom, and her brows jumped at the sight of me.

"What's wrong?" she asked, coming right to me, right into my space.

I shook my head once. "Nothing. I think I'm just tired—too much touristy stuff today, I guess."

I wasn't about to complain to her that the room was full of vulgar idiots. She'd come here to do a job—charming people for some reason or another, which I dumbly didn't even remember.

"I don't buy it, Holder," she said softly with a half-smile on her glossy lips.

Something about that dulled the edge of my frustration.

I grabbed for her free hand and slid the other one along her neck and into her hair. "Some of the guests here are idiots."

She chuckled, even though her eyes were flickering all over my face, likely trying to read where this intensity was coming from. "That's almost always true."

"How do you stand it? How can you stand people speculating about you and every part of your life?"

I wanted to press my lips to hers, to back her up against the wall and run my hands over all that dark green velvet. But I stayed standing right in my spot, watching as she responded.

One bare shoulder shrugged, and my heart skipped a beat at the sight, my eyes sliding along the slim line of her collarbone and up to her neck. My thumb stroked along the side of that graceful column, and I pushed my hand a little farther into the hair at the back of her head.

"You just do. I try to keep the main thing the main thing, and all that... it's not the main thing." She squeezed my hand and then dropped hers.

I stepped back to give her some space, reluctantly letting go of her.

"You ready to go?"

I nodded. She led the way, and I placed my hand on her back again. She stopped by the organizer's small circle and said thanks but we had to run. She waved to a few of the people she'd chatted with, and then we were moving to the exit. A whirlwind of people scuttled up to her to say one last thing, get her attention one last time, her wide smile flashing at everyone.

And then, I remembered I was supposed to kiss her. Here. Tonight.

I slid my hand around to her side and tucked her body a bit closer as we approached the doors, but stopped her right in front of them. We could see the crowd outside the restaurant on the sidewalk and the crowd gathering inside shoving to the front to watch her leave.

I turned her to me, there in front of everyone, and ignored the fizzing in my chest. She blinked, realizing what I was doing, and stepped closer. I leaned down, pulled her flush against me, and kissed the hell out of her.

Really. I'm not being arrogant. It was a great kiss. I didn't leave the Earth and start floating above myself, letting sensation fill me and overwhelm every sense like our kiss earlier, but it was damn good and would have looked like a passionate kiss between lovers.

After a minute or so, I pulled back. My eyes took in the woman in front of me, looking thoroughly kissed, her chest and cheeks a touch red, even in the dim lighting.

"Ready?" I asked, admittedly feeling incredibly smug.

She nodded, biting her lip to hide the smile I knew wanted to escape.

We pushed through the doors, the flashes burning our eyes, and the shouting began.

"Whit! Whit! Over here! How does Jamie feel about

your relationship with Ben?"

"Ben! How do you feel about Whit and Jamie working together again?"

"What's it like dating a soldier, Whit?"

"When's the wedding?"

It was amazing how entitled everyone felt to the personal details of her life. It hadn't bothered me early on, but the stiffness registered in my neck, in the pull between my shoulders, as we hurried into the waiting town car.

I pulled the door shut behind me, and before I could do anything else, she pulled my face to hers, and her mouth was on mine as we sped away. She slid her hands from my cheeks to my neck and scooted closer as I savored the feeling of her fingers gliding into the short hair at the back of my head, of her smooth lips moving with mine.

Finally, I pulled back. My pulse was pounding, and I could barely find my voice. "We're gone. No more cameras."

I watched as her eyes flickered back and forth between mine, her chest rising and falling in a torturous way in that sweetheart dress, and then, it happened.

Whit Grantham didn't pull away, tidy up her hair, and replace her lip gloss. No.

She shook her head just once, like she'd decided something, and then she pressed her cool hands against my neck and guided my head back to hers. She nipped at my top lip, then the bottom, while my mind resembled something like a record scratch, scrambling to make sense of what was happening.

This wasn't for the cameras. This wasn't for the PR. This wasn't to clarify that she wasn't cheating on me, hadn't done anything wrong.

No. This was for her.

And let's be honest, for me, too.

CHAPTER TWENTY-TWO

Whit

If someone had looked inside my mind six months ago and made a list of the things that lit up my brain and made me *hungry*, made me come alive, those things would have been:

1. Performing my own music
2. Writing music
3. Eating grilled cheese sandwiches

If someone made a similar list today, that list would be

1. Performing my own music
2. Kissing Ben Holder
3. Talking with and being near Ben Holder

That's right. Kissing and talking to and being near Ben

Holder had handily supplanted both writing music *and* grilled cheese.

I know.

This was big, making me not entirely sure what to do with myself. I was pretty sure he wanted to be with me as much as I did him, but he'd tried not to come on too strong. And I appreciated that. My life was one long series of people coming on too strong—for autographs, for connections, for what I could do for them.

Funny enough, I wanted to do whatever I could for Ben, but he didn't seem to want anything from me. We'd gotten word I wouldn't be doing the football half-time show— they'd had a Country act two out of the last three years and wanted to go pop. Ben had been sorry for me, but when I'd made it clear I wasn't upset, neither was he. He hadn't pouted at the loss of something I'd dangled in front of him as an incentive like I thought he might have.

He wasn't concerned. He just wanted to celebrate *me* when I succeeded, or let me feel however I felt when I didn't. It was the strangest thing.

My parents had never celebrated anything. Birthdays had been a nice dinner with dessert, usually a flourless dark chocolate cake too decadent for a child to enjoy. Even when I met their expectations and got into Juilliard, I received little more than a *well done*.

When I won the contract at the end of *SouthernStar*, I was fairly certain there'd been wailing and gnashing of teeth, the neighbors (if the people living miles down the stately country road could be called neighbors) calling in the professionals to deal with the great Grantham disap- pointment. The show was vulgar and beneath me, and certainly beneath them. We simply didn't speak of it.

And that was one of many reasons why I had auditioned under a fake name and had kept it since. Not entirely fake, but different enough that my parents didn't have to acknowledge me, nor did I them.

So Ben turning to me and saying "I'm so proud of you," or demanding to toast me after the Grammy nominations—those things were catnip for me. It was pathetic, on one hand, that his applause and congratulations meant so much to me when I was constantly surrounded by people who lauded my ability, awarding and celebrating and marking the milestones of my career. On the other hand, he didn't do it because he'd been hired to.

False, said my inner voice of reason. And it was false, on one hand.

Technically, he'd agreed to be Team Whit for a few months. And he was getting travel and hotel rooms and concerts and *access*.

But anytime I was with him, I could tell those were simply not why he was there. He was there for *me*, for some reason, and that both excited me and unnerved me. It proved confusing, his insistence on choosing to support me and show up when so few people did that without holding out a hand and asking what was in it for them.

Maybe I was trying to make something into nothing.

I probably am.

But I couldn't ignore the fact that being with him, even just talking, lit me up. And funny enough, it made me want to write—it'd had me writing—like I hadn't since he'd told me his story and hadn't even known it was me.

Oh, about that.

Yeah. I knew I needed to tell him. I couldn't quite pin down what was stopping me.

Well, actually, I did know.

I was worried. Ben was so decent, so sweet, with just

one thing that he really struggled with. The same thing I'd ultimately shared with the world in the form of a song. The same song that, when I was nominated for a Grammy, he'd toasted me for.

Would he hate me? Would he feel betrayed? Would he even care?

I hoped he wouldn't. But the longer I went without telling him, the higher the likelihood he'd feel betrayed by me—by a woman he didn't know, but to whom he'd spilled his rawest feelings after the most traumatic time in his life.

Yeah. I should worry.

That wouldn't have mattered so much to me a month or so ago. But this tour had forced us together in the most irretrievable way imaginable. I could no longer pretend that my heart didn't beat faster at the sight of him. I could no longer pretend that when I closed my eyes, he wasn't the fantasy that populated my mind. I could no longer pretend that all I wanted him for was fulfilling a sham contract to be my fake boyfriend.

I wanted him to be mine, really mine, and I wanted to forget about everything else.

How to get to that place, I had no clue. It'd been three days since I'd kissed him in the car, no audience, and he *must* have gotten the message that I wanted him for *him*. Right?

But he'd been friendly, sweet. He'd done everything a dear friend would, but he'd made no move to be close to me or alone with me.

To be fair, it hadn't been all that possible. That night, Nikki'd left a message for me with a long list of to-dos once I got back from the cocktail party, and Ben had excused himself to lie down. He'd passed out on his bed, and I'd kissed his forehead before I turned in without him ever knowing.

The next day, we'd loaded tour busses, and the madness had resumed. I'd performed that night, then we'd been back on a bus to the next city, this being the window where the shows were closest together.

The day after that, we'd hardly seen each other while I did a photo shoot and packed in a million other marketing events.

But tonight was Christmas Eve, and we didn't have anything until late tomorrow when we'd hop back on the bus and travel south to Pennsylvania. Tonight we were in New York City, one of my favorite cities, and I didn't want to do anything but sit and look at Ben and ask him if he liked me.

Maybe I could send him one of the notes like kids supposedly did in grade school. Pull a George Strait and ask him to "Check Yes or No." He was a George fan—he'd get it if I just played the song, right?

I dragged my hands over my face and wondered what to do. Ben was, most likely, planning to spend the evening with me. Wasn't he? And then, I realized... what if he was missing home? What if he was missing his family and wishing he was with them in Alabama instead of with me, contractual girlfriend and occasional kissing partner?

I smoothed back the edges of my hair, making sure it was still secured back in the stylish ponytail Damon had done earlier for my visits to the morning shows and then a handful of label events. I was exhausted, but I hadn't seen Ben all day, or really in what felt like days

I knocked on the door to his bedroom.

"You decent?" I hollered, partly hoping he'd say yes but end up topless at the very least.

No answer, so I knocked again.

"Come in," his deep voice came through the door.

I slowly opened the door, eager to see him. He sat on his bed, back against the headboard and a pile of pillows cushioning him. He had headphones dangling from one ear, the other side apparently removed—probably why he hadn't heard my first knock. He wore jeans and a short-sleeved shirt that hugged his shoulders and chest, but still looked comfortable. His hair was messy, and he had what looked to be a three-day beard, which meant he was as scruffy as I'd ever seen him.

In a word: delicious.

His eyes had tracked me moving into the room, a confusing mix of hungry and remote. My stomach had twisted into knots by the time I sat on the edge of his bed next to his feet.

"Hey, Ben," I said, trying to act all kinds of casual and no-big-deal about how fluttery seeing him relaxing in his natural state made me.

One side of his mouth quirked up into a smile. "Hey, Whit."

Just hearing him say my name made me smile, but I tried my best to keep it under wraps. "What're you listening to?"

His gaze flickered to his phone, and he pulled out the headphones so I could hear. The last verse of Waylon Jennings' "Just to Satisfy You" came on, and I laughed. "You do love Waylon, don't you?"

"I do, but why do you say that?"

Then I realized he'd told me he loved Waylon last year, not in our current relationship. And it was the perfect opening. I imagined myself in that moment, a fleeting vision, taking his hand and pressing it to my lips and saying, *"You told me once..."*

But I didn't do that. No, I cowered, the trill of fear that lined my rib cage stopping me from taking the chance.

"You seemed to love 'Nashville Bum,' and I've gathered you prefer old Country, so it makes sense." I smiled mildly, hoping that sounded legitimate, hoping he couldn't tell how uncomfortable I was lying to his face.

"You're right. I do prefer the old guys. And women, for that matter. It was just different a few decades ago, you know?" He sounded genuinely troubled.

He tapped his phone to turn down the volume so the next song, a George Jones track called "Walk Through This World with Me" accompanied the conversation without interrupting it.

"Yeah. I loved Patsy Cline and Loretta Lynn. That's what got me started wanting to perform."

"Really? Did your family listen to Country?" he asked, wrapping the cord of his headphones up and slipping them into a little baggy.

It didn't surprise me he didn't have wireless ones—nothing about Ben was flashy or demanding to have the newest and best stuff.

"Uh, no." A light chuckle covered the discomfort.

He tilted his head to one side like it would help me see him better. "You never told me about your family."

"No, I haven't."

"What's the story there? Obviously, it's not your favorite subject, but at this point, I hope you know you can trust me," he said, ducking to catch my eye.

I rolled my lips between my teeth and let out a forced breath. "My parents had me trained in classical music—

piano. I went to Juilliard, but dropped out after a little over a year to go compete on *SouthernStar*."

His mouth dropped open a little, then snapped shut. "Juilliard?"

"Yeah. I was good." An understatement, which he could tell if the grin on his face meant anything.

"I'm sure you were. So what'd they say when you dropped out of school?" He leaned back and rested his hands behind his head.

"Um... not much. We haven't really spoken." I studied the clean white stitching on the comforter beneath me.

"That was..."

"Four years ago, about."

He swore under his breath, then wrapped his hand around my arm.

"Come here," he said in that low, sweet voice.

He pulled me over to him and tucked me into his side, my head on his shoulder, arm between my body and his, my body and legs stretched out next to his. He pulled my other arm over his belly and then set his hand on my wrist. "Tell me."

I tilted my head up to see his face, and he stared back at me. He nodded, urging me on wordlessly.

"My legal name is Eleanor Whitley Ford Grantham."

CHAPTER TWENTY-THREE

Whit

He smiled. "That's pretty."

"It's a mouthful. But it's nice enough. When I signed up for the show, I used Whit... I'm not even sure why except that I knew I wanted a degree of separation from my parents and their disapproval. I knew they'd be disappointed by me leaving school, and they wouldn't understand me giving up their dream for me in favor of my own dream."

The arm holding me to him squeezed me tighter, and that big, solid hand ran up and down my back. That moment of sweetness and solidity grounded me, and for the first time, I didn't feel as much dread as I'd expected at revealing my big lie—well, one of them—to this forthright, genuine man.

"When I got to the show, they didn't like the angle of me being a rich kid classically trained in music, so they left the details blank, but over the years, the label and even Nikki have dropped hints as though I came from poor, Kentucky roots. If anyone has ever made the connection to the wealthy Granthams of Louisville, they haven't exposed me yet." That familiar mixture of disappointment and regret churned in my belly.

"You don't need to be ashamed because you came from money, Whit."

"I know. I'm not, really. I never was. I'm ashamed of my family because they're unfeeling and embarrassed by me." My voice became a whisper. "And it makes me so angry, I can't stand to think of them."

His soothing hand ran over my back for a minute while I stuffed down all that anger and disappointment, knowing the *poor me* feelings weren't going anywhere useful. "So that's my sad little story that only you and a few others know."

"Why does Flint call you Whit, then? He introduced you that way, anyway."

He'd tucked his chin into my hair, and something about that, feeling his breath on the top of my head, made warmth spread through me to my toes.

"It's actually always been my nickname with the cousins. Only the older generations ever called me Eleanor. But my parents enrolled me at school without indicating a nickname, and all the class rosters said Eleanor, my room-mate had been given the name Eleanor... so only the people who really got to know me there knew me as Whit."

"I hate to say this about anyone, but your parents are crazy."

I hugged him the best I could. "Thanks."

His stomach tensed like he was going to say something more, but he stopped and let out a slow, silent breath.

We sat like that, quiet in each other's arms, his phone playing old Country by Willie Nelson and Merle Haggard and all the good ol' boys until it died.

"Do you want to go out tonight?" he asked, his hand now stroking along my arm.

I took a slow breath. "Not really."

"You know it's Christmas Eve, right?"

I could hear a smile in his voice.

I sat up right next to him and studied his face, let my hand float up and touch the curve of his jaw, letting the prickly-soft hairs of his new beard tickle my fingers. "Are you missing your family?"

"A little. We never did have huge celebrations because my dad was often gone, so it's not unusual for us to be apart." He pressed my hand closer to his cheek and leaned his head into it.

That simple action made my heartrate triple, the beats tripping over each other in rapid succession so I got breathless just sitting there, touching his bristly cheek. "I'm sorry you're missing them. Maybe someday, I can apologize."

"I'm sure they'd love to meet you." His blue eyes seemed somehow more blue, and infinitely more intense.

"I'd like to make it up to them," I said, my voice useless. I glanced down at his lips, swallowed, flicked my eyes back to his.

He wore that half-smile that killed me now. "Don't feel too bad. I'm right where I want to be."

His eyes moved between mine, and we both knew it was coming. We both felt it was long overdue—of course, only I felt that, I couldn't confirm, but when he leaned up just as I moved down, I knew it. Our mouths were inches apart, approaching each other so slowly, like we were in danger of frightening the other one off, my heart downright lurching toward his, throwing itself again my ribcage like it had to escape, had to get to his heart, or it'd expire.

Or maybe that was how I felt about our lips meeting, finally, after days of missing him. Just as our mouths touched, through the sweet shock of sensation in the smoothness of his lips and the slight tickle of his beard on my chin, the hotel room phone rang, the worst sound I'd ever heard, and we both jumped apart.

I put a hand to my chest, trying to calm the riot there and steady my breath, and he chuckled and ran a hand through his hair. He frowned at the phone on the bedside table and then answered.

"Hello?" His voice was nothing short of decadent, all gravelly and rough.

I couldn't hear the answering voice, but I leaned up fully, straightened my dress. It was nothing fancy, but I'd wanted to look decent and festive. I wore a brighter green T-shirt dress, totally inappropriate for New York City on a snowy December night. But I'd never planned to leave the hotel, so who cared?

"Yes, Mom, I'm having a lovely Christmas Eve," he said, arching a brow at me and widening his eyes like he couldn't believe she'd called him on the hotel phone.

I gave him a bright smile and excused myself so they could have some privacy. I needed a minute and didn't want him to feel bad about telling her he missed her.

Far sooner than I expected, he came to find me in the living room, curled up with a book I'd been staring at for a few minutes but hadn't read a word of.

"Everything okay?" I asked.

"Yep. She got worried when I didn't answer my phone. After the last year or so, we have an agreement that I will always answer within a half hour if it's after work hours. If I don't, she gets worried."

Something sad or guilty flickered over his face, and that familiar pull to him, the desire to hold him and kiss away all the hard things he'd dealt with, tugged at me again. It didn't work that way, sure—I knew it, but it didn't change me from wanting to try.

"So when you didn't answer, she hunted you down."

"Yeah. I sent Bea the itinerary so at least someone would know where I was... just in case, you know? They like to know what I'm up to, but Bea is the least likely to blab since she barely talks anyway."

"Why?" I asked, curious about Beatrice. He'd mentioned her a few times, but he mostly talked about Bridgette.

"She's just shy. Very, very shy. Introverted, not big on people or... most things." He smiled to himself and sat next to me on the couch.

"What'd she say when you told her we were dating?" I wanted to know what he'd said about all this, but didn't know how to ask for those details.

"She was quiet, but didn't seem surprised, which is sweet. Bridgette was a bit more incredulous—had a lot of questions."

His cheeks flamed adorably, and I set my book down and turned toward him to face him.

"What questions did she ask?" I was snuggled into the couch now, knees and dress tucked under me, one elbow propping up my head on the back of the couch, the other hand resting on my knees.

I wanted him to take that hand. I wanted it to be his to take.

"She hit me with a whole list. Who, what, when, where, why, how."

I laughed as he listed them.

"Yeah, she's nosy."

"She sounds like a very engaged big sister."

He nodded. "She is. She still worries about me... I know Bea does too. But I can finally tell them I'm not worried about me—at least, not in the way I used to be."

I took his hand in mine and folded our fingers together. "How do you feel about that?"

"I understand why they worry. I do. I know I was in a bad place, and they needed to worry about me, or I gave them a reason to. And Dillon's sister Bec, she's someone I worry for. I know that the time passing doesn't necessarily erase that worry."

"That's wise of you. Are you close with Bec?" I asked, working to keep my tone neutral.

"I don't think Bec is especially close with anyone. Thatcher and I have tried, but I know being with us hurts her in some way, reminds her of her brother and makes her feel the loss even more. She doesn't seem like anything's wrong, but when you talk to her, you can see it. You can *feel* the ache in her, even if she won't let you acknowledge it."

I studied his face for a moment, wishing I had the strength to stop myself from asking the next question. "Do you love her?"

CHAPTER TWENTY-FOUR

Ben

My face had to show my surprise.

"No. Well, maybe in some ways, because I loved Dillon as a close friend and some of that has transferred to her, I guess. They were twins—look a lot alike, but I think part of me feels that brotherly love for her. But I—my interest in her isn't like that."

I held Whit's gaze steadily, making sure she understood. Making sure there was no chance she'd think I was interested in anyone but her.

"I'm sorry you worry for her. That must be hard," she said, her voice soft and smooth.

I took a long, slow breath. "Yeah. It's frustrating—there's no good way to help someone when they refuse to acknowledge their need for help. Until then, I'll pray for her, and show up whenever I can."

Whit's eyes sparkled back at me. "You're a good man, Benjamin Michael Holder."

My stomach dropped out at her saying my full name.

I raised and dropped a shoulder. "I'm all right."

She chuckled, and then her face turned serious again. "Why was your sister so shocked you were dating me?"

"You're A-list. It's pretty rare to meet someone like you to begin with, but to date someone like you... it doesn't happen to normal dudes."

"You're not exactly normal, Ben," she said, like that was something I would know.

"What do you mean?"

She let go of my hand and crossed her arms over her chest. An unusual thing for her, which I only realized when she did it, and it seemed so foreign to me.

"You are exceptional."

I opened my mouth to laugh, or refute her, but nothing came out. My eyes were wide as I searched her face, no response emerging.

"Don't look so shocked. You are. You have been through incredible hardships and personal lows, but you've worked to get out of them. And I can't tell you how much I respect your openness about that—that you don't try to pretend the things you went through didn't matter or didn't change you. That's amazing."

Her breathing had elevated a bit, and her arms tucked even more tightly together.

"It's nice you think that." I wasn't sure what else to say. My gaze moved over her, trying to figure out the deal with those crossed arms. I much preferred us holding hands. "Why are you all tied up now?"

"What?"

"You wrapped in on yourself. You have your arms

crossed so tightly around you, I bet your lungs can't fully expand. What's up?" I sat up on the couch, leaned toward her to get closer, right in her face, for some reason.

She swallowed and looked down at her arms like she hadn't realized that's how she was sitting. "I, um... I didn't want to touch you."

She shot me a false little smile.

"Why?"

My heart knew before my mind did, though. It was warming up, getting ready for the sprint.

She started to speak, then stopped herself. Her cheeks were flushed and made a stark contrast to her usually very fair skin and her green dress. For a woman with incredible lung capacity, she was breathing in shallow, useless breaths.

"Because all I want to do is touch you."

The words broke out, as if against her will. She smashed her lips closed and blinked at me.

It took me only a second or two to react.

I reached around behind her, cupping the back of her head, and brought her face to me before she even got those arms uncrossed. My hands slid along the smooth hair pulled into a long ponytail, and my lips crushed against hers. Another second, and she had her hands on my rough cheeks, running into my hair, over my shoulders.

I sat taller, and she leaned toward me so our bodies pressed against each other, both instinctively seeking to close the gap between us that, now that I thought about how long it'd been there, was unfathomable.

For minutes that moved in slow motion and yet felt like we were skipping ahead, we reveled in each other, kissing like it was our first and last kiss, every part of me wanting her, searching for her, needing her. At the tipping point—

the one where things would progress past the line of stopping if we kept going, we both pulled back.

I guessed I looked as wild-eyed and well-kissed as she did.

Good grief, she's gorgeous.

It was nearly painful to sit there next to her and give her space to breathe—give myself space to breathe before I ripped off her dress and made her part of me.

"We should take a breath," I said reluctantly. *Oh, how reluctantly.*

The tilt of her head held a question.

"We should. Or this will be way more than either of us signed up for," I explained, wishing I didn't care, that I hadn't made myself promises in the last year that mattered to me.

"I—" she started, but stopped. She took a deep breath and tucked a stray hair behind her ear. "I'd like to talk about that."

"About..." I wasn't about to put words in her mouth.

"About what you signed up for. And what we're doing here. I feel like things are different now." Her eyes were riveted on my face, watching for any reaction.

Unfortunately for her, I had an incredible neutral face. It wasn't all that neutral—really, it was the opposite of severe. Just a resting smiling face. My mouth naturally turned up, the smile lines just getting started at the corners of my eyes, my general demeanor all saying *I'm here for the party*. It was something I'd perfected over the years.

I'd always been pretty much *that guy*. The good times guy up for a game, a prank, a drink, a kiss, a drive, whatever. And when I wasn't, I didn't allow myself to show it. People always commented on how laid back I was, how up for anything I was, and I wanted it to stay that way.

But Afghanistan and Dillon's death had cut that out of me. I wasn't the up-for-anything guy all the time anymore— guess I was doing a decent enough job showing that to people like Whit since she'd commented on how amazing I was at being real. I wasn't sure that was my goal, but I was tired of pretending everything was dandy.

With all that, though, I did still have one hell of a neutral face. It gave me time to process, to weigh things, and to let myself decide whether I was going to ride the laid-back train, or whether things would need more of my attention and emotion.

"Okay. Tell me your thoughts," I said. A little cheap, yes, but she was the person in the position of power, both because of who she was and how I felt about her.

I wasn't about to flay myself wide open for her if she just wanted someone to mess around with. I may or may not have held my breath for what would come next.

She squinted at me, then a wry smile curled her lips. "I think you like me. I like you. I think we're kissing in a hotel room with no cameras because we like each other."

The breath came out on a chuckle. "Your observations are sound."

"And I think it would be easy for us to just *date*-date instead of fake-date."

Impressive. She was so direct. I'd expected more tiptoeing.

"Just like that, huh?" I asked, trying to be casual when all I wanted was to pull her close and spend the rest of the night like that.

"Pretty much. We're adults. I think it's kind of lucky that we like each other." She clasped her hands together and rested them in her lap.

I liked the idea, no denying that, but what if...

"What happens when you get sick of me? Being friends is easier to maintain, and easier to break off when the arrangement isn't doing what it's intended for. If we date and something goes wrong before it's good for you, what do we do then?"

And maybe a large part of me was wondering what happened when she realized how little I had to offer her. I worried for how awkward she'd feel when she realized she didn't admire or respect me the way she thought she did once I was out of the Army and had no idea what came next.

"Good question. I guess we hope it doesn't go wrong?"

Her small smile warmed something cold in me, setting to thaw what had been frozen in doubt.

I reached for her then, pulled her gently to me, and kissed her lips. "I'm not about to turn you down. But I don't think we should start by going for broke. Let's go easy. It feels like if we go all out, it might blow up sooner."

Her brow wrinkled, and she pursed her lips, clearly not agreeing with me. "If that's what you want, that's okay with me."

"Okay, good. Since it's too early to go to bed, what do you want to do?"

"Any chance you'd want to take a walk and see the tree?"

CHAPTER TWENTY-FIVE

Whit

This man was out to test my patience in a way no one ever had.

He didn't walk like a New Yorker. And even though I'd only lived here a year, I still had it in me. Wandering around New York City that night, the streets flooded with people visiting Rockefeller Center and gazing at the Christmas tree, all of it—he moved slow in every possible way, like he was forcing me to stop and take notice of my surroundings instead of plowing ahead toward a goal.

How utterly maddening.

But worse, definitely, was his insistence to move slow with *us*. I could sense he had *reasons* for that, though his stated reason that moving our relationship at a slower pace would avoid a faster burnout—that made sense, I had to admit.

But a soon as he'd said it, a weighty sense of dread and disappointment had settled around my shoulders. The startling thought, *what if I don't want it to end at all?* had flashed through my mind. It made no sense. We'd only fake-dated. We weren't in love.

The thing was, though... I thought maybe I could love someone like Ben. I'd never had that thought. Not with the guy I dated at Juilliard, not anyone I'd dated since getting big, and certainly not with Jamie Morris, as endearing and beautiful as he was.

Ben was the first one, and something in my mind had known it from the first time we'd talked.

There it is again.

I needed to tell him, definitely. At this point, we could laugh it off. I could just say, "Hey, Ben, this is so crazy, but one night at Black Smoke Café, I sat by you while you downed whiskey and confessed your darkest fears and pain to me without knowing it was me. And then I wrote a song about that, and it got really huge. You know the one. Cool, huh?"

Yeah. That'll go just fine.

I'd had several chances to tell him lately, but I'd backed away. But it wasn't a Christmas Eve conversation, was it? Clearly not.

After we'd walked to the tree and come back, then sat on my bed and ate room service, we snuggled up and watched *The Holiday* and laughed at Jack Black. We parted with a far-too-sweet kiss, and that was that.

Christmas day was strangely busy, and I wasn't sure what Ben did for most of the day. Soon enough, we were back on the road, then another concert, then another, constantly in the bus, and finally in Nashville for two nights, and it was New Year's Eve. This was the last I'd see of him until this mini-tour wrapped up. An annoying sadness descended on me at the mere thought of saying goodbye to him a full week and a half before I'd be back and the tour completed.

I had to remember this—he lived in Nashville; I lived in Nashville. We'd been able to see each other every week or so before the tour, and we weren't even dating then. We'd be just fine.

That was ignoring the fact that his job could send him away. In a very real way, Ben could become entirely inaccessible to me. We hadn't talked much more about his work. Last we'd spoken about it, he'd seemed unhappy and unsure. I had no idea what it looked like to get out of the Army. The one and only person I knew in the military was my cousin Reese, and he'd put in almost twenty years. He was going to retire.

Now Ben and I were at a swanky party in some fancy hotel or building or something—honestly, I hadn't paid attention on the call with Nikki earlier and hadn't really even noticed when Ru had pulled up to the door and Ben had settled his hand low on my back as we'd walked in.

It'd been an insane day. I was supposed to be very present this time of year, and it exhausted me, but I hadn't been around quite long enough to just do what I wanted. I envied stars like Adele who'd established from the very start that people didn't have access to her at all times.

Smart woman.

But Johnson liked people who were *engaged*, and that appealed to his desire to see his soundtracks and songs win big awards. It was also a big expectation in Country, I'd found, in a way that it wasn't so much for others. Or maybe that was my own self-imposed ideology, but there you had it.

Ideally, I'd snag an Oscar here in another couple of months, but I had no sense of how competitive Jamie's and my song was. That should help things, get me closer to some of the autonomy I was still waiting for in terms of being irresistible for projects I wanted and decisions I could make but usually wasn't allowed to.

We'd been at the party for an hour already, and my feet hurt. I wanted nothing more than to head home and sleep in my own bed for the night. Preferably with Ben nearby.

"Ba-by *girl*, you're looking fine tonight," Colton Danes said as he sidled up next to me.

It was an industry party chock-full of photo ops and posing with fellow celebrities. I'd managed to evade Danes thus far, but my luck had evidently come to an end.

"Hi, Colton." No warmth or welcome were present in my greeting.

I looked around for Ben—he'd been snagged by someone who was not likely to let him get away easily. Ben had one arm crossed over his chest and tucked under the opposite arm's bicep, that arm hanging by his side with his drink idly swirling, his head ducked and nodding as he listened.

My heart got a glowy, sweet feeling as I looked at him. Regretfully, I turned to face Danes.

"I keep askin', and you keep sidesteppin' me. When're we gonna make some sweet music together, baby?"

He tried to crowd into my space, but I literally side-stepped him to create a bit of distance.

"I'm not sure. I hate to say it, but with making up these tour dates, my schedule's just crazy. You know how it is when the dates gets delayed."

And yeah, he did. He'd been arrested for DUI during

his last tour and had had to cancel a few dates while he dealt with that teeny tiny problem.

"Ah, I see how it's gonna be," he said with a smile, like he knew better. He stepped to me and put a hand on my arm, his eyes lingering on my chest. "Why don't you let me convince you to make some time for me?"

A warm hand slid around my waist, and Ben pulled me to his side. "I'm sure Whit'll let you know if she's interested in working with you."

I resisted the urge to give Ben a surprised look because I wasn't mad he was getting rid of Colton Danes, but I was definitely not sure how he'd gotten to me, or where this side of him came from. He was so casual, laid back, and not at all possessive. Part of me liked that, though I wouldn't have minded if he showed a little more jealousy. But in the end, that would make for a lot of useless drama because I was surrounded by people paying me compliments and sometimes literally proposing to me. For anyone I dated, they had to get that.

Ben did. But apparently, he didn't like Colton Danes touching me, and I was certainly in agreement.

"Oh, big soldier man comin' over here to lay it down. All right." Danes gave Ben a lazy glance, then turned and dipped his head to me like he was sharing a secret, though he spoke at full volume. "When you get tired of this no-talent Boy Scout riding your tailcoats and looking for hand-me-outs, you give me a call."

He tossed up a peace sign like that was an acceptable way to exit an adult conversation, and off he went.

I let out the giggle that had welled up in my throat and curled into Ben's chest, my face right at the lapel of his jacket. "I'm guessing he meant coattails and hand-outs."

Ben brought his other hand to my back and hugged me to him. "Yeah."

The word sounded hollow. I looked up, fully expecting to see an amused smile on his face, but his features were serious, his brow pinched in the middle as he watched Danes walk away.

CHAPTER TWENTY-SIX

Ben

I pulled up in front of Reese Flint's house and turned the keys of my truck, giving myself just a minute to get my head on straight before going inside. Between Flint and Erin, I'd end up spilling my guts about Whit. I was also probably in for an inquisition about my future with the Army.

It was time. I'd been dreading facing Flint on this and letting it be final, dreading what he as a friend and mentor would think about me abandoning the life I thought I'd live. Abandoning him and everyone who'd gotten me through the last year and a half.

"Hey, stranger," Erin said as she opened the door.

"Hi, lovely. How's my favorite redhead?" I leaned in to hug her just as I heard Flint grumble.

"Paws off my woman, Holder," he said, but took me

roughly by the shoulders and clapped me loudly on the back.

He wasn't delicate, wasn't smooth, and wasn't particularly touchy-feely, but we'd never shied away from our friendship once it had been forged.

"I have no designs on Erin." I shook my head as he ushered me in.

The woman in question moved into the kitchen where the delicious scent I'd smelled upon entering the home intensified.

"Nothing fancy today. Just some beef stew and homemade bread." She took a large ladle and stirred a pot on the stove.

"It smells amazing. Based on everything I've ever eaten that you've made, I'm sure it'll be great."

Flint handed me a beer, and I took it, even though I wasn't sure I wanted one. What I wanted most was to get the grilling over with and move on to talk about them.

"All right. Let me have it," I said, leaning my backside against the counter and crossing my arms.

Flint took up the same post across the kitchen from me, to Erin's left.

"Go ahead, then. You tell us," he said, that stern face no less intimidating than it ever was.

"I went on tour. It was a great experience. We got pretty close. I like her a lot." I studied the edge of my bottle, then took a swig.

"Okay. And now tell me about how you were fake-dating her, but now, you're really dating her. Let's start there."

Flint folded his arms, and Erin shot me a look like *you better buckle up for this.*

"I didn't realize you knew about, uh, the agreement." I shifted, widening my feet to get a better grip on the floor.

I willed the heat that threatened to rise to my cheeks away, not wanting to show him anything more than he'd already seen with his eagle eye.

"I called Whit after Thanksgiving," he said, like that wasn't news.

He grabbed his bottle and nodded toward the living room. I followed after him and sat on the couch. He and Erin sat together on the loveseat, as usual disgustingly cute and endearing.

"Why would you do that?" I asked, kicking my feet up.

"Because I wanted to make sure she wasn't messing with you." He leaned forward and rested his elbows on his knees. "And then, she confirmed what I'd feared—that she was."

"She asked me, I agreed to it. She wasn't messing with me." I did my best to keep the defensive edge to my voice smoothed out.

"But that's just it. You weren't paid, and you got nothing but time with her. I know why, too. She's magnetic, she's charismatic, she's basically walking, singing, guitar-strumming catnip for any red-blooded person with eyes who likes women." He was sitting straight up now, his jaw firm.

"So in your mind, your famous Country-singing cousin was preying on poor little old soldier Ben and his masculine urges?"

Erin bit her lip to hide a smile, which earned her a glare from me. She was staying out of this, but clearly enjoying the volleys.

"Not quite that simplistic, but basically? Yes."

"I'm fine."

"I see that you are. I also heard you say you're really together. Tell me what that means."

He had his executive officer voice on, the one that had bossed the entire battalion around for a year. He'd moved out of that position, but God help him, he couldn't resist using it when he was demanding information from me. And like a good underling, I responded to it.

"We realized we liked each other as more than friends. We decided we'd bag the agreement and just enjoy dating."

It was simple enough, and if he'd been so concerned that I was getting used, he should be happy about his.

He scowled and clenched his jaw. "That easy, huh?"

"Just tell me what your problem is, all right? I can't read your mind, and I don't know why you're pissed at me other than for dating your cousin, but you're not really the type to get all falsely protective of a woman who makes her own choices, so I'm not sure where this is going."

Flint stood, so I did too. We faced each other, nearly eye to eye except for the four inches he had on me. It was as close to eye-to-eye as we got.

"I'm not worried about Whit."

That crashing humiliation I'd been lucky enough to avoid lately came rushing in. "Don't."

Flint shook his head, and Erin ducked back into the kitchen silently. "I'm not implying anything here. I'm just worried about you. Dating someone like Whit isn't simple. It's a huge deal, and it's particularly big for someone who's been single and celibate for over a year."

I swallowed and folded my arms across my chest. "I get that it's a big deal. I never would have thought I had a chance if it hadn't happened the way it did—her, like you said, basically using me, though I was a willing participant. It was a chance to say *yes* to something that seemed a little like an adventure. I haven't had much of that in a long time."

We watched each other, those kind eyes staring back at me and making me wonder what I was missing.

He pulled in a slow breath, let it out. "I get it. I do. And I love my cousin—maybe more than anyone else in my family but my mother. But I'm concerned this tour created a false sense of intimacy. I'm worried you're going through a lot—yes, still—and it's a bad bet to date someone whose life is constantly the subject of gossip. I don't want you sucked in, and I don't want you hurt."

Part of me loved him for being my big brother, my mentor, my dear friend. Another part of me wanted to kick his shins and run out the back door without a word.

"I'm not breakable."

Flint scoffed. "Of course you are. Everyone is."

"I mean about this. I like her, she likes me, we're dating. I know tabloids are going to talk. I'm not worried she's going to cheat on me, and I'm not going to get the news about our relationship from the Internet. If I get confused, I'll talk to her."

"You seem to have it all worked out." He pressed his lips together.

"Whit's great. I'd be an idiot not to see where this goes."

That was true, but his concern, his pushing about this, made me pause. I wouldn't think about it now, wouldn't question myself or her now, but he was someone I listened to, and I'd have to let myself listen later, by myself, when I could hear.

"She *is* great. As are you. I hope you don't lose sight of that," he said, those gray-green eyes looking at me, impressing me with the thoughts.

"Thanks."

"And the other thing..." he said as he walked to the kitchen.

"Go on, get it out."

He turned and shot me a look, one eyebrow raised. "Okay. Where're you going?"

He walked right up behind Erin, pulled the hair from one side of her neck, and kissed her just behind the ear. He must have said something low enough I couldn't hear, because she turned and kissed him, a light blush on her cheeks.

I formulated my thoughts like I'd been doing for weeks, months, and took a seat at the small table in the breakfast nook where we'd eat. We never ate in the formal dining room.

"I don't know where I'm going," I admitted.

Flint carried two plates with bowls settled on them, steam rising from inside, to the table. He set one in front of me, one in front of Erin's spot, then returned to the kitchen and grabbed the third. He returned with the last bowl, and Erin carried a steaming loaf of bread and a crock of butter.

"That's not the worst place to be," he said as he sat down.

"It's not easy. I know that feeling, as you know," Erin said, giving me a look because I had indeed been aware that she wasn't sure what she wanted, even months ago, or at least hadn't known how to get it. "But I think Reese is right. It's not the worst place."

"I'll agree to that. I'm fairly certain I've been in the worst place," I said, then cleared my throat.

Erin patted the back of one hand, and we all mumbled agreement to my statement.

She blessed the food, and then we dug in, Flint groaning so loud, I might have been concerned for him if I hadn't seen him eat Erin's food countless times before and have the same response.

Frankly, it was indecent.

"This is great, Erin, as always," I said, taking another bite of the piping hot stew.

She was an amazing cook, and I'd never had anything less than delicious made by her. It was all the more satisfying that she'd been able to pursue her dream of cooking for people. She'd been building a small clientele around the area for a year or more, but had only just started working on a website and some branding.

"I'm glad you like it." She smiled.

"Ben, not to beat a dead horse, but your time is running out. If you're going to drop your packet, it's going to have to be soon. I bet you get an RFO in the next sixty days," Flint said between spoonfuls of stew.

The knot in my shoulders tensed, the small semblance of pleasure I'd had with my friends and the meal vanishing. He was right. I'd get a Request For Orders to my next duty station, most likely the schooling for the next promotion I'd get in the army to captain, any day. If I was going to get out, I had to drop my packet—officially notify the Army—before moving and going to that school, or I'd be obligated for more time.

"I know."

"I hope you know that I support you, whatever you want to do," he said, his voice gentle, but not pitying, thank God.

"Thank you. I appreciate that. I think I've known what I want to do for a while now, but actually making the call and ending something I thought would be my life for twenty years or more... it's terrifying."

My throat felt dry, my eyes itchy. I took a long drink of my water.

"We'll be here. You'll land on your feet. You've got training and skills, you've got a degree—"

"A useless degree, yeah—"

"It doesn't always have to be dead-on. A lot of jobs only need you to have *something,* and then you can get in the door and get going."

I snorted back a laugh. "That's based on all your experience out in the civilian world?"

He put his palm to my forehead and pushed my head back as I laughed.

"I don't have to have a job in the civilian world to know how it works. I'll admit my primary frame of reference is the Army, but I do know people in other industries. And on that note, if I can help in any way..."

"Thank you. I know. The problem now is I have no idea what I want to do. I know pretty clearly I don't want to stay in, even if saying that makes me want to cringe at the thought of betraying the people I've served with." I folded the napkin and set it on the table.

"That's a myth. You can't stay in for other people. That burns off faster than gasoline. It's not a reason to stay," Flint said, catching my eye.

"I think I've realized that. I just... I don't know what's next."

CHAPTER TWENTY-SEVEN

Whit

"No, thank you," I said as diplomatically as possible.

"What do you mean?" Nikki said, her voice calm, but the little twitch at the side of her cheek told me she was getting tired of me. This happened daily, but it was early to be there already.

"I mean what I said—*no, thank you.*" I poured steaming coffee into a bowl-sized mug and let the too-warm feeling heat my hands as I cupped it.

"That's not a response. Try again," Nikki clipped.

I felt it. It'd been inching its way to the top of me, about to spring loose, and Nikki was the one who kept poking at it. My restlessness, my irritation, my general feeling of being *off* was about to explode all over her.

I wasn't a diva. I never had been. But I was stubborn; I

could be inconsiderate in my single-mindedness, and I knew that.

But times like these, when someone who worked *for* me couldn't take a beat and understand what I was saying... *Lord help me.*

"Okay. I'll try again." The coffee cup went on the counter. I drew in a slow breath, willing the ragey righteousness to calm. "No, thank you, I do not want to perform with Colton Danes at the Grammys."

Her jaw hardened, and I could practically hear her grinding her molars into pearly rubble.

"Whit. Use your brain for a minute here. They want a Country medley, and you're going to do it. You say no, you're going to look like the biggest diva out there. You don't need that on your list of questionable qualities."

My hand was on my hip now, and if I'd had the presence of mind to be chagrined, I might have been. Instead, I lost the tether on my *off*ness.

"Nikki. *What. The. Hell.* Are you talking about? Am I a convict? Am I some notorious lech or drunk or princess? Am I some kind of criminal and I don't even know it? Why can't I say *no* to something that would have me cozying up to that spineless creep?" My voice hadn't raised—not much —but I was spitting mad, and she could see that.

She pressed her lips together and stretched them into a sour smile, the expression one I'd seen before, but maybe not with that glint in her eyes.

"Let me explain this to you so you understand. I'm doing my job—a job you pay me for, and which I do well. You have a reputation—whether you've done anything to actually deserve it or not—that you cheated on Rock and Roll's beloved son. As you pursue working with Johnson, a man who is notoriously old-fashioned, you have to do *every-*

thing I say. *You* made the goals. *You* asked for this to be carried out."

She took a breath, and neither of us spoke.

"I'm sick of this. There's no way rumors should affect my career like this." I stared down into the black coffee in my mug.

"Yeah, well, there's the price of fame, right?" Her bitterness rang clear and had me checking her face.

"Is there anything we need to talk about... beyond this?"

It wasn't uncommon for us to disagree, or even to fight a bit. But lately, the edge between us had been sharper.

"It's fine. I'm just stressed." She gathered up her notebook, computer, and phone. "Am I telling the Grammys yes?"

I let out an audible sigh. "Fine."

She left minutes later. I plunked onto a stool and let myself turn over the last half hour, trying to figure out how it'd ended with a fight and me still performing with that nightmare of a man Danes.

Nikki *was* right when she said I'd set the goal up—I needed to work with John Smith Johnson because working with him, more than anyone else, would give me opportunities I wanted. If I ever wanted to transition to soundtrack and scores, he was my way in, and I needed his wholehearted backing.

To get there, I had to play the game. I had to do what needed to be done, and if that meant tolerating a few rehearsals and sharing the stage with Colton Danes, I could do it. At least a bunch of other people would be suffering along with me.

Ben probably wouldn't be too happy about it, either. But he'd understand. And it wasn't like it was an intimate duet—that was saved for me and Jamie, which didn't seem to rankle Ben in the same way, but maybe that was only because they hadn't been in the same room together.

I wondered what would happen when Ben and Jamie did meet. They'd both been through a lot, and a large part of me thought maybe they'd become friends.

At that thought, my friend and my boyfriend meeting, a pang of longing for Ben hit me. We hadn't even used that term—*boyfriend*—but that's what he was, and I hoped he'd think of me as his girl.

I rolled my eyes at myself and gulped down the last of my coffee, then rinsed the mug, set it in the dishwasher, and wiped down the sink. It was time to face Kendra and my workout. I'd see Ben soon, and after more than a week apart, I wanted it to be good.

~

Ben

Strumming guitar traveled down the hall and into my mind, right to the place where I felt joy and pleasure. Knowing I might get to glimpse Whit in the act of practice or creating had my feet moving faster. Kendra had let me in, mentioning Whit was upstairs practicing in her room.

I kept moving to her doorway, feeling that same sense of the forbidden while approaching the entrance to her space. I'd been in there before in the whirlwind of the first month of our dating but hadn't been back since—hadn't been back to her house, in fact, since we actually started dating.

I hadn't stopped thinking about Flint's concerns for me and his cousin. He seemed so sure she would hurt me, but I hadn't felt that. My own doubt over why she'd want me was real, but I didn't know if I could broach that subject with her without sounding weak and whiney. I'd just climbed out of the hole where I felt weak and sad and scared so often, so not exactly chomping at the bit to get back there, especially in front of Whit.

I stopped in the doorway, leaning against the frame to enjoy the view. Whit sat on her sofa in jeans and a T-shirt, looking out the window at the wintry blue-gold light of the afternoon, her fingers strumming the guitar. I could hear faint hums, but she wasn't singing words. The sounds she made, the focus, the cant of her head to one side—all of it had me feeling a hopeless kind of drop.

When the last chord sounded, she let it resound, then gently laid her fingers atop the strings to quiet them.

"That's beautiful," I said, meaning everything about the moment.

She set aside the guitar and jogged across the room to me. She pulled me into her arms and hugged me—warm, solid, sweet. How I'd missed her.

"Hey, you. How long've you been here?" she asked, but before I could answer, she pecked my jaw, my cheek, but regrettably stopped before she reached my lips.

I smoothed a hand over her hair, which was still a little wet underneath. "A few minutes."

"You should have said something," she said, pulling me after her back to the couch.

"Never."

Just as she bent to grab the neck of her guitar, I swooped a hand around her waist and pulled her back to me, twisting her around and pressing her against me. She wasted no time cooperating—she rose to her toes, wrapped her arms around my neck, and met my lips with hers.

She pulled away and looked at me, my pulse thrumming in my ears just standing next to her.

"You're so pretty," she said, her voice breathless.

A loud laugh escaped me.

"Thank you. So are you," I said, letting my eyes sweep over her in appreciation.

Her smile was bright.

"Was that a new song you're working on?" The notebook with unintelligible scrawl on it lay next to her mechanical pencil, close to the guitar.

"It was. Just a melody so far. The words are just out of reach," she said, a little frown on her face.

"Is that how you see them? Something you have to grab for?"

She flopped down on the couch and pulled me down next to her. "Sometimes. Some songs are right there, all at once—just... the whole thing practically unraveling itself for me as I write it. But others are more elusive. This one's doing that to me. I've had the melody, and I keep thinking if I play it, the words will come, but they're stuck."

"That sounds frustrating. Any of your Grammy nominees the easy kind, or are those all the blood, sweat, and tears kinds?"

It was a fascinating process, and the fact that she really did do the majority of her writing was one of so many things I liked about her.

She looked up from her guitar, her fingers moving over it easily, picking out some tune I didn't know, until I did. The melody of "Stolen Moment" came through.

"This one. This one hit me like a bullet train."

She kept strumming, and I'd never wanted anything as much as I wanted to hear her sing that song for me, right this moment. "Will you sing it for me?"

Her head had been ducked, but she looked up at me and gave me a sweet, relaxed smile. Then, her playing intensified, a fuller sound vibrating out of the instrument of which she was clearly a master.

The words floated over us, all sense and meaning feeling new, stronger, more personal as she sang the words to *me*. Every part of me wanted it to be for me, wanted her to feel that way for me, even if I'd dispatched the brutalized part of me months ago.

She held the last note in a pure tone, then let the guitar finish the song. She dampened the strings and took a deep breath, not looking at me for a few minutes. When she finally did, the look on her face made something in my chest twist and sigh.

"I've sung that song probably a thousand times in the last year, and that was definitely the most intense." She wiped her mouth and set the guitar on the stand.

"Why?"

"The song's about you. It's exactly about what you've been through, and singing it to you, it's just... intense." Her voice a little shaky, she smoothed her hands over her pants, tucked a strand of hair back from her face, took a sip of water.

I'd felt that, the intensity, and I'd felt it was about me—it related to my experience, or it could. It was a song I knew many soldiers valued, and I was no different.

"It's incredible, Whit. It's an amazing song, and I'm honored to have you play it for me."

Her brow creased, two lines marring the expanse, and she started to speak. "No, it's actually—"

My phone rang. It was my mom.

"I'm sorry," I said while showing her the phone.

"Don't apologize. Say hi to your mom for me."

She gave me a too-bright smile I couldn't decipher as I tapped the phone and answered.

CHAPTER TWENTY-EIGHT

Whit

The moment had passed. He chatted with his mom, even put me on the phone. When we hung up with her, the time for confessions was gone.

I'd tried to tell him—I *had* told him, but he hadn't gotten it. Of course he wouldn't, because it wouldn't make sense to him, but the swirling disappointment in me was twofold. The familiar sadness for him ever having been in that dark place, so dark he couldn't recall it, and the secondary and now much more powerful feeling that I was too cowardly to own up to using him and his words.

Pathetic.

"Thanks for talking with her," he said as he tucked his phone into his back pocket.

"Of course. She seems great." Based on who Ben was, and on her attentiveness to him, she must be. My mother and I hadn't talked in years. Literally *years*.

He nodded, a small smile tugging at one corner of his mouth. "She's pretty great. She's strong, determined. You remind me of her in that way."

I stood and shoved my hands down into my back pockets.

"I remind you of your mom?" My brow quirked at that.

"You do, in that you're strong and a little bull-headed, but in a way that means you go after what you want. Bridgette's similar, though there's nothing *little* about her determination to get what she wants." He leaned his elbows on his knees and looked up at me.

I closed the distance between us in a few steps. That little sideways look he was giving me, those bright blue eyes, those lips, that face... I wanted to be right in his way.

"Hmm. I'll choose to take that as a compliment."

He settled his hands on my hips as I came to stand in front of him.

"You should. It is." He looked up at me.

I inched closer and set my hands on his shoulders, let my hand run over the long column of his neck, the curve of his Adam's apple, the once again smooth edge of his jaw.

I swallowed, then said, "I kind of miss your beard."

A pleased smile creased his cheeks. "My leave beard was good, wasn't it?"

His warm hands pressed into my lower back, then slid up and down my back.

"It was."

"But the nice thing about this is, now when we kiss, you won't get beard burn."

I was standing so close that when I looked down at him, his face was directly below mine.

"Is that a fact?" My voice came out low and sultry in a way I hadn't planned.

He nodded, then leaned up just as I leaned down. The kiss was slow, building in a purposeful way, our universe of two completely unaware of anything other than each other.

Until the phone rang again, and I wanted to maybe murder someone.

He pulled back, took a slow breath, then let his head fall to my chest, which was rising and falling rapidly, still caught in the moment.

"I'm sorry," he said, then looked back at me as he let his hands drop away from me.

My body felt colder now that it was no longer in his hold, and I wanted it back.

"Take it if you need to. I'm usually the one getting inconvenient phone calls." A forced chuckle accompanied the words, with little humor in the frustration I felt like a fever.

"What's up?" Ben said into the phone, then shot me an apologetic look.

I took the moment to pick up a few things around the room, tuck away my writing notebook, and then ducked into the bathroom to give him privacy. A few minutes later when I came out, he was talking more heatedly.

"What do you want me to do?" he asked the caller as he went back and forth in front of the couch.

As he paced, he nodded, silently agreeing with whoever was talking. Then, "she won't respond to me. She won't respond to you. I'll ask Erin if she can get a hold of her, but short of showing up at her place, I don't know what I can do."

I stood by my massive bed and leaned a hip into the high, soft comforter that covered the sheets. My attention focused on my phone, it occurred to me maybe I should leave, but just as I reached the doorway, he told the person he'd call them later.

"I'm sorry about that," he said again, his voice a little rough with frustration or some other emotion I couldn't quite pin down.

I turned and walked to him, but stopped a few feet shy. "Everything okay?"

He looked at me, then at his phone, and dropped his hand as if in surrender. "Not really. You know Bec? My friend whose brother..."

"Yes. You told me about her."

"Well, my buddy Thatcher is worried about her. He can't get ahold of her, and I'd mentioned to him the other day that she hadn't returned any of my messages in the last ten days or so. That's unusual, and so the combination has sent Thatcher into a tizzy. And he wants me to track her down." He crossed his arms over his chest and rocked back on his heels.

"How can I help?" I asked, finally letting myself go to him.

I pulled on his crossed arms until they fell, then wrapped my arms around him and pulled him close. I rested my head against his chest and hugged him with everything in me until his arms came around me.

His long inhale, then his slow breath out, moved his chest under my cheek.

"You're doing it," he said in a small voice, one that sent a twisting sensation full of compassion and affection for him through me.

Affection?

Was that it, really? It seemed inadequate, but before I had a chance to examine it, he spoke again.

"I should probably go help him look for her. And I'm

sorry to say it, but I don't think you should go with me—I think we may be finding her in a bad place, and she won't respond well to someone she doesn't know." His arms were still locked around me.

My heart sank at the thought of not helping him. Also, was it because she didn't know me, or because I was *me* and she *would* know me? I couldn't control that now, and the most important thing was for Ben to help his friend.

I leaned back to find his eyes, the set of his face, mournful.

"I'll come with you. I can stay in the car, or whatever. I don't want you dealing with this alone."

"Thatcher's going to meet me. I won't be alone."

"Okay. Please just... let me know she's okay, and you're okay..." A strange amount of worry filled my voice. My heart hovered near fluttering, but not in a fun way at all.

He hugged me to him, kissed my hair, and pulled back to drill those blue eyes straight into mine. "Don't worry. I'll keep you posted."

It was minutes after he'd gone before my heart slowed. The adrenaline, the fear wrapped up in worrying for someone I didn't even know, proved surprising. I hadn't ever had a friend in such a bad place I was worried about them like this, and now, I was worried for Ben's friend, someone I hadn't ever even met.

And what did it say about him that he would drop everything and go search for her, someone he wasn't related to and who he was only sort of friends with, from what he'd said?

He refused the title of hero flatly whenever the press tried to saddle him with it, but in this moment, as I sat wringing my hands, I couldn't help but feel he was. He was, both for what he'd done to try to save his friend, for surviving the journey to get back to a place where he could function, and for insisting on being there for the people he loved.

His compassion, his empathy, his *heart* were beautiful. And damn if I didn't want to be one of those people.

CHAPTER TWENTY-NINE

Ben

Bec was fine.

Thank God.

I glared at Thatcher who had his arms crossed, his back hunched into himself as Bec all but yelled at us.

"Just because I don't respond right away doesn't mean I'm about to harm myself! Just because I have chosen not to return your calls..." She glared at Thatcher, her eyes so full of anger, I would have withered if I was him.

Which, he kind of was.

Hands on her hips, the dramatic pause lingered, and then she continued. "And don't think I don't know what you thought had happened. I am not suicidal. I am not even depressed. I am making some big life decisions, and I will thank you very much to *mind. Your. Own. Business.*"

Thatcher shook his head. He was visibly upset, not

unusual when it came to Bec, but I was surprised by just how little he was locking it down. "We—"

"I don't want to hear how you've taken on the job of watching out for me. I don't want that. I lost my brother, and I didn't sign up for two more."

She stomped her way over to the bar of her kitchen where she deposited her empty wine glass. She turned back to us and folded her arms, as though waiting for us to leave.

"You aren't going to tell us about these big life decisions?" I asked, genuinely curious, and hoping we could move out of the fury and into a normal conversation.

"Definitely not." Her chin jutted out proudly, just like Dillon used to do.

Good grief, he was an arrogant ass.

It was one of those moments where remembering made me smile and ache at the same time.

Thatcher took a breath, let it out, ran his hands over his face. "Bec, please—"

"You need to leave. *Now.* And I will talk to you both at some later date when I don't feel like the most likely result of our conversation will be my incarceration for murder." Her voice still shook with rage.

"Okay, we're going. But if you don't call within a week, we're coming back," I said as a not-entirely-mock threat.

That made her dark eyebrows flash to her hairline. "You will do no such thing, Ben Holder. If I have to call your fancy little girlfriend and have her chain you down, you know I'll do it. Do not mess with me on this. I will call you when I'm good and damn well ready, and you'll be just dandy with that, clear?"

I let my brow furrow and tucked my lips between my teeth to keep from smiling. This was perfect. This was what

I wanted to see—she was spitting mad, take no prisoners, Bec-with-a-vengeance, and she was fine. Not healed completely, but she was good.

"Yes, ma'am." Out of the corner of my eye, I caught Thatcher nodding.

I moved to her door and opened it, but turned back to her. "You know we love you, and that's why we're here?"

Her shoulders slumped a little, and she looked me in the eye when she said, "I know it."

Her eyes flickered to Thatch's and held there, both of them locked in a moment I didn't fully understand, but had begun to lately.

Thatcher clenched his jaw, and with a little nod to Bec, followed me out of her place.

He shut the door gently behind him, and we walked to the parking lot where we'd parked next to each other in the visitor parking area.

I stopped in front of my truck and surveyed him. He was lost in his own head. "You okay?"

He started nodding immediately, like that was the answer his mind had commanded him to give, but his mouth wouldn't comply. "I don't know, man."

We'd promised to be honest with each other, and for him to say that much was truly saying something. He was one of the most positive, sunny-side up kind of people I'd ever met.

"I just got it in my head she was in trouble. I tried to talk to her when she got back from her trip at Christmas, and she blew me off, and then I couldn't get ahold of her, and when you told me you hadn't heard from her either, and Erin hadn't seen her in weeks, I..."

"I know. And it wasn't without some merit. It's okay to be worried about a friend. But I wonder if you're feeling—"

The sharp shake of his head, the bitter frown on his lips, stopped me short.

"Nah. No. Let's not go there. Not now." He pulled his keys out of his pocket and let them clink together into his palm. "I'll see you at church?"

"Yeah. See you tomorrow."

I climbed into my truck and strapped my seatbelt as he pulled away, then messaged Whit to let her know everything was fine. Thatcher barely braked as he left the lot, and a grim kind of smile settled on my face. This was all so messed up.

Whit suggested I come back over since we'd ended up finding Bec and resolving the issue (or more accurately, getting kicked out of her crappy apartment halfway between Fort Campbell and Nashville) more quickly than I could have hoped, and of course, I obliged.

The half hour drive back was full of questions about Thatcher and Bec, thoughts about Bec and whether she really was okay, and wondering what her life decisions were. She'd been stuck, paralyzed in the same job, the same apartment, since Dillon's death. Erin had told me she'd asked Bec if she'd ever leave the area, and how she thought Bec was considering it. Would she finally leave, and would that signal an acceptance of her loss? I wanted that for her because I knew what it was to try and keep acceptance at bay.

When I reached Whit's house, I felt bone weary in a way I hadn't in a while. I'd managed to smile and feel good about leaving, had talked myself into being glad about Bec's anger with us for banging on her door like we were FBI and she a hunted fugitive, but the farther away from it I got, the more drained I felt.

Whit swung open her giant door, a soft smile on her

face, and I walked right into her open arms knowing there was truly no place I'd rather be.

CHAPTER THIRTY

Whit

Ben was clinging to me.

Clinging.

And it felt so good to be there for him, to be ready to take on any burden he wanted to share, to physically comfort him. To feed him.

"Are you hungry?" I asked, pulling away just enough to see his face, that smiling mouth looking uncharacteristically sad.

"Not really, but I should probably eat something, huh?" he said, gently stroking my back.

He released me, and we went to the kitchen where I got out the fixings for grilled cheese sandwiches and tomato soup.

"You having some too?" he asked, collapsing into the chair at the counter.

"Yes, I am." My stomach rumbled in anticipation.

"Wow. Throwing it all away for me, huh?" A smile lingered in his voice.

I set up on the counter across from him, sliding butter over one side of each thick piece of bread then slicing sharp cheddar, and responded as I did. "I was actually planning on us having this tonight. This is sort of my last cheat meal until I'm done with awards season, and then I'll take a breath."

His lips pursed, and I shook my head at him.

"Don't make that face."

"What face?" he said, clearly surprised I'd noticed his disapproval.

"That face that says you think I shouldn't worry so much about what I eat. I'm not starving myself, and though I admit to sometimes feeling deprived, I know the difference. My mom was—" I stopped, surprised I'd ever started talking about my mother.

I didn't discuss my parents, not ever. Ben knew the basics, but I didn't want them to have more of my life than they already had.

"You mom was…"

I dumped a container of tomato soup into a pot on the stove and turned on the burner. "She was very specific about how we ate, even when I was young. It was all very healthy, very measured. I only remember having pizza a handful of times in my childhood, and *never* at my own house."

"That's just… hard to imagine. I feel like I was thirty percent pizza growing up, just based on the sheer volume I consumed at any given point."

A laugh cracked out. "That's a lot of pizza."

"I bet it was overwhelming to go to Juilliard and have so many options," he said, leaning his elbows on the counter.

He had no idea.

"It was. I gained ten pounds the first month, then lost fifteen... I had no idea how to manage myself. I'd literally been spoon fed, never had a choice about what I ate. It was almost a relief to hire Kendra to make my meal plans and make those decisions for me. Of course, she's much more interested in my overall health and less concerned with my physical appearance, though of course, that's her job too. But I trust her, and I feel good when I stick with her plans."

He started to speak, then stopped himself. I gave him a questioning look, and he grinned, then spat it out. "Do you wish you didn't have to worry about it?"

"I don't worry about it anymore, but I did have anxiety related to food, particularly when I first left home. I had anxiety related to a lot of things. As crazy as it sounds, I am so much less anxious now than I was then—even with the paparazzi and invasions of privacy and never knowing how my music will be received."

I set the buttery sides of our sandwiches down on the griddle, and they sizzled deliciously.

"Why, do you think?"

"Because I knew that path—the path my parents set me on—wasn't *mine*. It was *theirs*. And I'm not saying there's anything wrong with wanting what your parents want for you, but for me, I'd had to suppress so much of me, even to the point of feeling ashamed that I wanted something else. Once I let that go and took the leap, it was better. It's easy to say now, of course, but I think even if I hadn't won, if I'd just ended up slugging it out at bars and honky tonks in town, I'd have been happier than I was before."

I heard him slide his chair back from the bar, but went about my business lifting the edge of the bread to see if it was toasting up right. When I glanced over my shoulder, I saw him leaning against the counter next to me.

"I'm glad. I know it has caused a rift between you and your family, but I'm glad you feel so sure you're where you want to be." He eyed the griddle and seemed mesmerized.

"What are you thinking?" I asked as he stared wide-eyed and entranced by the melting cheese.

He broke from his daze and looked up at me with an odd look. His voice was small and unsure as he said, "I was just thinking, I didn't expect you would cook."

I barked a laugh, not expecting all that staring and intensity to be rooted in my cooking skills. "Well you're mostly right. My cooking extends about as far as you can go on a hot plate. Beyond that, it's the barest minimum, or someone else makes it."

"Well, you seem to have grilled cheese down."

I flipped the sandwiches and stirred the soup, then turned off the burner. Nothing worse than a scalded tongue.

"That I do. I won't be modest—my grilled cheese is the stuff of dreams. It's why it's my first and favorite cheat."

I collected plates, napkins, bowls, and spoons, then dipped out soup into each bowl. After a quick check of the sandwiches that showed they were—as I suspected—perfect, I pulled those to my wooden cutting board, sliced them diagonally, and set them on the plates. I dropped a dollop of unsweetened whipped cream and some fresh chives over the soup, and voilà.

"Go sit," I demanded while wiping my hands on a towel and then delivering the two plates with bowls and sandwiches to our seats at the counter.

For a few moments, the only sounds in the kitchen were the crisp bites into buttery, toasted bread, my completely indelicate groan of appreciation at the flavor of the melted cheese and bread combination, and Ben's unsubtle snickers as he devoured his food.

"I didn't think I was hungry," he said as he sat back and set a hand on his abdomen. "But that was perfect."

A sigh of satisfaction drifted out. "It was."

We cleaned up the kitchen together and moved to the living room. There was nothing like snuggling up on the couch with a fire after a long day, and I'd been looking forward to curling up with this handsome man all day. I'd been worried sick while he was gone, but finding Bec had taken no time at all, and he was back.

We settled into the corner of the large couch and he pulled me close, one arm around me. We sat and watched the fire I'd built just to have something to do when he'd left flicker and jump in the stone hearth.

Part of me still felt jittery, like *I* was the one who needed calming. Maybe I knew that was a warning sign—that my upset on his behalf was a signal my heart had gotten involved and there was no going back. I'd certainly felt nothing for Jamie other than mild, human-decency-level concern when his family member had gotten sick and he'd had to fly home toward the end of our time dating.

Which reminded me.

"Plans tomorrow?" I asked, hoping this wouldn't take him too off-guard after the night he'd had. But I didn't want to wait any longer to tell him.

"Church, but that's about it. What about you?" he asked, his voice drowsy and low.

"I have a meeting in the afternoon..."

One brow lazily arched. "On a Sunday?"

"Uh, yeah. I was hoping you'd come over for it."

His eyes opened more fully, not looking so tired.

"It's uh... Jamie Morris? Remember him?"

He waited a beat, maybe for me to drop the punchline, then shook his head and looked at me like the crazy person I was.

"Yep. I remember him," he said with a chuckle.

"So, he's coming over while he's in town. We're going to run through our song because he'll be on tour in the UK and Europe right up until the Oscars..."

"That's a good idea." His voice sounded totally neutral. Not one single hint as to what he thought.

I turned sideways in my corner seat, easily the best spot on a sectional couch, and let my legs cross over his. We sat perpendicular to each other, and I crossed my arms and squinted at him in an exaggerated move that had him shaking his head and hiding a smile.

"Are you expecting me to be jealous? Or... what?" He peered back at me with the same mock-suspicion.

"I don't know. No? Or... I really don't know what I expect. But your non-response feels like a response." That didn't make sense, but I didn't know how to say what I meant, so I just kept rambling. "Or maybe it really is. Maybe you are the one and only person on Earth who has completely neutral feelings on the subject of Jamie Morris."

More dramatic pausing, then, "More than anything else, I think the operative question here is, what are *your* feelings on the subject of Jamie Morris? Because those are the feelings that will inform my feelings."

His arms were crossed now, and he'd given me a wide-open opportunity to tell him if I wanted Jamie or had any other thoughts on the matter.

I hid a grin I couldn't stifle by ducking my head and pressing the back of my hand to my mouth to buy me time. "I feel friendly feelings toward him. Sometimes when I'm being petty, I feel jealous feelings toward him. Sometimes, I feel pity for him."

The question flickered across Ben's face at that.

"He's kind of your typical tortured soul musician. It's not an act. The miraculous thing about him is he isn't a jerk, and he isn't a user. But he's pretty unhappy, and that gains my sympathy. I think that's why we tried to date—to fill each other's gaps. But we're friends, nothing more. I'm sure you'll see that reflected in our dynamic together, and I honestly think you'll like him a lot when you meet him, if he'll let his guard down with you."

Ben's gaze slid over my face, taking in my no-make up and messy ponytail, dipping to my T-shirt for just a moment before he jerked his eyes back to mine. "I'll be here."

CHAPTER THIRTY-ONE

Ben

What a weird thing, knocking on Whit's door and knowing that inside would be one of the biggest rock stars on the planet.

Let's set aside the fact that I was currently dating one of the biggest Country stars out there, that I got to hold her hand and eat grilled cheese at her kitchen table and fall asleep with her tucked under my arm on her ridiculously comfortable couch.

Yeah, never mind that because *no big deal*, right?

But I was actually kind of a fan of Jamie Morris.

In fact, pretty much everyone I knew was. He was just *good*. His band was good, his voice was good, and his songs were good. He hovered somewhere between the singer song writer and the rock star in that he wrote his own songs and had an awesome voice, but a darker edge than the solo acts usually had, which gave him a sweet spot where men wanted to listen, and women fell in love.

He toured like a banshee. I'd seen him in concert before deployment a few years back—dude was amazing live.

So knocking on that giant wood panel again felt more than a little surreal. Nikki opened the door and ushered me in, her phone tucked against one shoulder and her head. She jerked her chin toward the living room, and I nodded in thanks then walked around the corner to find my girlfriend, Country star Whit Grantham, sitting cross-legged with her guitar in her lap, jotting notes down in her notebook

Along with Jamie Morris, musical icon and rock god, breaker of hearts and stealer of souls (okay, maybe that was a bit much), holding his guitar just the same, his long-ish hair in one of those man-buns that only musicians can make look anything other than *trying-too-hard*.

Ho. Ly. Sh. It.

My heart rate reached a canter and kept on mounting, my palms beginning to sweat. Jamie Morris was the first to look up and notice me, and Whit must have seen his casual nod to me, because she turned around and rewarded my presence with a blazing smile.

Oh, I like her, my dumb heart thought at the sight.

"Jamie, this is my boyfriend, Ben." She set aside her guitar and came to hug me, kiss my cheek, tug my hand in the direction of Jamie Morris.

"Good to meet you, man." Jamie Morris stood and offered me a hand.

In an other-worldly moment, I stretched out my own hand and watched myself shaking Jamie Morris' tattooed one, his strong grip grasping mine, then dropping it. He then backed up to sit on the couch and settle his guitar back on his knee.

I hadn't spoken and cleared my throat. "Nice to meet you, Jamie Morris."

Did my voice sound weird? Or was everything kind of weird right now—that strange tilt of the afternoon sun coming through Whit's shutters, the flickering firelight, the recessed lighting in the ceiling, and was it hot? It was definitely hot in here.

"Wait, are you... is this really happening?" Whit yanked on my hand until I faced her, that gorgeous face full of amazement. "It *is*."

My face flamed at her statement, and I ducked my chin, pulling a breath in through my nose to calm myself and get a break because I was embarrassing myself.

"You have at no point shown even the barest *hint* that you cared about celebrity. You were hardly even surprised when Reese introduced me. And now you're speechless?"

I let out a strangled cough-laugh-bark thing, trying to cover my embarrassment, my nerves.

"I'm a fan. So sue me." I must have been giving her the most pathetic look of all time.

Her wide smile looked so completely pleased, I couldn't feel bad. I did not, however, take another glance at Jamie Morris, who I was man enough to admit was a super good-looking guy and all the more so in person. I could see why both of my sisters had been obsessed with him when he debuted his first album years ago. Hell, I sure had been.

The thought flashed across my mind: *how is Whit not in love with this guy?*

"You've met every single big name in Country. You've met all the living legends in Country... I just, I'm blown away. I didn't even know you liked Jamie."

A snicker came from the general vicinity of Jamie

Morris, and then he spoke. "It may surprise you to find that a lot of people like Jamie."

Whit shot him an annoyed look. "Yes, I know, Mr. Grammy himself, but please. I'm not kidding you. This man right here—" she gestured to me with a thumb over her shoulder, "—has met everyone. Half the time, he seems like he doesn't even realize the person is famous. The other half, he's practically *rude* to the person."

"That's not true!" I had to say something in my defense.

"If it's Colton Danes, it's true," Whit said.

"Obviously Ben's a man of discerning tastes," Jamie Morris said, and when I met his eyes, he gave me an approving nod.

Somewhere in my head, I recognized I would likely never think of him as simply *Jamie*—he was Jamie Morris, and that was that.

"It's not hard to feel a bucket full of disdain for Danes. He's constantly hitting on you, so how am I supposed to act?" A wave of irritation ran through me at the memory of the multiple times I'd come upon Danes hitting on Whit in front of his own date or me.

Whit set a hand on my arm and squeezed so I'd look at her. Her eyes were soft as she said, "You do just fine with him. I wouldn't change a thing."

I found myself smiling back at her, my heart beating to a rhythm she set in me anytime we made eye contact.

"Can I get you some water, Jamie?" Whit asked, not looking away from me.

"Please."

Lazy strums of the guitar filled the air around us as she took my hand and pulled me out of the living room through to the kitchen. When she got there, she dropped my hand and faced me, crossing her arms.

"So..."

My cheeks grew hot again, leaving me only mildly irritated that she'd pulled me away and I was now blushing for the second time in less than ten minutes. "So."

"You're a Jamie Morris fan." She cracked a half-smile, but smothered it by pressing her lips together.

"I am."

"How did you never tell me this?"

"It was irrelevant." I let my eyes flick around the kitchen to avoid hers, but that was pretty impossible.

She blinked slowly and eyed me from under her lashes.

"Okay, fine. It wasn't exactly on the top of my list to admit that I'm a moderately big fan of your ex-boyfriend. That just seemed weird." I shifted from foot to foot, unable to find a comfortable stance.

She watched me for a moment, no change in her expression. Then she swallowed, and all at once, reached out, pulled my face to hers, and crushed herself against me in a kiss. Just as suddenly, she let me go. "I like you a little too much, you know?"

I was perplexed, thrilled, and now mildly turned on with a side order of still-awkward and over-excited that Jamie Morris was still sitting in the other room, strumming what must be one of his infamous practice guitars.

"Too much?" I asked, my voice coming from some other guy.

She just smiled, grabbed my hand, and said, "Come on, let's go hang with your idol."

CHAPTER THIRTY-TWO

Whit

It was startling to realize how opposite Ben and Jamie were physically. In some ways, I saw them as similar in that they'd both been through hard things, had both suffered in some way, though Ben had come out of it, and Jamie... who knew if he'd ever make it out.

We played our song a few times, and Ben sat, rapt, watching Jamie. If I didn't know how much he liked me, I'd probably be jealous. That, and I knew how good Jamie was—that was why I'd pushed Nikki, my manager, and everyone else I knew to get me paired with him on this project. Turned out he'd wanted me for it, anyway, which was its own kind of dream come true.

Where Jamie was dark, Ben was light. Jamie's hair was long and usually pulled back away from his face but for a few strands that fell moodily over his eyes. Ben's hair was close-cropped into a military-approved cut.

Jamie had ever-present stubble, sometimes a beard. Ben could grow an impressive beard as I'd seen over the weeks of the tour and his leave period when he hadn't been required to be clean-shaven, but most of the time, his face was shaved close, and even at the end of the day, the five-o'clock shadow was just a suggestion since even his beard hair was still a blond color.

Both men had presence. Jamie had presence because he felt a little like a black hole, all energy and attention collapsing into wherever he sat—that angled, brooding face, those dark blue eyes, the tattoos. Even his energy seemed intense.

Ben's presence was lighter, easier, comfortable in a way that snuck up on you and you didn't realize you required it to be at ease until it was gone. He wasn't just a simple man with no problems like he sometimes projected— I'd realized he had incredible depth to him, and he was constantly processing the world around him, working to be at peace with his past, with what might lay ahead in his future. But he didn't generate that restlessness Jamie did, and I hadn't realized how much I liked Ben's calm and confidence until this moment, sitting on my couch with the two men.

No chance Jamie and I would get back together, so the comparison was moot, but of course, it was hard to avoid with them both sitting in the same room. Jamie and I never would have gotten far—he wasn't emotionally available for much, and though we did care about each other, I think we cared about each other in the same way we did now—as friends, as fellow artists whose talent and drive we respected.

Seeing Jamie there was a reminder of how lonely I'd been for so long. It's what we'd seen in each other—that aching longing for love and companionship, and yet, we couldn't provide either for the other person. For him, I suspected that whatever in his past tormented him and seemed to drive him also kept him from real connection. And for me, in my heart of hearts, Jamie and I just didn't connect.

He was beautiful, talented, driven, honest, and respectful. But he was also closed in so many ways.

Ben was open. Ben had been open with me since the very beginning, and I knew what I owed him. I owed him honesty about the song, and then honesty about my feelings, because that's what he'd give me.

"You guys sound so good. Seriously. I can't imagine what other song would win," Ben said, looking back and forth between us.

"Thanks. I guess we'll see." Jamie was still picking away at his strings.

"I hate waiting. I hate the build-up of this season with one show after another, getting dressed up and parading around while you're so nervous, you just want to puke."

I set my guitar aside and rubbed my hands down my jeans. The flare of nerves from just thinking about the Grammys, which were fast approaching, rattled me. I'd have to fly out in two weeks, a few days early, but hopefully, Ben would join me. We needed to nail down the details.

"You get nervous?" Jamie asked, eyeing me even as he plucked out some elaborate melody I didn't recognize. Maybe it was one of his newer songs—I hadn't heard it.

"You don't?"

"No. Award me, or don't, whatever."

A surge of irritation hit me immediately.

"That's easy for you to say. You win every award every time. It's easy to be casual when you know you're going to win and have a decade-long track record to prove it." I stood and flipped my notebook closed as he answered.

"It's also easy to win if you decide you don't give a damn."

I turned to look at him, but he'd dropped his head back down to focus on his guitar.

Ben arched a brow at me, and I rolled my eyes at him. Then I said the words I knew would provoke Jamie. "Maybe someday I'll get there. Maybe you have to be an old man before you can stop worrying about such things."

Jamie's head shot up, and he let loose one of his heart-breaker smiles. *Deadly.* "Whatever you've gotta tell your-self, little one."

"Sizeism is beneath you, Morris. I'm going to get a snack."

I retreated to the kitchen and thought about the two men in the living room, so different, and yet, if Ben could get over his starstruck freeze, I knew they'd be friends. He'd already loosened up in the hour we'd spent together, so maybe he'd be able to talk now if I left them for a moment.

I wasn't sure what had happened in Jamie's life, but if he and Ben became friends, Ben could be good for him. He'd be good for Jamie like he'd been for me.

Well, that wasn't quite right. Ben was fast becoming everything for me, and I wasn't about to let him be that for someone else.

CHAPTER THIRTY-THREE

Ben

"So now you're best friends with Jamie Morris, is that what you're telling me?"

Thatcher shook his head with a wry smile, and a little tug of satisfaction pulled in my chest.

He'd been just shy of miserable since last weekend when we'd left Bec's. For that matter, it'd been weeks, as he'd been fairly morose before that run in, in all likeliness because Bec had refused to return his calls.

I used phrasing like *just shy of miserable* and *fairly morose* because calling Thatcher *actually* miserable or morose would ring false. He was one of the most positive, kind people I'd ever met, and he had a way of looking at things that made political spin look like it was standing still. Not that he ignored hard things, but he was one of those maddening people that could seemingly find the *blessing* in everything.

Damn him, I'd thought so many times. But lately, I knew he was struggling to find those blessings, to keep that positive spin.

The thing Thatcher didn't know was that I knew why he cared so much. It was easy to see, had always been easy to see from the day Dillon had introduced me and Thatch to his twin sister.

Not sure what kind of messed up thinking he'd gotten himself into over it, but he didn't want me knowing he felt something for her, or worrying, and he seemed to think he didn't want Bec to know, either. I wondered if she did. And I wondered how she felt.

Sometimes, it felt like assuming Bec had feelings at all, maybe other than wanderlust, hunger, and anger, was futile.

"Yes, basically, I'm his new best friend."

I pulled my ID card from my computer, slipped it into my wallet, and stood. It had been a long week, and we were heading to a movie. Whit had *stuff* all weekend, and I doubted I'd even see her, though I was going to try to find time, even twenty minutes, because the thought of going another day without touching her or hearing her voice made me feel restless and wrong.

"You're such a jerk," Thatcher said, a good-natured frown on his face. "You end up finagling your way into a relationship with one of the hottest Country stars of all time, and now you're friends with *Jamie freaking Morris*."

"Hey man. Power of positive thinking, right?" I joked, grabbed my bag, and we were off, leaving the battalion headquarters behind.

The crazy thing was, it was sort of true. I mean, no, I wasn't best friends with the guy, but yeah, we'd gotten along. We'd talked about music a bit, and then he'd asked about my life in the Army. He'd actually done a USO tour to Afghanistan the winter after I'd left, and so, in a strange confluence of my Army life and my musical idol colliding, we'd talked about Bagram Air Base and how stupid and surprising it was that it got so cold even though the region was mountainous and so it shouldn't be such a surprise.

The guy was genuinely nice.

And the music he and Whit made—wow. It had been more than a little mind-blowing to be sitting in that cozy living room listening to the two of them casually start and stop their song as they adjusted, made plans for their all-acoustic version. It'd be a guitar duet, both of them playing and singing.

The finished product sounded astounding, the song so full of emotion, I would have choked up if I hadn't been hearing it on and off for an hour by the time they were done. I suspected it'd get me when they played it live.

Any fears I might have had about Whit and Jamie being involved, or one of them pining for the other, were removed after that afternoon, and I knew that was why she'd wanted me there. She could have sworn up and down, though I'd never asked her to, and she'd never offered. I could admit to being glad I'd seen them interact, could see the friendly, almost brotherly way they spoke to each other, and then the very professional and focused way they functioned for the majority of the time Jamie was in the house.

(And see? I'd made such progress. He was officially *Jamie* now, not Jamie Morris, so I felt all kinds of worldly with that.)

The immediate challenge, after I got over the holy-crap-that's-him moment of thrill and embarrassment at meeting him was recognizing that the guy really was as pretty as he looked, but even more so in person. I didn't use the word lightly when saying the dude was *potent*—between the face, the hair, the tats, and the guitar and voice… it was hard to imagine a woman being in the same room as him and not falling all over herself to get his attention.

But not Whit. And frankly, I'd seen as many men and women tripping on their tongues in front of her to know she had that kind of effect on pretty much everyone *she* met. It was overwhelming to be sitting there with both of them as they first started playing, almost stifling to be there with their beauty and talent filling up the room.

Until I relaxed, and listened to the songs, and let myself smile at their banter—more ribbing than flirting. In the end, it'd been reassuring, which I still liked to tell myself I didn't actually need, but knew I probably did. Especially if they were going to go on stage and sing that song together in a little over a month and the resulting fire that would light in the tabloids and gossip blogs because of it, I probably did need the verification that there wasn't anything between them.

"Really though, how's it going with your woman?" Thatcher asked.

A small thrill shot through me. *Your woman.* I liked the sound of that.

The truth was, I didn't think Whit *was* my woman. The strange thing about dating someone like her, someone famous and familiar to everyone she meets, was that she wouldn't ever just be *my woman.* She was a public figure, and everyone wanted a piece of her.

But I had the biggest piece. Didn't I? I knew she cared about me, knew she liked being around me, but I just wasn't sure where we'd go.

I'd always been someone who had a sense of where he was going. Things lined up, I had a plan, I worked hard, and voilà. College. ROTC. Commission. Army. Tada.

But now that was coming to an end, and fast. I'd have to drop my packet soon, or the Army would force my hand by putting me on orders to career course, and if I did that, I'd be sucked in for another few years. I'd gone past the point of debating with myself about that. I was done here—just knew it.

The thought hadn't fully formed, or maybe I hadn't *let* it form yet. But I was beginning to feel the inklings of an idea for what came next. I hadn't told anyone—wouldn't, until after looking into it more. But the first sprouts of hope for what came next in that regard had started germinating.

And then, there was Whit. Looking at what came next with her was completely opaque. I had no idea where we were headed, and the more time we spent together, the closer we got, the more shared experiences and intimacy we built, the more I realized I might want *everything* with her.

"She's amazing. Super busy with awards season coming up. She's got Grammys next week, and Oscars end of February, and a few other things I'm not even sure about. I barely see her right now, but when I do..."

The cheesy grin on my face must have looked obnoxious, especially to someone essentially in agony over a woman he thought he wasn't allowed to be with.

But Thatcher was the best kind of man. He grabbed me around the neck, hugged me to him with one of his massive arms, and said, "Nobody deserves happiness more than you, my brother."

He shoved me away roughly, and that action helped me swallow the lump in my throat. *Same goes for you*, I should have said.

I *would* say, and soon.

CHAPTER THIRTY-FOUR

Ben

Nikki, once again, opened Whit's door when I knocked later that weekend on Sunday afternoon. Whit'd been swamped all weekend, then I'd been busy with plans I'd made thinking she'd be busy, and now, here I stood, taking whatever scraps were available.

Fine, that sounded a little poor me. But the weekend without her had made me realize I didn't like being without her. And that reality had me confronting the awful truth that I would almost always be without her if we were together, if we continued dating and let our relationship progress. She'd always be this busy, touring, living life at a clip I could hardly imagine.

"Ben, good to see you. I need just a minute of your time," Nikki said, not actually looking at me, but focusing on the phone in her hand, her fingers a blur over the screen.

"Sure. Everything okay?"

"Perfectly fine, just want to update some documents and debrief a bit."

She turned and walked abruptly into the dining room, so I took that as a sign to follow her.

While she spoke—something about the tour going well and being pleased with the latest buzz—I checked my watch, mentally counting the hours I'd steal with Whit before she needed to sleep and I'd have to go.

"So just sign there and on the next page, and we're good."

I scribbled my signature where Nikki indicated, and she gave me a nod which signaled the conversation was over. Relief flooded as I nodded back despite knowing she wouldn't see and began the hunt through the house to find Whit.

I knocked on her door, and she answered a moment later, long hair wet and dripping over one shoulder.

Oh, and in a towel.

My gaze ran over her—the wet hair combed away from her face, the little droplets lingering at the dip in her collar bone, the towel tucked in on itself at her chest and ending mid-thigh, leaving the miles of her legs exposed.

I swallowed, looked back to her eyes, expecting to see an amused smile, or maybe even some frustration with my so clearly objectifying her. But none of that was there. No.

She was all fire, her lips slightly parted, her eyes almost glassy with heat, the color in her cheeks darker now. She moved back and opened the door wider, and I stepped inside, renewing the vow I'd made to myself, promising myself that I wasn't the kind of man who'd take what he wanted in that moment, demanding my fingers not reach out and pull the towel away and watch those little drops of water continue their journey down a body I wanted to the point of pain.

I walked past her, hands clenched and shoved into my pockets to keep them from acting on their own, and made my way to the couch, where I stood and looked out the window. Then I realized her drapes were open and she was standing there in a towel, so I jerked them closed.

Mercifully, when I turned around, she was gone.

Whit

Had a man ever looked at me like that?

Ever?

Yes, of course I'd been wanted. I'd been looked at and told I was desirable—sometimes with flattering language, sometimes with words so debasing, I needed a shower and a therapy session after.

But that moment with Ben...

I took a shuddering breath and blew it out, counting. I slowed my heart, calmed my mind, pulled up my jeans, fastened my bra, pulled on a T-shirt. I towel-dried my hair and combed it, ran the towel over it again.

I shouldn't have answered the door. Honestly, I'd thought it was Nikki with a reminder. I'd finished my training session with Kendra and jumped in the shower so I'd be ready for Ben. I was fast enough to run a few minutes early. Somehow, I'd forgotten that he almost always ran early, and I hadn't been expecting him to come right to my door. But Nikki had been distracted, had probably just sent him up, and it wasn't like he hadn't knocked.

The worst part was, I didn't want him to clench his fists and walk away. I wanted him to let himself have what he so clearly wanted—what we both did. Maybe that was the difference in how it felt to be looked at, and how it felt to be looked at *by him.*

I shook away the thought, knowing that wasn't going anywhere helpful. We hadn't talked about it directly, and though I wanted to, we had other things to deal with today, and admittedly, no time to take that other path, as much as I also wanted to.

"Hey." I moved across the room to where he was staring at the closed curtains.

"You need to close your curtains. Some creeper with a long-range lens could have seen you," he said, his shoulders hunched and arms crossed.

"Okay."

No point in arguing with him—no point in reminding him that the hedges, the trees, the fence around the property, that all those things would keep people out, and if they didn't, the blinds would, and if they didn't, the fact the window was a good thirty feet from where I was standing and the angle wouldn't work would prevent someone. None of those things would matter, and it wasn't worth arguing.

He must have been surprised by my lack of comment, so he turned, his gaze sliding over my jeans, shirt, face, hair again, not all the heat gone from his look. He held out his hand, like he needed me to agree to his touching me. If only he knew how much I agreed.

He took my hand in his warm one and stepped to me. He set the back of my left hand into the palm of his left one, then ran his right finger over the callouses.

"I love your hands." He sounded gruff.

My voice, usually my power tool of choice, lost itself somewhere as his eyes and fingers studied my hand. I'd always loved my hands, too. I'd known from a young age they were the key to making music—first piano, then guitar and violin and fiddle.

"They've been insured since I was eight."

His head lifted, and he raised a brow. He knew enough about my parents that he wasn't all that surprised. His finger tip traveled from the pad of my index finger to the base of my thumb, traced up to the end of my middle finger, then the dip in my palm. His gentle exploration of my hand was sending every sense and thought flying around my head.

"So many expectations piled on you," he said, almost like he was talking to himself.

I swallowed, nodded, watched.

"And now?" he asked, his voice still that low, toe-curling rumble I'd rarely heard from him.

This version of Ben Holder was the stealth one, no doubt. Less casual, less controlled, and one hundred percent irresistible to me.

"Still are." I wasn't sure if he was talking about the insurance, or the expectations. I wasn't sure if I was, either. Both were true.

Slowly, he brought my hand to his chest and pressed it over his heart, where I could feel the muffled thump of his heartbeat. He held my hand there with both his hands and just looked at me, almost too long, until he said, "I hope you know, whatever happens this week, I'm really proud of you."

Tears immediately pricked my eyes, making me press my lips together hard to fight off the answering sob yearning to be released. He was so sweet, so unconditional, and it was beautiful and destructive to me.

I pushed against his chest and let my hand drop when he released it, then summoned a smile and cleared my throat. "I need to tell you a bit about next weekend so you know what to expect."

I sat down on the couch, and he followed.

"I'm all ears."

"I'll be leaving Tuesday, I think, or maybe early Wednesday—honestly, I'm so jumbled right now, I have no idea. I'll be in rehearsals the rest of the week, and then I think Nikki has you flying in Saturday. You said you had to be back for Monday, right?"

He nodded and grabbed my hand, making my heart race again as though it had ever calmed in the first place.

"Okay, so because of that, you'll leave on a red eye that night. I'm sorry about that, but it was the only way we could get you home before work on Monday thanks to the time change. I'll head back Tuesday night or Wednesday. Usually we do a little press tour the day or so after if I win..."

And not to sound like a jerk, but I knew I'd win. Out of six awards, I'd win something. If the duet with Jamie and I won, I'd be accepting since he was on tour and wasn't making an effort to come back for the show. Which, by the way, was perfectly typical of him—no wonder he didn't get nervous.

"That all sounds reasonable. What are you performing?"

"I'll be in a kind of Country medley with a bunch of people." I rattled off the list of names, burying Colton Danes' name in the middle. I wasn't going to give that guy the time of day enough to worry about him, and with eight of us performing, I should be able to avoid him on stage.

"I'm looking forward to it. I'll get my tux—"

"Oh, I hope you don't mind, I got you one. I actually need you to go get it fitted. I had your sizes and stuff, but it's custom, so you'll need to have them finish it up in person."

He blinked twice. "Okay. Should I maybe have been on some kind of workout regimen to prepare for this?"

I bit my lip and smiled at him. "No. You're perfect."

He raised that sardonic brow at me. "Perfect, huh?"

"For me, yes." A sappy smile lingered on my face. That smile fled when I saw the answering frown on his. "What?"

"I wish it were true, that was I perfect for you, Whit." His voice held notes of sadness and regret even as he tried to keep it light and playful with a half-smile.

"What makes you think you're not?" I asked, clasping our hands together and placing my other hand on the jumble of fingers.

Instead of a casual smile or a pithy reply, he took a long, slow breath. A jolt of alarm went through me, and my heart willed him to speak, to say anything, so I could reassure him how wonderful I thought he was.

"I don't see how I could be. You're this... force of nature, and I'm a guy who likely doesn't even have a job come summer."

He studied our hands resting on my thigh, the creases bracketing his frown making me want to smooth them away.

"No ideas on what's next?" I asked carefully.

I was walking a tightrope with this conversation and did anytime his future job prospects came up. I wanted to know, wanted to hash it out with him, but had no clue how to make sure he knew I didn't *care* what he did. I could find him a job in the industry if he wanted, probably in a heart-beat—he was charming, good-looking, and smart, so he could jump into just about anything. The way he'd adapted to me, my life, the tour, all of it—he could handle anything.

And that was without the factor of his Army training, the pressure and leadership he'd had to withstand. But none of those were things I felt I could say without sounding like it was important for me that he had a high-paying job. I didn't give a flying moon pie about his income, or what title he held. I loved that he'd been a soldier only because it'd clearly shaped him. But I wanted him to find satisfaction, to find that relief I felt whenever I stood on stage and strummed my guitar.

"I may be coming up with something. It's in the earliest stages of ideas, so I've got some more things to figure out before I tell you about it," he said, and I could have sworn I detected a nervous tint to his words.

I squeezed his hand. "I can't wait."

"I'm definitely ready to feel like I have a plan again. I don't like feeling my way around in the dark like this. And not knowing what I'm doing makes going to work even harder than usual right now."

"Just normal days are hard?"

He let his gaze wander over my face, catch on my lips a moment, before he answered. "Most of them are right now, yes. The new commander is pretty bad—just negative, trying to make us all super hooah—super intense. But it's a down time of the year, and it's making me forget all the things I do like about it."

"Tell me those things."

"I like the people. There are a bunch of idiots, sure, but then there are the best people I've ever known. Dillon was one, and I hate that he's gone, but because of him, I know Bec, and Thatcher. And you know your cousin... Flint is *it*, you know? He's the best kind of person, even if he is a crotchety old bastard."

His genuine smile sent a fall of longing and joy through me, a crazy mix of satisfaction at seeing that beauty on his face and the desire to see it stay there.

"I'm glad you have Thatcher at work. And hopefully a few others?"

He nodded. "Yes. There are a handful of others that are like brothers to me. It's one of those things that military life does that few other jobs would. When you go through the things we went through, there's a bond that will always be there. We're like brothers, even though many of them, I wouldn't choose to spend time with outside of work anymore. It's hard to explain, but... that's one of the things I don't know how to walk away from."

"If you leave, you're not walking away from the people, right? You'll still be their brother, their friend. You'll still talk to Thatcher, you'll still support Bec, and I am sorry to tell you, but I think Reese has added you to his rare collection of things he won't let go of, so you're stuck there," I said with a teasing smile.

He chuckled. "Yeah, I'll never be rid of Flinty, that's true. You're right—it's not like I'm trying to burn it down. I just need a change. I've been talking with my therapist about this—trying to figure out how to make peace with doing the right thing for me while still allowing myself to process some of the other feelings." He stopped and rolled his eyes. "I swear it was easier when I pretended to have my crap together."

I leaned over and put an arm around him. "You not

having your crap together is one of my favorite things about you," I said, not able to keep back my laugh.

"Oh, the truth comes out!" He pushed me away with a playful nudge. "Enough about me. Let's game plan so I can see you before you go because I'm one of those pathetic boyfriends who likes to see my girlfriend more than once a week."

CHAPTER THIRTY-FIVE

Ben

I was now the owner of a bespoke suit.

I'd sent Bridgette a photo of the guy with his teeth full of pins crouching at my ankle while I stood on a pedestal in front of a mirror because I knew she'd freak out. And of course, she had, sending me a barrage of messages until she'd given that up and sent me a video call so she could watch everything in live action.

I looked *good* in that suit. How I'd feel next to Whit in some crazy formal gown, I had no idea. I wasn't sure if I'd walk the red carpet or what, but there'd definitely be a thorough briefing of what to expect before we loaded into the car.

Whit would fly out early Wednesday morning, so once I got off work Tuesday, I rushed home to see her. I'd been feeling more and more needy—terrible timing, really, since I was also seeing her less and less. Why hadn't I felt so desperate for her when I'd basically been living with her?

I knew why. This had all been, mostly, before we were really together. It was when we were no longer *fake* together that I let myself want her, need to see her, look forward to being with her. The only thing that had kept all of my interest, excitement, and desire for her under wraps had been the fact that we'd agreed we were friends and I was helping her. Once that had gone out the window, well... it was a miracle I had maintained any sense of calm since then.

In a way, it was good we couldn't spend all day every day together. There'd be no way to play it cool then, and if I knew something about Whit, it was that she didn't like people falling all over her. I'd gotten that sense the first time I ever saw her when I'd been momentarily speechless other than gushing out her name.

And so, the hour or so we'd had on Sunday had me eager for a few more minutes with her before she passed out to get a few hours of sleep in anticipation of her early flight. She'd be busy all week, and she'd also be busy all day next Sunday for the award show, so this was potentially my best shot to have some quality time, even if I wanted both the quality *and* the quantity.

But, beggars can't be choosers.

She opened the door, and I kid you not, my heart skipped a beat at the sight of her. I'd seen her two days ago, but still, seeing her standing there in sweatpants, a T-shirt, bare feet, and hair in a ponytail, clearly in her comfort zone, had my heart hammering in my chest.

"Hey, honey."

A small thrill shot through me at her calling *me* honey.

"Hi." I then rushed her, kicking the door closed behind me and tossing her over my shoulder.

"Ben. *What are you doing?*"

She was laughing at the unexpected move, and I had to admit I liked the feel of her on my shoulder as I trotted into the living room and gently tossed her onto the cushions of the couch. I crawled over her and boxed her in, my knees on either side of her hips, my hands pressing into the cushion on each side of her head.

I brought my face close to hers and stared her down with squinting eyes.

"I missed you," I said, enjoying her hands now coasting over my back under my shirt.

"That was a nice way to greet me. I'll have to add some weights to my routine so I can do the same to you next time," she said, letting one hand slip to my side and pinch my rib.

"Ah!" I squawked, and jumped up so she couldn't reach me.

"No. No, come back, I didn't mean that to make you go. It was just for emphasis."

She laughed again, and the beauty of that sound floated around me, more beautiful than any song.

"That sounds like a line. I'm not sure I can trust you. My ribs are very sensitive."

She chuckled again. "So I gather."

Overly-cautious, I approached her and sat down next to where she lay, then leaned over her torso with one hand to the side of her head. "You are obnoxiously pretty, you know that?"

She bit her lip, all kinds of adorable and coy, and she knew it.

"I know you know it," I said.

"I don't always know you think so." She let her eyes flicker up to the ceiling above me.

"Really?" She wasn't one to fish for compliments.

Her returning look was shy—which meant she was serious. That was insane. She blinked up at me, and that rare vulnerability she kept tucked away crept through.

"Are you really asking me if I think you're pretty, Whit?" My voice stayed gentle, low, so she wouldn't take it as a criticism.

I wasn't completely sure she wasn't messing with me, and I wasn't about to start spooning out compliments from the bucket I carried around if she was. Even with that flash of anxiety I'd seen after she'd said it and looked away, it was simply hard to believe.

See the weekend, when she opened her bedroom door in nothing but a towel, and I nearly evaporated into a cloud of desire.

Her brow furrowed a bit, but she didn't speak. The look on her face broke my heart, and I didn't understand it. How could she doubt any part of her was beautiful? Of course it had to come from her parents, and maybe from the sycophants attracted to fame, but...

"This is probably something you should know about me. I get insecure before award shows. I know it's stupid, and I know nothing about *me* has changed, but being on parade is unnerving. So much goes into how you look, and the photographs circulate for years—they pop up at the grocery and every Internet site for weeks afterward. It's exhausting, and I'm not immune to comparing myself." She reached up and grasped my arm where it rested by her head, her small, strong hand warm against my wrist.

"Scooch," I said, nudging her with my hip. She moved so her back rested against the back of the deep couch, and I lay down beside her. We both propped heads in hands and leaned on our elbows so we were facing each other, eight inches apart.

"That's only human," I continued. "I'm sure it's difficult to stay focused on yourself when others compare you, and then when you're walking the red carpet or sitting in the seats, looking around at all these people whose jobs it is to look beautiful."

With my free hand, I traced her dark brows, the curve of her cheek, along her chin, and stopped at her perfect lips.

I pulled her chin toward me while leaning in and set a soft kiss on her mouth. I could see the barest of smiles on her lips, even though they hadn't moved.

"It's brutal. And I'm naturally hard on myself. I know this, and I always prep with my therapist. I'm excited you'll be with me, too, but the small, scared part of me imagines you seeing Taylor Swift and becoming the boy in her next song." For some reason, she swallowed the last word, like she wanted to cut herself off—maybe she'd been too honest.

For my part, I couldn't help but shake my head. "Taylor doesn't do it for me."

Her blue-green eyes danced. "No?"

"Nope. Not really at all, but certainly not if I'm there with you."

I could hear my voice had done that low, kind of gritty thing she seemed to respond to, and I knew I had a smug little grin on. But I wasn't quite done. "You understand that I am completely gone for you, right? Pretty much always have been."

My heart raced as she drew in a surprised breath.

"There's no way that's true."

"What do you mean?"

"I remember you being kind of shocked to see me at Reese's, but otherwise, I don't think I've ever seen you... I don't know." She moved her attention to something behind me, clearly not wanting me to see too closely.

"So you think that because I didn't act dumbstruck like I did with Jamie, or fall all over myself when we were fake-dating, that I'm not into you?" I set a hand on the rise of her hip and shook her a little to try and lighten the mood.

She gave me a regretful grin. "Yes?"

"Whit, darlin', I don't want to date Jamie Morris. Playing it cool gets me nowhere with him. If I'd been a bumbling tongue-tied mess when you asked me to that first thing in October, would you have asked me again?"

She pursed her lips. "No. Admittedly, I would not have."

"Exactly. And you wouldn't have let me take you on the tour of post if I'd been all over you the very first time we met. In fact, my little stuttering greeting was a fraction of the disbelief I felt, but some beautiful part of me for which I will forever be thankful recognized that the only way to impress you was to act like you didn't impress me."

She still just watched me.

"And if I told you how brain-meltingly beautiful I find you every time I see you, whether you're dressed up or lounging next to me on the couch, or if I told you how more than once, your voice has brought me to tears, even before I knew you, would you have wanted to sign a contract for me to be your fake boyfriend?"

She swallowed, her face all serious now.

I dipped my head and told her one last truth. "And if I told you that I want you so much, sometimes when you're near me, I find it hard to breathe, that my mind curses myself for ever making a vow of celibacy that keeps me from having you every way we both want, would you believe me?"

She studied my face, her cheeks flushed and her breath coming fast, just like mine. Then, out of the clouds and tearing us away from that fraught moment, she loosed a wide, brilliant smile. "So you think I'm pretty amazing, huh?"

I shook my head and didn't stop as I appealed to the ceiling. "Lord save me. What have I done?"

CHAPTER THIRTY-SIX

Whit

Low of me—I was better than that. I knew I was, and yet, Ben's incredibly persistent reassurance was exciting, and *good grief*, did it make me feel good. Happy.

No. More than happy. Even with the awards coming and the stress tugging at so many parts of me, even though I could genuinely say if I didn't win a thing, I'd be fine.

Yeah—just fine. I wouldn't be *happy* I didn't win. That wasn't in me, and it never would be. But I'd be just fine, and a big part of that thinking stemmed from having Ben in my life. I'd been more alone than I'd ever realized until he came along and showed me—not only how lonely I'd been, but how wonderful it was to be with someone who I could just *be* with. I didn't have to be on, I didn't have to be working, I didn't have to produce, or charm, or create. I could laugh and show him the good *and* bad.

And last night had been the bad. I knew it. It had been fishing, and I should have been more ashamed than I was. But he'd handled it beautifully, not calling me manipulative, but generously giving me what I needed, even if I was pained to admit it.

The bonus, too, was that now I knew a bit about his boundary, one that was clear even though thus far, it'd been unspoken. He'd made some kind of vow, and I'd bet it had something to do with his friend's loss, or something.

We'd need to talk about that specifically. I wasn't sure how I'd handle this closeness without actually getting to be fully together, because I was attracted to Ben in a way I never had been with anyone else. I wanted him in a way I never had anyone else.

I hadn't dated many people. I dated one kid at the private school I went to in high school, though my freedom at that time had been so limited because I was practicing for six hours or more a day. In retrospect, I can identify times I'd had off, but during those years where I was starting to feel the suffocating effects of my parents' insistence on piano and inability to talk about or hear anything else from me, I'd felt cornered. Relationships had been essentially impossible, and the kid hadn't been interested in the limited access plan I was on.

And over the course of the last few years, I'd dated on and off, but I wasn't someone who could connect with a person on a first date at a restaurant when everyone was listening in. Jamie and I had snuck up on each other by working together, but that relationship never went very far physically, and I think we were both glad for that since we enjoyed an easy friendship that wouldn't be possible otherwise.

Maybe that was the magic of how I met Ben—I met him

outside of the Nashville spotlight. And then, we'd spent time together in a casual setting, no date pressure, and it had been him showing me about his world at Fort Campbell, not me talking about music or taking him to an event.

Whatever the case, Ben was the person I felt the most for, and it was equal parts exciting and terrifying.

I want you so much, sometimes when you're near me, I find it hard to breathe, that my mind curses myself for ever making a vow of celibacy that keeps me from having you every way we both want.

Was he *trying* to seduce me? Clearly not, but between the fire-laced look the other day in my room and his words last night... I didn't like the feeling that my heart was being held in someone else's hands, and that was how I was beginning to feel.

Not completely, of course. I'd added in my songwriter's embellishment. But I was on increasingly shaky ground with myself as I continued to care for Ben, but hadn't told him about the song.

When he left last night, I knew I should have just told him. I wanted him to know. And my stupid remark about him liking Taylor Swift who'd write a song about him... could I have been a bit more on the nose? "Stolen Moment" wasn't a dating song, but it was a kind of love song, and I wished I'd told him the night we met. Or the next time I saw him. Or on tour. Or any other chance I could have taken that I'd wussed out on.

Now, I'd backed myself into a corner, and it welled in me, what I was going to do, and I prayed he'd be okay with it.

"Whit, honey, tilt your head up," Amanda said, one finger on my chin to assist.

I was dog-tired, and just sitting up in the chair was

killing me. I'd let myself float around in my head for the first half hour of hair and makeup, but the time had come to tune in.

I let out a long sigh and resisted the urge to slump. I'd not slept last night, and I don't sleep on planes—I just can't. We were done with rehearsals and heading out for some promotional shots the show would use the day-of, so I needed full hair and make-up. I wanted to go to the hotel and sleep for a day. Somehow, the drive up to the awards was making me drag in a way I didn't usually.

Ben and I had been messaging through the day—my only highlight. I felt greedy for his words, his face, his voice. I wanted him in front of me, wished he could have come with me for the whole trip.

I understood why not. I did. But I couldn't help wondering if maybe he could find something more flexible after the Army so maybe he could just... come with me all the time.

Whoa.

I'd been having more of those thoughts. More of those future-focused thoughts that betrayed what I already knew but wasn't ready to admit.

"And open," Amanda said, her minty breath wafting over my face as she finished brushing on eyeshadow. She stood back and looked back and forth between my eyes, held up a brush to one side and the other, measuring the liner. "Good. You can't tell how exhausted you are."

I frowned. "Thanks."

"You're burning that candle at both ends, my friend. You've got to sleep tonight and every night until the show, okay?" She flipped the brush over a finger and slid it back into her makeup tool belt, much the way an old gunslinger might have done his pistol.

"I know. I'm not trying to, but it has been insane. And the only time I've been able to have with Ben is late. So it's not a bad thing he's not here 'til Saturday." I inspected my hands in my lap, hoping she wouldn't see how pathetic I was, missing a man I'd seen less than twenty-four hours ago.

"Aw, honey. That happens when you're in love. You'll get through it to the sweet part—past the tortured part, and he'll be here with you for Sunday, which is perfect." She sprayed a setting spray on my face, and we waited a moment for it to dry.

She chattered on for a few minutes about the rest of the day, the rest of the week's schedule, a friend she was seeing while we were in LA, and a few other things I couldn't hear because my heart and mind were circling that statement like sharks.

That happens when you're in love.

Was I *in love* with Ben?

Was that what this feeling was?

Ben

I hit *send* and sat back in my chair. What an insanely easy process to end one's career.

It sank in, this giddy, terror-filled sensation that filled out my rib cage and crawled up into my throat. I popped up from my desk and stalked to Flint's office. With one knock, I walked in without waiting and claimed the seat in front of his desk.

He took his time acknowledging me—typical. He could either be so absorbed in whatever he was working on or be intent on making a point about barging in without waiting for his invitation, but either way, it was just a matter of time until he'd deign to acknowledge me and we'd get on with it.

"And how are you today, Lieutenant Holder?" he asked from behind his computer screen, not yet giving me his full attention.

"Just submitted the packet. I'm done May fifth." Saying it out loud sent a galloping sense of relief and excitement through me.

Flint appeared from behind his desk, a small smile on his face. Then he stood, so I did too.

"Congratulations."

We shook hands briefly, and if we weren't at work, he'd probably give me one of those obnoxious, almost-painful back-pat-hug things he did. I'd look forward to that.

"Feels good to have it done. I guess they'll approve it and process it and everything, but as you've mentioned, there's nothing to keep it from being approved at this point."

There was always the fear something would happen, that they'd say I owed more time or something, but I hadn't done anything to incur additional obligation, so there wouldn't be.

"You should be all set. I'll look forward to seeing the official word come through." He sat back down. "Get the door for just a minute?"

It wasn't so much a question as a direction, a command. That was certainly the Major Flint I'd become acquainted with in the last few years.

I closed the door and took my seat before he spoke again.

"So what's your plan?"

He'd been asking me that question, in one form or another, for nearly a year and a half. Ever since we'd been back from Afghanistan, I'd had no idea how to put one foot in front of another. I'd rarely had an answer for him that was something I could act on and be proud of beyond "wake up tomorrow." In the beginning, that had been the best answer I could give him, all I could commit to, and it had been what he'd wanted from me.

And now, I had an answer, and it felt surreal. "I think I'm going back to school."

Flint nodded, like he'd known it. I'd roll my eyes about that later.

"Any idea what for?"

"I've got to narrow it down. Maybe counseling, or social work. Something where I'm doing what my therapists did for me. I'm not about to pursue a PhD—I'm not that into school—but I want to help people. I think that's something that has changed for me. I guess, in the tritest sense, I want to pay it forward."

"A worthy endeavor, for sure. And I know anyone you spend time with will benefit. You can be proud of what you've done here—in the Rambler Battalion, and in your company, and in your time in the Army over all. You can be proud of who you are now, and that you're finding what's next."

"Thank you. I know you know this, but I'll say it now, and I'm sure I'll say it again at some point. I owe you too much to repay. I—" I cleared my throat, banishing the emotion for the moment to get this out. "I'll never forget it."

Flint's jaw flexed, and he nodded. "You don't owe me. Don't believe that for a minute. If nothing else, you helped me get my head on straight about Erin, and for that, to you, I'd be forever grateful. But you've been a friend to me, even when it didn't make sense and when I'm not the warmest guy."

We shared a knowing look, because that was saying it lightly.

"Anyway, we're good. And I suspect Erin won't let me lose touch with you, even if I try."

I chuckled at that. "I think you're right."

"Or, if you keep dating my cousin, I guess I'll never be rid of you."

Inevitable, of course, but I'd thought maybe we weren't going to work around to the subject of me and Whit after all the emotional thanksgiving.

"Well, I hope I do keep on. I'm flying out to be her date to the Grammys this weekend."

I couldn't suppress the smile that covered my face just thinking about it. I'd be nervous, but I was mostly excited to be with her.

"Saw the leave form." Flint, though, didn't seem as excited. "You ready for all of that? As soon as you're out with her at something like that, your anonymity is gone. And there will be judgement and speculation and cruelty. Are you ready for that?"

He wasn't saying it to scare me away or to try to school me about Whit's life. He'd visited her, seen glimpses of it, and I'd gathered maybe she'd confided in him once or twice about the pressure she felt.

He didn't say it because he didn't want me with her—I didn't think so. He said it because he knew I hadn't always borne pressure well, and was checking.

"She's worth it," I said, a gentler smile on my lips.

Flint laughed once, an amused little sound, and then his eyes filled with a smiling pity. "Ah. So that's how it is."

CHAPTER THIRTY-SEVEN

Whit

If this guy didn't back up off me, he was going to get an elbow to the ribs, and I would not be responsible for any cracks or breaks.

We'd been rehearsing for twenty minutes, and already, Colton Danes had bumped into me, or come up behind me trying to look all cozy. The last straw was when he came up and set a hand on my hip and his chin on my shoulder, standing close enough that his whole body was pressed against my back.

Not cute. Not funny. Definitely not welcomed.

I kept my outward smile, not interested in making any more of a scene than this could turn into, and kept my attention in the direction of the choreographer who was explaining something I couldn't focus on, and I said in a low, lethal voice, "If you don't back up and stop touching me, we're going to have problems."

His smooth, crooney voice—which should have been pleasing, but I found to be grating since I knew what was behind it—came too close to my ear. "Aw, baby, you know you like me bein' close."

I took an exaggerated step forward, tearing myself away from him, then turned to look, gave him the best *do not touch* glare, and moved closer to one of the other performers. After the meeting, I'd planned to approach the choreographer and ask if there was any way to have Danes share a mic with someone else, but she'd disappeared before I got off stage.

I could manage one more rehearsal and the actual performance. He was unlikely to make any moves when the cameras were live, but if I got a chance, I was going to talk to him and make sure he knew I had no interest. Maybe I'd been too polite. Maybe I'd smiled at him too warmly once.

Or maybe he was just an idiot.

Whatever the case, I'd make the lines clear.

A car was waiting for me outside the arena. I let my eyes shut on the trip. Though it should have been short, the traffic in LA made the two-mile drive turn into something like twenty-five minutes. I dozed off and only startled awake when the car came to a stop.

"Miss Grantham, we're here."

The driver was someone I didn't know, and that was fine. I liked having Ru, but he was dealing with an ailing parent and had taken a leave of absence.

The driver held out a hand, and I happily took it. I was toast and didn't know if I'd even be able to get food in me before passing out. Between still being on central time despite having been in LA for a few days, and generally feeling exhausted, plus not sleeping well thanks to nerves and everything floating around in my head, I was usually asleep by eight. That meant I was up early, but I didn't mind.

Somehow, I woke still exhausted, but was able to get a workout in with Kendra over video chat and feel some semblance of normalcy. I was eating meals planned out for me and delivered to my hotel room, another small mercy in itself—I could eat whatever was on the plate, and I should eat all of it, and that was that.

By the time Saturday rolled around, I was nervous and trying not to bite heads off the people who asked me questions or tried to make small talk. I knew the nerves, that I was going to feel better in forty-eight hours, but I couldn't lock down the feelings.

Feelings are exhausting.

So many darn feelings. I was nervous—wanting to win. Mildly sad, like always before a big event my parents wouldn't even be watching, or more specifically, would be actively avoiding. It felt spiteful verging on cruel. Maybe it was. Always good fodder for my therapist, though, who every so often encouraged me to reach out to them and see if they were open to a relationship with very clear boundaries, but I hadn't done it.

I didn't want the judgement—didn't want to see their disappointment. I didn't want to walk out of my childhood home, if that's what one would call it, and feel that bone-deep loneliness.

But then there was Ben. Ben helped. Ben made that loneliness nearly non-existent, and if I had him, maybe if I even walked out of those double French doors that hung at the main entrance, I wouldn't feel the same way. I'd never had someone like him in my corner.

Reese would have been, but he'd been gone with the Army for most of my growing years. For some reason, he'd tried in the last five years to see me, know me, and be near me. Likely because we had the parental alienation in common, and he'd seen glimpses of what it was like growing up a Grantham.

The truth remained, I didn't have close friends—a few people from Juilliard, but in the end, I'd been there so short a time, I hadn't made strong bonds. I'd always had my mind on escaping, and part of me did regret that. I wished I'd appreciated the opportunity, but I saw it only for what it was for my parents and not what it could really offer me.

Ben was more than just someone to fill the loneliness, and the sizzling anticipation of showing him off to everyone in the world in just a few days filled me with new hope.

$\sim$

Ben

I pulled the door of the restaurant, the bell jangling loudly and causing an elderly couple in the corner to glare at me. I was meeting Bec and Thatcher for brunch before my flight to LA. Bec had messaged me and Thatcher and said she was ready to make peace, and she'd fill us in on her plans. We were told not to ask any questions—that she wouldn't be responding unless we couldn't make it.

Normally, I wouldn't have wanted to meet up the day I was flying, but my flight was later—I wouldn't get to LA until evening, unfortunately. I don't know who booked the tickets, but since it wasn't me, I couldn't complain. They were getting me there to support Whit, and they were getting me home to avoid the ire of LTC Baker who'd made it clear, in no uncertain terms, that he would not sign off on me taking leave for even *one* day during the week, despite there being absolutely nothing on the training calendar.

So, one more point in that guy's bucket, and one more thing I wouldn't be sad to leave behind.

The hostess greeted me and led me to the table where I saw, from about fifteen feet away, Thatcher and Bec. Bec looked furious, evidently her natural state lately, and Thatcher's back was to me, the set of his shoulders and neck tense, his spine straight as a steel beam.

They didn't notice me as I approached.

"You're not my brother," Bec said in a voice full of venom.

"Trust me, I know that." Thatcher's voice was hard.

Bec's jaw clenched as her eyes flicked up to take me in. "Ben's here."

Thatcher straightened further and turned as I walked closer to stand directly at the table.

"Everything okay?"

"Just fine. I've actually got to head. Good luck, Bec," Thatcher said, with an abruptness I'd never seen before.

He stood, slid out of the tiny booth, and gave me a false smile.

People did that all the time—gave different smiles out like greeting cards, all false sentiment and empty promises. But not Thatcher. Seeing that thin stretch to his lips, the tension in his eyes and jaw... Bec better plan on talking.

"Have a great time tomorrow, and fly safe. I'll be watching." He patted me on the back as he passed and didn't look back as he left, the bells jingling behind him.

I kept my attention on him as he exited the place to give Bec a minute, and frankly, to buy myself some time to recover from witnessing them at each other *again* and seeing Thatcher so visibly upset.

I plunked down into the booth seat, bouncing a little in the process.

"How were they going to fit all three of us at this table?" I asked, desperate for something that wasn't *so what's the deal with you and Thatcher?*

"They were going to bring a chair for the end," she said, her voice calm, if a bit subdued.

"Ah." Could the waiter maybe bring me some water, or a basket of chips, or something?

"We didn't touch the chips, if you want them." She nodded to the little red basket of fresh tortilla chips and the bowl of salsa. Rosita's had the best chips of all time.

"Great." I quickly shoved enough chips into my mouth to be comical, and also to keep me busy while looking over the menu.

The waiter came. I ordered their huevos rancheros because they were bomb and then turned my attention to Bec.

"So." I folded my arms on the table and waited.

Her focus flickered from one place to the next around the room, and she sipped her water. "So. Thatcher asked me to meet him a few minutes early. We got into it, and now you're on your own."

"What does *got into it* mean for you and Thatcher?" I asked, chomping another chip despite it being nine-thirty in the morning.

"It means he came early to talk me out of what he somehow found out I was planning to do. I don't know why he thought it'd be more effective without you, but he apparently did." She crossed her arms, her legs, and leaned back in the booth.

"Okay. Tell me about that, then."

She took a deep breath. "I got a job in Europe. At a base

in Germany for their ed center. The perfect GS job popped up, and I applied, and got it, and I leave next week."

"Next week? That's... soon."

I really hoped someone was recording this for posterity because my conversational prowess was at an all-time high.

Bec snickered. "Yep. Nailed that one, Holder."

The unimpressed look I shot her made her laugh out loud.

"Tell me more," I said just as the waiter brought our food.

"It's going to be amazing. It's actually a lateral move, but I've heard once you get into the European system, it's a bit easier to move around over there, so hopefully, something will open up, and I can promote. But I get access to the base resources, though I have to find my own place, which I have some good leads on. I have a few friends who've done this, including my old boss, and I've been in contact with her."

She sliced through a fried triangle of dough. This place served sopapillas as a brunch item and they. Were. Mind-blowing. If I hadn't been about to be in a tailor-made suit in front of millions of people escorting one of the most beautiful women in the world, I would have ordered those.

"That sounds like a perfect opportunity for you. I can't think of anything better, really." I'd expected bad news based on all the tension wafting from the table when I came in.

"It is. Erin's been telling me I should think about getting out of here—away from Tennessee, away from Fort Camp-bell, for over a year. For a long time, I felt like that was a betrayal. I felt like moving away was a kind of moving on that Dillon would never have, so it wasn't fair for me to do."

She focused on her meal for a moment, taking a bite, chewing, and if I knew her, composing herself so the emotions that seemed buried so deep wouldn't try to surface.

"I understand. I've felt that way, even about my own stuff. I can see why it would be difficult for you."

"I think I finally realized that all my traveling and getting away was my attempt to have little glimpses of life outside of here without the risk of actually moving, and without the guilt of it. But the last six months or so have made me realize I don't want to be stuck here, physically or mentally, for the rest of my life."

Her lovely brown eyes met mine, and I saw it there. The fear, the longing, the hope.

If she felt her travel had been more adventure-seeking and less evasion tactic, that was for her to decide. But, without a doubt, getting out of here would be good for her. She'd lived here for two years before her brother was killed, and now well over a year after. Watching her go through life without her brother, really her only relative she had in the world she saw regularly before he passed, was like watching something brutal and violent you couldn't stop.

I felt nothing but relief that she was taking this step. "Why is Thatcher so upset about this? I would have thought he'd be supportive."

She set her fork down and wiped her mouth with her napkin. The patches of red at her cheeks deepened, and it shocked me to see she was blushing.

"I'm not sure."

I swallowed a particularly delicious bite. "Really?"

"Really. He nearly blew up as soon as I said I was leaving next week. He's been hounding me for weeks, wanting me to check in with him and let him know I was okay. He's got it in his head I'm this fragile creature who needs... something from him, and I don't. I think he got upset that I made that clear. He's acting like he's trying to do what Dillon might have done for me—be this disapproving big brother. It's really irritating."

I couldn't help the grin that jumped to my lips as she said that.

"I don't think that's quite it." I had to be careful here.

"What do you mean?"

She tucked her short hair behind her ear, and that small action made me wonder when I'd see her again. We were a strange mix of close and not close at all, but we'd had Dillon in common for long enough now that I thought we'd stay in touch.

"I mean, I don't think it's as simple as him wanting to fill Dillon's role. I know Thatcher cares about you, wants you to have a great life. I'm the same—I want you to have a full life and not be hobbled by the loss you've experienced, even if the grief will never leave you."

Her face darkened, and mine must have, too.

"I want that for both of you, too," she said, her voice low.

Nothing but that drop in tenor and the slight shake of her fork would have betrayed any emotion. Bec kept a lock down on herself like I'd never seen when it came to the feelings surrounding her brother, and the fact that her voice and her hand shook told me just exactly how unsettled she was by the conversation with Thatcher.

"I hope you'll talk to him one last time before you go. I hate to think of you guys parting on bad terms, and you know it'll tear him up."

She had to know it would, even if she didn't fully know the extent to which it would.

She nodded, her face sullen. "I know. I'll... figure it out."

I reached across to where her hand rested on the table and patted it. "You will."

I smiled at her, and she smiled back, and this time, it was a small but real one.

"Enough about me. Let's talk about you dating the princess of Country music and not even telling me," she said with an accusatory brow.

"I haven't seen you. You may have noticed that I kind of freaked out about that, seeing as how I joined Thatcher on the hunt for you a few weeks ago. So it's not like you've been available for updates on my love life."

"*Love* life?" she asked, her eyes wide and piercing as she watched me.

I took a bite, let myself chew and swallow carefully, returning her stare.

I wasn't sure what she saw there, but she broke into a broad smile then, all teeth and sparkling eyes. "Good to know, my friend. Good to know."

CHAPTER THIRTY-EIGHT

Whit

"Hello?"

"Ms. Grantham, we have a Mr. Holder here, who says he's supposed to meet you?" The nasal tone of the head of Reception came through the hotel room phone just as I walked in.

"Yes. Please send him up immediately," I said, breathless with the elation that hit at the news that Ben was there.

Ben's here!

I paced back and forth, wondering just how slowly the Reception people were moving if it was taking him *this* long to get from the lobby to my room.

Our room.

I hadn't changed out of the clothes I'd worn all day, a short halter dress and sleek ponytail, requisite stage and camera makeup, heels—I needed to shower, let my hair dry, and get to bed soon. I'd hoped he'd get here sooner, but no doubt the traffic had kept him away.

We'd messaged a few times a day since I'd left. I think he was giving me space and I was giving him space, too. I didn't know why, but I just wanted him *with* me. He was calming, even as he set my insides to fizz.

Finally, the knock on the door came, and I practically sprinted to get to it, checking the peep hole to see him turned sideways, probably chatting with the guard stationed in the hallway. My belly flipped, and I pulled the door open.

Ben Holder stood there, a bag in each hand, jeans over gray and red Nike tennis shoes, a rumpled long-sleeved T-shirt, and his hair clean cut on the sides and a bit longer on top like he'd worn on the tour. It hadn't been all that long since I'd seen him, but he was absolutely gorgeous. Almost to the point that I didn't know what to do with him, except that I'd been waiting ever since we'd said goodbye Tuesday night for this moment.

"Hi." I grabbed his arm since his hands were full and pulled him into the room.

I set his bag to one side, and he hung his garment bag to his left on a hook meant for a jacket, though that was fairly ridiculous for LA unless it was a rain jacket.

We both had the same idea.

Our arms wrapped around each other, and the relief washed over me as he pressed me to him, leaned back just a bit to lift me off the floor. Then his mouth was on mine, and the relief turned to a new sense of urgency. He bent just slightly, put his hands on the backs of my thighs, and pulled me up—like it was nothing, mind you—and held me with my legs circling his torso and my head now a few inches higher than his. His arms locked underneath me to hold me in place, and I urged him closer, my hands around his neck.

With a groan, he turned and my back gently slammed against the wall as he pushed closer, let his hands run over my cheeks, my neck, skate down my body as I did the same, relishing having him in front of me, savoring every touch and breath and taste.

The phone startled us both, and he pulled back, giving me the most delectable look shaded with desire and a laugh.

"Guess you should get that," he said, his voice all gravel and grit.

"Probably should. You never know." I cleared my throat and let my feet meet the ground toes first as he released me.

My body was thrumming with adrenaline now, making me wonder how I'd ever sleep.

"Hello?"

"Bedtime, princess. You need eight hours tonight—you're going to be in for a long day."

Nikki's voice was no more or less demanding than usual. She had a way of delivering good *and* bad news with a kind of business-like monotone. Most times I'd greet bedtime, if I hadn't already been asleep, with delight. Tonight, it felt like punishment.

"Yes, *mother*."

"My timing is usually impeccable. Tell Ben hi, and don't let him keep you up all night," she said, and that thought brought even more heat to my cheeks.

I clicked the phone down into the receiver, silently marveling at the fact that hotels even had room phones anymore.

"Everything okay?" he asked, still standing where I'd left him.

"Yes. That was Nikki with my *go to bed* call. I have to be

up early, and she seems to have guessed you'd be getting in late and that might distract me from my bedtime."

I grinned as he looked down, almost shyly, though clearly pleased with me, or himself, or us—whatever it was, that smile made me hungry for more of them.

"I don't want you to be too worn out. Let's get you to bed," he said gamely, and moved to get his bags.

I took a moment to look around the room. The suite was big, but in the end had only one bedroom and a living room. While I was a big name, I wasn't someone who demanded the presidential suite when showing up for an awards dinner, nor did I want to spend the money to pay for it for the week I was there, so I took something far lower on the totem pole and didn't mind that a bit.

Ben seemed to notice that at the same time I thought it and looked at me.

"Where should I..." His Adam's apple bobbed as he swallowed.

"So... that's sort of up to you." I gave him a bright, cheesy grin. Not natural, for sure, but I didn't want him to feel pressured. "You can sleep with me, and by that I mean sleep—" I gave him my most earnest look, "—or we can fix up the sofa out here, which extends to a really nice bed."

He gave a kind of resigned sigh and just looked at me. I couldn't tell what he was thinking, but he seemed to feel defeated, and that, as with most things having to do with him, made my pulse race. I trotted over to him and hugged him around the waist as he stood there holding the bags. With my arms still around him, I looked up at him.

"I don't have an ulterior motive. I went with the one bedroom because you're only here one night. If you are uncomfortable, I will get you a separate room right now, no questions asked, and no drama. Please don't feel—"

"I'm fine, Whit." He dropped his bags and ran his hands over my back, through my long hair. "I have every confidence that we can share a room, as we've done many times. I'll take the couch so you can sleep without my snoring waking you up, and you can come wake me up in the morning so I don't miss a minute with you."

I ignored the drop of disappointment that he didn't opt to sleep with me, which felt embarrassing and a little sharp, but at the same time, he was probably right. I needed to rest well, and it'd be hard enough to do that knowing the day that awaited me, let alone if he really did snore.

"Do you really snore?" I asked, stepping back and picking up the garment bag so the suit I couldn't wait to see him in didn't wrinkle.

He gave me a smoldering look. "Wouldn't you like to know?"

I laughed then returned his look. "You know I would."

He practically gulped, and my toes tingled at the effect I clearly had on him. It was too sweet, too sensitive. I loved it.

I ran a hand over my chin, over the raw feeling left from kissing him with his five o'clock shadow.

"Sorry," he said, wincing. He smoothed his thumb over the undoubtedly red skin, frown lines bracketing his mouth.

"That's what makeup's for," I said with a smile. Amanda could cover up anything, and this wouldn't be a problem by morning. All it did was make me want to kiss him more.

"I'll be sure to shave before I give you your good night kiss," he said, the corners of his mouth turning up just slightly.

"If you must."

CHAPTER THIRTY-NINE

Ben

The crowd of people screamed from either side of the tinted windows, phones, flashes, everything shuttering as the driver pulled forward in the line of like limousines and town cars toward the red carpet.

Whit squeezed my hand, and I turned my attention to her.

Dazzling.

Not a word I'd ever thought before, but she was. I'd felt winded upon seeing her coming out of her room where I waited for her.

She had an old Hollywood wave to her long, dark hair, diamond earrings probably worth something north of what I'd earn over a lifetime, and a blazing red dress just shy of what would be considered scandalous on someone with a more voluptuous body. The dress plunged low in front, though not as low as some I'd already seen from the window, and came to a few inches above her knee. It was far more revealing as she sat, but I didn't let myself linger on the smooth lines of her thighs.

Nope.

The Grammys, I'd been told, were always a little more expressive in terms of fashion—not as uptight as The Oscars. Since Whit was performing, she'd be changing clothes before she took the stage, and somewhere, a car was delivering Amanda and Damon and probably Nikki to a backstage area where they'd assist in her change of costume and then back into her gown.

Whit's hand was warm, dry, and steady. I knew she was nervous—I could see it in the pull around her mouth, the perfect lines of her lips highlighted in a matching red of her dress, but they pulled flat just a bit.

"You all right?" I asked, squeezing that hand, relishing the fingers laced with mine.

"Yes. I'm ready." Her voice sounded sure.

She'd gone somewhere mentally in the last twenty minutes since we'd gotten in the car. She'd been nervous, even a little short, though not with me. Everyone understood—in many ways, her nerves were reflecting everyone else's.

For my part, I was nervous as hell. I wore a black suit that fit me better than anything I'd ever worn—I looked great, I could admit. If I made it out of this without sweating through the jacket, I'd reward myself somehow.

When Whit saw me, I'd rolled up my comedically dropped jaw while she'd just shaken her head and said, "You do clean up nice, Lieutenant Holder."

At that point, of course, I couldn't kiss her—her makeup had been applied and perfected, and I didn't dare face Amanda's, or Nikki's, or Whit's wrath.

I wished I'd had some great speech prepared, but I didn't. I wanted to tell her everything I felt for her, how amazing she was, but I wouldn't get it out right, not now, and not as we were pulling up to the red carpet.

"I'm proud of you," I said, feeling strangely emotional.

"Thank you for being here. It means so much to me."

One last ounce of pressure on our hands together, and then, it began.

The initial barrage of cameras overwhelmed with flashes in every direction, and the sound of shutters snapping—it almost sounded like gunfire. It occurred to me then that there was definitely a possibility for someone to experience trauma just from going through a gauntlet like this. But Whit's smile blazed as she stepped out of the car at the hand of the person opening—it'd been decided she'd go first, though I would have liked to be the one to help her out.

Then I came out, and it seemed everyone knew my name, all shouting for me like they were on my short list of friends. More screams were for Whit, and all the cameras, the microphones that waited in the first area, vibrated with energy and excitement.

We made our way through, my hand at her back as we moved, then watching as she hit the mark for the posed photographs, then I'd join her for an interview, avoid saying much at all, and we'd move on. The person escorting us through the gauntlet on the carpet was nice, and that helped me relax. Finally, we made it inside, and I could breathe.

Or I thought I could, but then we started mingling, Whit introducing me to everyone who was anyone in her industry. It was overwhelming. I kept it together, not lapsing into ridiculous fan-induced idiocy like I had with Jamie Morris, but I maybe said twenty words in that half hour of chatting.

I'd met just about everyone in Country music between the events we'd been to and her tour and socializing in the last few months, but this was different. This was everyone who was anyone, and it was names I didn't even realize I knew until I was shaking a hand. It was wild.

Mostly, though, it was amazing to see Whit in this environment, so clearly comfortable with herself in the context, so sure, and so alive. I kept the thoughts about my belonging there at bay, not wanting to betray any of my insecurities by turning inward.

When it was time to take our seats, I'd grown more than exhausted. I wasn't an introvert by any means, but making small talk, chatting with this many people, proved insanely draining. I was relieved to have a chance to sit down and watch a show.

Except I didn't find relief when I did sit, because I became obnoxiously anxious. Whit was nervous, just sitting quietly by me, and that made me nervous right back.

"Everything okay?" I whispered, ducking my lips to her ear.

She smiled tightly and nodded.

I pushed out a breath as the lights lowered and the opening act went on. It was amazing, exciting, impressive—all those things, but my mind remained on the small powerhouse next to me, a cocktail of anticipation, self-consciousness, excitement, and overwhelm making my head swim. Before I knew it, Whit was escorted back stage by a runner so she'd have time to get changed, and I was left to sit, nod politely, and wish I had my phone so I could look busy.

The lights went low, and the music began. Eight of the top Country stars were lit with spotlights as guitars and drums crashed and the song took flight. Four women, four men, all decked out in guitars and cowboy hats—Whit's transformation had my attention completely. She wore cut-off jeans and a tied up button-down sleeveless shirt with red cowboy boots and a white cowboy hat. What an insane shift from the polished, daring look, and yet, she was no less magnetic.

She looked at home up there, sharing spotlights and marching across the stage like she owned it. Toward the end as the group worked its way to the platform that had extended out into the crowd, Colton Danes, whom I'd done an excellent job ignoring by keeping my eyes squarely on Whit, slid his slimy hand around Whit's waist and pulled her to his side, his fingers on her bare stomach.

It'd been a while since I'd felt rage, but there it was, crawling up my throat and nearly steaming out my ears. I might have launched out of my seat if I hadn't been gripping the sides of my chair, if I hadn't seen her cock her hip to the side and bump him away from her, and if he hadn't complied with that less than subtle hint.

I could feel eyes on me, could practically hear the questions the reporters would ask as we left, but as long as she was okay, I'd be okay. After what felt like an hour, she was back in her red dress, her hair, make up, shoes all looking as though she hadn't just been performing her heart out on stage for a six-minute medley and ending it by getting groped by a fellow performer.

I turned to her immediately. "You okay?"

I bent to look in her eyes and saw only determination there, which was a relief, if a bit confusing.

"I'm just fine. He knew better, but he won't get confused after tonight."

I had no idea what that meant, but she seemed settled, so I wasn't about to push it, especially when the applause had amplified as more presenters walked out and the award for best song was going to be announced.

Before I had a chance to get light-headed, there it was, someone saying *Whit Grantham for "Stolen Moment!"* Somehow, my body knew it should stand, knew I should hug Whit, kiss her cheek, absorb the smile and joy radiating off her in that moment, take in her words as she said, "Forgive me for doing it like this."

I sat down as she reached the podium, adrenaline shooting through me as she took the award and envelope, hugged the presenters, and then stood at the thin microphone that popped up out of the stage every time an award was announced.

"Thank you so much for this honor," she started, her voice rich, beautiful as always, a slight tremor of nerves or adrenaline, maybe even emotion.

She continued, thanking all of the people who'd helped on the album, who'd influenced her, all so rapidly, I could only understand a third of the names.

"Finally, I have to say thank you to the soldier who inspired this song. Without his vulnerability and willingness to share his pain, this song wouldn't exist. I'd like to say thank you to all our men and women serving, for how much they give up, and for those who make the ultimate sacrifice."

She took a breath and found me in the audience, and my thudding heart pounded so loudly, I could hardly hear.

"But today, I'd especially like to thank my boyfriend, Lieutenant Ben Holder, who is, in fact, that soldier who inspired this song. My heart has always been yours."

The room exploded, people cheering and standing, a few around me clapping me on the back as Whit was escorted off the stage, her focus straight ahead.

I heard nothing—not the sound of clapping or

comments as people shook my hand or smiled in my face, offering me congratulations.

Minutes ticked by, and my mind was all white paint in a white room, just bright and harsh and bland and empty.

On what? Why were they congratulating me? And why had the floor dropped out from underneath me? What did it mean when she said I was him?

It was metaphorical. It had to be. It must have been, because we'd never met—I hadn't talked with her before Flint's house, and the song had already been out then.

Or had I?

I sat down, feeling my hand shake and tucking it beneath my thigh, my heart continuing to pound like I was running, racing, with Whit still nowhere to be seen. I waited through a commercial break, through another award announcement, and finally, I had to get space, still not breathing right, still not making sense of anything, my skin nearly crawling from the confusion.

My mind was empty as I went through the motions in the bathroom, that same white room, then as I made my way into the hallway and toward the door to the theater.

"Ben," came her voice, and I turned.

I took her in, beautiful, flushed, concern in her eyes, but I couldn't tell why it didn't impress me like it normally would have. I had no idea what I was doing here.

"Please talk to me," she said, her words slow and level as she approached.

She put a hand out to touch me, then must have thought better of it as she pulled back and let it drop to her side.

"I don't know what to say," I said, welcoming the approaching numbness because I couldn't begin to process what her words meant, what I was doing here with her in a room full of people I didn't know as the date of a person I certainly didn't know.

"I didn't want to tell you that way. But I've been too—"

I waved a hand, stopping her. "Let's just get through this. Then we'll talk."

CHAPTER FORTY

Whit

Ben was barely meeting my eye, not touching me, not talking. I didn't want to push him, but the look on his face, even in the darkness with the spotlight in my eyes, had terrified me.

I didn't know I was going to say it—not for sure—until Colton Danes had slid his hand around my waist, and that had been it. That had been the straw, both for me kneeing him in the balls back stage, which he'd fully earned after I'd spoken with him *and* the choreographer the day before, and for me telling the world that Ben had been the inspiration for my now award-winning song.

Ben had looked completely blank. And now, he still seemed stunned. He wasn't even cold, just completely empty, like he wasn't even in the building. I won two more awards and accepted the one Jamie and I won for our song— a good sign for our Oscar hopes, people had clucked backstage as I exited, and I wished I could have cared more about it.

But my mind was on Ben as I quickly realized he was simply shocked—he hadn't yet become angry or even confused. Each time I'd won, he'd stood, smiled, kissed my cheek, a consummate professional under pressure, in the end, and I'd kept my thanks short and sweet, only listing names I'd memorized in preparation, and waiting for the end of it.

Every minute that ticked by, the distance between us grew until, when I finally heard the click of the car door and the driver speeding away from the flashing lights and screaming fans outside the venue, I knew his mind was sifting through my words, trying to make sense of everything.

"Please say something," I begged, not hiding the desperation in my voice.

"I can't think of anything," he said, no edge to his voice, just emptiness.

The panic at that sound, the sound of *nothing* in his tone, not even anger or confusion, choked me. "Do you have questions? I can tell you. I went into the bar that night and was getting a drink before I sang. And you said—"

"I don't need to know. That's not... I don't want to know."

My pulse pounded in my neck, my ears full of the rushing sound of my blood. How could he not want to know?

"I should have told you so much sooner. I should have told you that day at Reese's," I said, feeling heartsick and rushed.

Somehow, LA traffic had given way in honor of my

crisis, and we had maybe five minutes until we got to the hotel. And I knew what would happen then.

"Yeah."

God, help me.

Was it all down to this? Had my cowardice dissolved any chance I had with him, all because of this stupid secret that shouldn't even matter? This was insane. This, between us, was so much more than this small thing. I should have told him, but Ben was generous and reasonable, and part of me had always known he'd forgive me for not telling him sooner.

So what was *this?*

My mind scrambled for something more—how could I explain, and how could I tell him how much the conversation meant, how much it influenced me? How could I say those things *now*, like they weren't excuses for lying?

Before I came up with anything, the car stopped, the door swung open, and we were shuffled into the lobby by security, then into the elevator, then down the hall to the room. When the door clicked closed, the silence was unbearable.

"I'm so sorry. You can't know how sorry I am." I moved in front of him to gain his focus, to make him talk to me.

He'd been standing, staring at his bag packed and ready to go on the couch. He turned to me, his movements stilted. "I'm sorry, too."

"Why?" I asked, stepping closer to him.

"For being so drunk I didn't remember you. For being the other end of a conversation that influenced you so much, you wrote an award-winning song about it, and not remembering a damn word of it." His face showed a hint of his anger then, his disgust—at me, or himself, I wasn't sure.

"No. No, that doesn't matter."

"You're right. That's not the issue."

Something cold had entered his voice, and if I'd felt any sense of alarm before, it had been foolishness. That nothingness in his voice had been better than this new edge.

"Okay," I said dumbly, my mind screaming with unspent words.

His eyes searched back and forth between mine, grazing over my face, down over my dress, then back to my eyes. He kept looking, and I prayed he could see the regret I felt, the sorrow for hurting him in any way, how much I cared for him.

And then, finally, he spoke.

"I hope it was worth it," he said, less cold and more resigned.

"Worth what?"

"I hope all this, you and me. I hope it did what you needed it to, Whit. I hope you get everything you've been wanting."

"I don't—"

"Congratulations on your wins."

He stepped around me, grabbed his bags, and was out the door before I could form a sentence.

I should have chased after him, but my feet wouldn't move. I don't know how long I stood there, looking at the empty place on the couch where his bag used to be.

He was always scheduled to leave tonight, but this wasn't how I'd planned it. He'd left to catch his flight, but one thing was all too clear: I'd lost him.

CHAPTER FORTY-ONE

Ben

I changed out of my suit in the bathroom at the airport. In my worn jeans and sweatshirt, I felt more like myself. Inconspicuous, uninteresting—just another guy heading somewhere. Nothing remarkable, exactly what I was looking forward to feeling.

My flight left LAX just before eleven, and I got home just shy of five the next morning. The four-hour flight had been a sleepless one. I'd closed my eyes, tried to sleep and knock out so I wouldn't let the thoughts creep in. Staying numb wasn't healthy, wasn't productive, wasn't going to help me in the end, but it was a matter of self-preservation.

The reality was this—I loved Whit Grantham, and she'd used me.

She'd told me she would, and she'd held up her end of the bargain, with me the fool sitting on a plane ride home after she'd made her big play, feeling more hurt than I had a right to, more used than I ever had, and even though I hated admitting it to myself, betrayed.

Somewhere along the way, I'd fallen, and I'd thought maybe she would, too. I'd thought the contract, the tour, the arrangement had all fallen by the wayside over Christmas when we'd shared our feelings. I'd thought we were really, actually dating.

Hadn't we agreed to that?

We had, but maybe that was just another level of her betrayal that I couldn't fully digest yet. I wanted to believe she'd felt something for me—maybe she'd gotten caught up in our chemistry, in the tour, like Flint had feared, and then reverted back to her brutal pragmatism that would get her where she wanted to go once it'd worn off.

Every time I shifted in the too-small seat, the low lights of the cabin casting an eerie glare over my fellow red-eye passengers, the more I ran through the series of our relationship as I'd seen it.

We met at Flint's. I gave her a tour of post. I liked her social media. She messaged me, and I responded. She invited me to an event as a friend. Then another. Then, she proposed the fake relationship, and I agreed. Then on the tour, we discovered genuine feelings and bagged the fake for real. Then we dated, grew closer, and I'd fallen for her like a chump.

But to her, none of that was true. She'd known me and some of the most personal things about me, for over a year before we ever met. And she'd had time and time and time again to come out and say so. She'd chosen not to, and all I could think, even though I hated myself and I hated her for even thinking it, was that she'd waited until a moment like last night to get the biggest impact. Because the story of a drowning soldier coming home, of the singer-songwriter loving him from afar—how beautiful.

But the story of that love now come to life, in front of everyone's eyes, now *that* was a story. That was something people would talk about for years, would inspire movies, would inspire more songs, and would likely nab Whit that spot at Johnson's table she'd been so desperate for.

It was a blow. That's all it was. I'd get past this, I knew I would. But for now, for the rest of this plane ride, for the rest of this week as I went to and from work and avoided talking about what everyone I knew had to have seen on my face if the camera had cut to me when Whit was talking, I'd let this pull toward numbness win.

~

Whit

The victory lap.

That was what my team called the chock-full schedule of the next few days. I was shuffled from one interview to the next, and it took every ounce of energy not to let everyone see how little I cared about this.

It didn't make sense that Ben's leaving on a flight he'd always planned on taking would have thrown me like this. I kept convincing myself we'd had a disagreement, that I'd see him when I got back from all this insanity, this weird LA bubble that took over when I was in Hollywood and couldn't think straight.

I wouldn't let myself think of him, so withdrawn as he congratulated me. I couldn't think of that beautiful face, the sadness in his eyes even as he said entirely without malice, *I hope you get everything you've been wanting.*

That was what had me curled on my side, feeling like my insides were rotting, when Amanda came in to start my touch up for the evening schedule. I'd been busy from six that morning until two hours ago. I'd come back to the room, eaten a few bites of baked chicken, and curled up here on this pristine white bed.

"Whit?" Amanda's voice sounded in the silent room.

I could tell she was worried. This wasn't me.

"Right here." My voice came out rusty from an early morning, a long day, little sleep.

"I see you there," she said, and sat gently on the side of the bed I faced so her hips came into view first. I looked up at her, and she said, "What's going on, hun?"

I started to wave her off, tell her I was exhausted, just worn out, it wasn't a big deal, but that look on her face told me she knew. *She knew,* and she was here, and even if she was someone I paid to put makeup on my face, she was probably the closest thing I had to a friend right now.

"He's gone," I said, more like sobbed, since now that I'd said it, it was true, and I couldn't pretend we'd just argued, or that I thought he'd see me again and let me explain when I got home.

Amanda covered my hand with hers and clamped down her jaw. She was supremely empathetic, and she'd be crying with me any minute. I didn't cry often—it wasn't a public sport. I'd been raised to avoid any shows of emotion, and maybe part of my British heritage had shared its *stiff upper lip* approach with me.

But this wasn't one of those moments. It wasn't a time where I could skirt around it and talk myself into waiting until I was alone, until I wasn't wearing a centimeter of mascara that would run despite it being waterproof and ruin my false lashes. I couldn't keep pretending that Ben was only a friend, or that what'd happened on Sunday hadn't been the end.

I couldn't pretend that I wasn't in love with him anymore.

"I knew he'd be upset about the song," I started, but my voice broke, and I turned my face into the bed to weep.

I felt Amanda move, and when the bed depressed again, she was shoving a tissue in my hand. I blew my nose, pursed my lips to help lock down the tears so I could tell her, suddenly feeling a desperate need for someone to understand.

"He can't be that upset about it. He's a good guy," she said now that I'd calmed and the sound of my crying wasn't filling the room.

"He is. He *is*." I was crying again, fat tears slipping down my cheeks as I sat up. "He's the *best* guy. And he wouldn't be upset if it was just that. He thinks I did it for show. He thinks I've been manipulating him this whole time."

I pressed my fingers into my eyes, trying to staunch the flow, until I realized I wasn't going to stop—no point in it now.

"Why would he think that?" Amanda asked, ducking her head to catch my eye.

"Because I did it in front of everyone, it seemed like it was trying to grab a headline, or make it seem like this big, cosmic love story."

Amanda set a warm hand on one of my knees curled up in front of me. "But isn't it?"

Her gentle voice undid me. I tried to hold in the sob, but

it slipped past my lips. I rested my head on my knees and felt Amanda's hand smooth over my hair. When I'd composed myself again, I took a deep breath before raising my head and looking back into her face.

"It might have been."

CHAPTER FORTY-TWO

Ben

I'd strategically ducked every attempt Thatcher and Flint had made at cornering me after seeing the look in their eyes—confusion, a little pity, concern.

I didn't want it. I wanted to move ahead, keep going, get to the next week and the week after that so I wouldn't feel so hollowed out. Time would help.

My therapist had listened. He'd let me get it all out. He'd asked me only two questions. *Do you think she cares for you?* And *Do you care for her?* For some reason, his refusal to be outraged on my behalf, even though that was patently *not* his purview, had infuriated me.

In some ways, it was a relief to feel something other than the sad, resigned feeling since I'd boarded the plane. Of course I had hurt, I had some anger, I had disbelief, but mostly, I felt like what had happened was what was always going to happen because being with Whit had been too good to be true.

But Dr. Cartan's two questions had stuck needles between my ribs, and I felt irritable the rest of the week with them running around in my head.

Did I think she cared for me? Sure. Probably some part of her. I did think we were friends, whatever else happened.

Great.

But where that also took me was that she clearly hadn't cared for me *enough*. Not enough to avoid a spectacle, not enough to tell me the truth, not enough to love me back.

What a fool.

I especially avoided Major Flint because I knew what was coming—he'd essentially called this. He'd warned me. He'd known my heart was soft and easy and just waiting for someone to give it the time and attention it needed. He'd known that the tour and hell, maybe even the fame, had drawn me in.

He knew his cousin, too. I'd been arrogant enough to think I knew her better than he did—that he was wrong about her. I'd had dose after healthy dose of humility in the last few years, and I'd wanted to be right about this, about her.

Damn it.

Bridgette texted me at least twice daily, begging me to talk to her, to tell her how I was doing, what I was thinking, what was going on, when she could come up to Nashville and slash Whit's tires. I'd responded to the first message telling her I was fine, that I was sad, but fine.

I didn't want to sit down in it with her, or with Thatcher, who looked like he was ready to hear my tale of woe whenever I wanted to lay it out for him. But I didn't want to. I wanted to one-foot-in-front-of-the-other until it didn't feel so empty right under my breastbone.

"Lieutenant Holder, I'd like to see you before you head out," Flint called to me as he passed my desk where I was gathering my things for the day.

I'd avoided everyone's subtle prods, the whispers and glances of more than a few soldiers who had to have seen the show and put the pieces together that Whit Grantham's boyfriend (though *former* echoed in my head) was *me*.

"Roger, sir," I said, praying this was something official and not the inevitable comeuppance.

I finished loading my bag, shutting down my computer, locking my file drawer, and then made my way to Flint's office. I ducked my head in, hoping to get away with that and not the whole sitting down and heart-to-hearting.

"Sir?"

"Plans tonight, Holder?" Flint said, not looking up from the planner set in front of him.

"Uh, not sure, sir. Probably something low key—"

"Good. Come to the house. Erin is making homemade pizza. I already told her you'd be there."

"Uhhh... I'm not sure I can," I said, my stomach clenching at the thought of an evening with him and Erin, sickeningly in love and determined to help me.

"Nonsense. I'll see you there in half an hour. I'm walking out in ten."

I pulled up at Flint's house to find Erin sitting on the back steps, evidently waiting for me, since she stood and smiled as I parked next to the garage. Flint's car wasn't home yet, but he was minutes behind, if that. I didn't have a full minute to take a deep breath and steady myself before Erin had pulled open the door to my truck.

"Come here, you," she said, that sweet voice at once comforting and a harbinger of doom.

I hopped down, and she pulled my shoulders into a rough, quick hug, then released me. "You okay?"

"Yep," I said with a curt nod, wishing that'd be the end of it.

"Okay. Come in and fix your pizza. Crusts and fixings are ready—you just have to build it."

She led the way to the door, then into the kitchen, and I had to appreciate her way with me, or really everyone. She was a tender-hearted person, incredibly empathetic, but she understood me well enough to know, or maybe she could just see, I didn't want to sit and talk.

She was good at giving me something to do, and topping a pizza after a long day with an unsatisfying lunch hitting bottom over six hours ago meant I was more than ready for food. That my dinner would be some of her food was an unexpected delight for the day.

Before I'd finished spreading the sauce over the home-made and shaped crust, Flint came through the door. I focused on my pizza as Erin went to greet him and ignored the pang their murmurs and Flint's low laugh caused.

"Beer?" he asked after delivering his keys to the hook where they stayed by the door and dumping the empty container he'd used for his lunch and coffee in the sink.

"Sure."

"Me too," Erin said, as she swirled sauce from a pan on the stove over a large pizza already sitting on a stone.

Somehow, we made small talk for a few minutes before Flint crossed his arms, leaned back against the counter next to Erin, and leveled me with the look I was all too familiar with.

"How was your weekend?" he asked, like it wasn't a grenade.

"Eventful."

I didn't want to drag this out, but I hadn't talked about it yet, except to my therapist, and that had been one big, pathetic whining tirade, and I didn't know how to even think about it any other way.

"Have you spoken with her since she got back?" he asked, and I wondered if he was avoiding saying her name for my sake.

"I don't know if she's back." That should make it clear I'd had no communication and had been off social media completely.

Erin glanced at me as she shoved one pizza stone into the top oven. "She is."

I sipped my beer, watched Flint's cat meander into the kitchen and start his path of weaving between each set of legs, begging for attention. The cat was shameless and endearing because of it.

"Did you know she wrote that song about you?" Flint asked, pinning me with that intense stare so I had nowhere to go.

"I did not," I admitted.

"No clue?"

I stretched my neck to one side, then the other. "You remember what I was like the first few weeks back. I put the black-out in black-out drunk. I'm pretty sure it was on one of those nights, and obviously enough, I don't remember anything about that week or two before I at least tried to stay conscious."

I'd paid penance for that time. I'd worked through it.

But realizing that I'd had an interaction with someone like Whit and had no memory of it created no small amount of shame in me.

Our interaction had been influential enough for her that she'd walked away and created something from it. Something meaningful. Something *I'd* found to be meaningful, and I'd had no idea it was about me.

No wonder it had always felt so familiar.

I'd walked away from it and probably puked my guts out the next day, remembering nothing but that I'd spent fifty bucks on booze and a taxi ride home. Maybe I even woke up to someone I didn't remember talking to, much less sleeping with.

That thought sent a fresh flash of frustration and fear through me. It could have even been Whit, and I never would have known. The very behavior that'd been the catalyst for my change, for the promise I'd made myself and that had kept me from sleeping with Whit, was potentially something that had had me with her without even knowing.

My cheeks were burning, but Flint and Erin gave me a moment to work through my thoughts before he continued.

"So you found out Sunday night? That's how she told you?"

"Me and everyone else watching."

I wished the bitterness in my voice wasn't something I actually felt. I wished the significance of her saying those words at that moment wasn't so huge—that it was just her telling me this secret she'd kept, and that was all we had to work through. Instead, it had been the end of our relationship, the end of anything real between us.

Flint cursed, which had my eyes jumping to him because he, as a rule, didn't curse. "I'm sorry, Ben. Truly."

"It's fine," I said, not believing it.

"It's not. You know it's not. I'm certain Whit knows it's not." He pulled Erin to him as she wiped her hands on a kitchen towel.

Erin looked at me with a regretful smile as she leaned into Flint. "She definitely knows. She has put on a good face in interviews, but she clearly knows—I can tell she's not all right."

Despite myself, a spike of alarm shot through me. "Is she okay? Why do you say that?"

She gave me a sweet smile. "She's just... it's hard to explain, but she seems different in interviews. And people keep asking her about you guys, and she's being very evasive."

A bitter laugh escaped. "I'm sure it'd be inconvenient if it came out we're not together anymore."

I would have liked that to sound harsh, sharp, but it only sounded sad.

"I know it's wrong she didn't tell you, but is it really something you can't forgive?" Erin asked.

I bought time by swigging my beer. "If that was the only issue, I could get over it."

Her brows rose while Flint watched with his eagle eyes. "Then what—"

"It was all for show. All of it. It started with a signed contract, and over Christmas, I thought we essentially shredded that and started off at the beginning of a real relationship. I missed all the signs that it was still fake. I was an idiot, and as angry as I am with her, I'm mostly just disappointed in myself." I set my bottle down and crossed my arms.

"What signs?" Flint asked. Demanded.

"Probably the biggest one was that her manager or PR person or whatever she is, Nikki, she had me sign some new confidentiality agreements and a few other forms I don't even remember. I'd thought it was because the old ones I'd signed when I'd agreed to the fake relationship were void or something, but now I realize it was likely because she was going to up the ante, and me going public with the information that our relationship was all for show wouldn't sit well after that big announcement she made."

Erin recoiled and looked at Flint. "That doesn't sound like Whit. She's dedicated and motivated, but I just can't see her using you like that. Why would she want you to think it was real when she already had the fake set up that you'd agreed to?"

I ignored Flint's clenched jaw. "That I don't know, nor will I pretend to understand. At this point, all I can say is I should have known."

"Why?" Erin pressed, God love her.

I forced a laugh, feeling no humor whatsoever. It was kind of her to seem so clueless.

"I don't know what she could have seen in me other than the story of it. The guy who inspired the song, and here he is, seemingly a good guy who has ties to her cousin, so she knows he can't be all bad, and he's decent-looking. Beyond the visual, I'm just a regular guy. I don't have incredible talent or money or even ambition. I certainly don't have military career aspirations, though I know she couldn't have known that to begin with. It just... makes no sense. And I knew that, but I ignored it."

That was the killer. I'd had those cow-eyed thoughts and shoved them away. I'd even sort of brought it up with her, and in retrospect, she'd done nothing to reassure me, had she?

It was all jumbled together. Every touch, every look. And how convenient for her that I was always the one putting on the brakes physically, so she didn't have to seem like she wanted that distance, though she'd never done much to force the issue. I'd thought it was her being respectful, but from this side of things, I suspected it was a convenience. She didn't have to sleep with me to get me to cooperate.

That's not how it was.

That still-hopeful part of me, the smallest shred, wouldn't believe that. I wished the rest of me could believe it—that she'd wanted me like I'd wanted her. That she'd cared for me in some real way.

That thought was the reason I knew I'd be okay. That little glimmer of something positive, and it came as a rushing relief for me. I wasn't tempted not to get out of bed, or stop going to work, or drown myself in so much whiskey I wasn't thinking about her all the time.

I *hurt*. I felt terribly sad. But I knew I could get up and do it again the next day, and for that, I thanked God, my therapist, my friends standing in front of me, and myself.

Flint practically growled, either at my expression, or what I'd said, I didn't know. "You're wrong about that."

The oven beeped, and he turned to help Erin removed the pizzas while I pondered his claim and what he meant by it.

CHAPTER FORTY-THREE

Whit

The speculation that Ben and I had split began immediately.

Apparently, some paparazzi had caught him leaving the hotel the night after the awards show, and even though that had always been the plan, and he didn't say anything to anyone, of course, they were wondering. They had no idea that he didn't know he was the soldier who'd inspired my song. No one knew, and no one knew what he thought I'd done.

It wouldn't have been news except that Ben had been photographed with a woman I guessed was Bec based on what I knew about her. There were pictures of them holding hands at a restaurant in Nashville, of them hugging, and even though I knew I had no right to be upset, and that there was nothing wrong with him having a meal with his friend, it added salt to my self-inflicted cuts.

I got home the Friday after the Grammys. I hadn't hidden out—I'd been genuinely busy, all kinds of interviews and photoshoots and PR that Nikki was drooling over. I'd kept it together when people asked about me and Ben. I didn't say anything—just that I liked to keep my private life private.

The fact that I'd shared a private secret on stage in front of millions of people made that whole concept ironic, but so far, no one had called me on it since the Grammy wins were decent enough news.

That, and the restraining order my lawyer had threatened Colton Danes with late in the week when he put his hands on me *yet again* in the hotel lobby.

But Nikki called Friday to say that the photos of Ben with a woman had surfaced, and now, the rumors had it that he'd been cheating on me all along, that maybe it had all been for show (*good guess*), and that I'd probably been cheating with Danes, were running rampant.

A week after that, a rep from John Smith Johnson called to notify me they weren't interested in working with me at this time. Nikki practically screamed at me when I opened the door to her late that morning, but I felt nothing but relief, and of course, that ever-present misery over knowing I'd ruined what was probably the best thing I'd ever have in terms of human relationship.

"How are you not more upset about this?" she yelled, pacing back and forth in my entryway.

"I'm done. I've made so many bad decisions in the last year to try to appeal to them, and I'm done. If they can't see through the rumors and nonsense, then I don't want to work with them. I'm a human woman who dates human men, and I'm also the target of more gossip than the average person.

That's not stopping, and I'm done cowing to them like I'm some sort of ruined woman in search of redemption and not a talented, successful, desirable option for their project."

Wow, that felt good.

"I don't know what to say," Nikki said, body still, eyes wide.

I ran a hand through my hair and wished she was someone who understood me a bit more intuitively. "Say you understand. Say I'm right. Say you agree and we won't pursue working with people who are so hypocritical and demanding."

She scoffed, and that was when I realized she and I were moving in different directions. But then, she solidified it.

"I tried!" she shouted, throwing her hands up. "I tried to protect you, tried to make sure you didn't get sucked in with him, that you kept your focus... I did everything I could for you."

"I don't blame you for any of this. You know that, right?" I took a step toward her, but her sneer kept me from getting closer.

"I'm sure you don't, nor should you." She stared at the floor a moment, and another—long enough, I thought about simply walking out of the room and leaving her to her fuming, but just as I was about to leave, she spoke. "I'll talk to you next week."

I didn't wait for her to let herself out. I felt so angry with her, with the whole situation, and still more than anyone, with myself.

I'd also begun to feel angry with Ben. Why hadn't he let me explain what happened, and why hadn't I told him sooner, or what made me do it when I did? Why didn't he want to know what had been said that night, or how I felt about him?

And why had he been at brunch alone with another woman, holding hands and hugging?

I felt ill. I wanted to curl up in bed and go to sleep and stay there for a week. I was exhausted, but mostly sad. I kept thinking I'd come to the end of the tears, but every night when I went to bed, there they came again. Fortunately, I'd managed not to cry in front of anyone other than Amanda that first time, so I counted that as a success.

Before I'd unwrapped a particularly lonely-looking chicken breast and broccoli that my housekeeper had left me for the night, the doorbell rang. I'd lost a few pounds, mostly from lack of appetite, but Kendra wasn't being too hard on me since I was still exercising and eating, and not, in fact, giving in to the desire to stay in bed all day and strum sad, half-finished break-up songs in the dark.

Maybe that happened once or twice.

As usual, I'd been too busy, and now, I was gearing up for the Oscars. I'd be heading to LA again in a few days. I felt no nerves, no fear, and I'd been wondering if feeling like your heart was torn out was the secret to not caring about awards. Jamie was on to something.

I took a deep breath, hoping I could maintain my calm and not fire Nikki out of pure frustration if she had any more accusations to throw at me. She'd been edgy and obviously frustrated with me. She'd already come over uninvited twice this week, and in the history of our working relationship, that wasn't unusual, but everyone else seemed to understand I needed space.

I could admit she was trying to do her job, trying to jump on the momentum of the Grammy wins and appearing at the

Oscars in a week, but I didn't have it in me to battle with her anymore. I'd decided that I needed to ask her to back off a bit, or I'd have to let her go, because I couldn't keep arguing with her.

When I swung the door open, it wasn't diminutive, raging Nikki, but my hulking, angry-looking cousin.

Thanks a lot, Saturday.

"What were you thinking?" Reese said, standing with his hands on his hips just inside my front door.

"Hello, Reese. Good to see you, too," I said, turning down the hallway while gathering my wits.

I didn't have to guess why he was here, or what he meant, but I had no idea how to explain myself. I had no idea how to talk about this with him. The fire that had been building in my chest to showdown with Nikki had died out completely.

I busied myself with pouring water in glasses, setting one at one end of the counter and then retreating to the sink to get a rag and run it over the gleaming countertop. I could feel his eyes on me, waiting, until finally, he sighed.

"Why, Whit?"

I dropped the rag at the side of the sink and turned to him. "I never meant to hurt him."

One shake of his head, telling me what I already knew— that wasn't good enough. "I told you to be careful. I told you to be up front and honest, and what else?"

This wasn't him being self-righteous. It wasn't an *I told you so*. It was genuine anger, and though it wasn't as simple and malicious as it seemed, I deserved it.

"Not to use h—"

"Not to use him. Yep. And what did you do?"

The pinch of emotion settled in my jaw, that growing ache that had me gritting me teeth before I said, "I know I hurt him. *I know I did.* But he doesn't know what really happened, and I haven't figured out how to tell him."

Reese's eyes bore into me, and I knew he could read the honesty, the devastation in them. He had to.

"You just tell him."

"I tried. That night, I tried to explain, but he couldn't listen. He was too... blindsided, I guess."

"Understandably."

"Yes. But now... I don't know what to do, and now, he's in the news with someone else—"

"You know better than that, Whit. He's not seeing anyone else. He's miserable."

It would have been consoling, if it hadn't filled me with dread.

"Is he... okay?"

He nodded slowly. "He's okay."

"I don't know how to fix it."

That was the truth I'd been circling around for weeks now—two full weeks. I'd texted him twice the days after he'd flown back to Nashville and I was stuck in LA and got no response. I didn't know if he'd even gotten them—maybe he'd blocked me. Or maybe he felt he had nothing to say.

Reese was silent then, thinking. He took a drink, set it down, and I wondered if my house had ever been so quiet.

"It has to come from you. It has to be in person. And you have to make him listen, because he's already talked himself into believing he has nothing to offer you."

"We talked about that. He knows what I think of him, that he's—"

"He doesn't know. And after what you did, he's adrift. He thought he knew, but then, when he discovered one lie, he thought he'd discovered a whole mess of them. And that's something only you can clarify for him."

I hated that he was right. I hated myself for ever lying and for revealing the truth in such a thoughtless way.

Well, not thoughtless. I'd thought about it for days before, and then nonstop leading up to the moment I'd done it, thinking it was right, just to realize in the moment how utterly wrong I'd been.

"I'm going home to enjoy the rest of my weekend, but if you'll let me, I'll give you one piece of advice about Ben."

"Please do." My sandpaper voice grated in my throat.

"Track him down soon, and don't give up. I know you might be inclined to give him space, but I don't think that's right in this case. He's done enough convincing himself he's wrong for you in the last couple weeks and it was his fault for falling for you... I don't think he'll be able to hear you if you wait very much longer."

I swallowed, nodded, pressed my lips together to keep myself from unleashing the sob rising in my throat. "I won't. I promise."

Reese left, and I walked around in a kind of numb daze the rest of the day, the rest of the weekend, savoring the moments I could be *off* and no one would skewer me for it.

Returning to LA had filled me with dread, because it had been the last place I'd seen Ben. If I had any question about what I felt for him, I knew now. These last few weeks, the count now at three since we'd seen each other, had taught me that I missed more than just being near him.

I missed his kindness, his strength, his easy smile, his honesty. Yes, I missed him next to me on the red carpet of the Oscars, which I walked mostly alone, though right after Jamie, so we posed for a few photos together.

"I know your secret now," I said between photos.

Jamie raised a dark brow. "What's that?"

"And back together, Whit? Jamie, arm around her." The

directions came from somewhere out front. We were used to it. Jamie slid a hand around my waist, my black ballgown fitting close to my skin before it flared out at my hips.

"Your secret for not caring," I gritted through my teeth, a bright smile glamouring the cameras.

"Oh, yeah?" Jamie asked, tilting his head down to catch the best angle.

"Okay. Thanks, Whit. Thanks, Jamie," that same voice said from behind the glare of lights and reflectors.

We both turned to continue on the carpet, Jamie escorting me. In some alternate universe, this might have been the fulfillment of a dream. No doubt it would have been for many men and women—having Jamie Morris in his stunning tux, his long hair tamed into a bun, looking for all the world like the World's Sexiest Man he'd been voted three times in the last few years, with his hand on their back, guiding them down a red carpet.

Dreamy. For someone.

"You have someone rip out your heart." I glanced at him just as he did toward me.

His dark eyes met mine, and I knew then I was right.

He nodded, a regretful smile on his face, and a knowing look in those depthless eyes. "Extremely effective. I had mine removed when I was quite young—does wonders."

We went about the motions of the show, our performance, our gracious acceptance of the award. The thrill of winning registered for just a moment before I remembered I had exactly no one to share it with. No one who was actually proud of me, who supported me, and who would have been just as proud without the win.

No one like Ben. And I knew I never would.

A bone-deep conviction that I had to try, at least once, to get him back and tell him how important he was settled in my chest. Reese was right—if I kept waiting, giving him space, collecting myself and hoping some miraculous plan would appear to me in a dream, I'd lose him for good.

And as much as I'd grieved in the last few weeks, I'd been grieving over my mistakes, and over hurting him. I hadn't begun to grieve the possibility that I'd *lost* him, not really. I couldn't face that, and I couldn't believe it. Not yet.

Not without one last try.

CHAPTER FORTY-FOUR

Ben

I was two hours into a *The Lord of the Rings* marathon when the knock on my door came. I'd gone to church, but skipped lunch, and no one had hassled me about it.

Thatcher had cornered me after, confirmed I was okay, and then let it go. Even if he couldn't acknowledge he understood what it was like to need space about something like this, I knew he did, and that was why he'd given the hood of my truck a double tap and turned back to the usual lunch crew.

So it wasn't likely to be Thatch, though maybe it was. Or it could be Flint, who'd been moody ever since pizza at his place. Or for all I knew, it could have been the landlord.

The knock came again, so I paused the movie and shoved my feet into my slippers to shuffle to the door. I pulled the panel open, and before I could do anything, even say hello, Whit Grantham had shoved past me into my apartment.

"Do come in," I said, shutting the door and turning to watch her take in the apartment for only the second time.

My eyes devoured the sight of her as my pulse pounded at being near her, having her in my space again, even as my heart twisted, crushed in on itself.

Fitted jeans, long sweater unbuttoned to reveal a T-shirt underneath, long hair pulled back into a braid. Regular make up. She was coming to me dressed down, not after an event or something public.

Though I'd made a point not to pay attention, the Internet liked to push her in my face using headlines in even the most news-focused places. She and Jamie Morris had won their Oscar last week—good for them.

"I'm sorry to barge in, but I need you to listen to me." Her gaze slid quickly over me, then bounced back up to my face. "Can you do that?"

My gut said *no*. Just hearing her voice felt like steel wool in my throat, but I would never forgive myself if I didn't let her say whatever it was she needed to. There was a chance it would make me feel worse—that she'd admit she never gave a damn about me and had used me all along.

But if there was a chance she'd say something to make sense of this mess, this wreckage, then I couldn't say no.

"I can." My voice came out low and steady, an excellent deception.

I held a hand out in the direction of the living room. We sat, me on one end of the couch, her on the other. I turned off the TV and resisted the urge to clench my fists and brace against the moment.

"First, I am sorry I lied to you."

"What about?" I asked, not to be malicious, but because

there had been multiple lies, based on my understanding.

She winced, but didn't protest. "I should have told you we'd met before when Reese introduced us. I should have told you right then that you'd inspired the song."

"Why didn't you?"

I'd only wondered that every hour since the big reveal.

"I was so thrown that you were *you* when you came to Reese's door, I just... I didn't say anything. And then you acted like you'd never seen me, so I figured you didn't remember, or hadn't realized it was me. I'd worn a blond wig that night, so that wasn't impossible." She inched forward where she sat, angled to me.

I nodded, cuing her to go on.

"After that, I just felt silly saying anything because we were hardly even friends. But then, we were friends, and I should have told you, but I'd already *not* told you, so I was scared of how you'd react." She pressed her lips together, her shoulders sinking. "And then, after we started really dating, I worried about the pressure it might put on you, and even more about not having told you yet. That just kept getting worse."

"What made you decide to tell me in front of millions of strangers?

That was the crux of it, and I needed to hear her say it. She'd used me, and in that moment, she'd made the final grab for Johnson, for the image and the story, and if she could own up to that, maybe I could really forgive her.

Maybe some part of this sadness would dampen.

She took a deep breath. "I'm not sure how to explain it. I've been trying to figure out what one thing made me decide, and I don't think there was one thing. Not really. It was a bunch of little things that had been building for a while. I had to tell you—I knew that. I had missed you so much—" Her voice caught, and she swallowed, her dark brows knitted together.

I'd missed her too. Before the breakdown, and since.

She continued. "At rehearsals, Danes was all over me, and I'd talked to him, his manager, and even the choreographer about that, telling them he had to stop or I'd have to walk. I'd thought he'd finally gotten the message, but then, during the performance..."

A growl of irritation escaped me.

"I know. He's got a screw loose, and my lawyer ended up threatening him with a restraining order, so don't—don't worry about that. Not that you were, but—"

"I was. I didn't know it was going on to that extent, but I was worried. I knew you were upset with that, and we had no time to talk, and then, it was the award, and then...."

She sat up straight. "I know."

"So Danes was one factor."

"Danes, I wanted him to get that *we* were more than casual—thought maybe that would help him take me at my word that I didn't want him. Stupid, I know. Then, missing you. And I'll admit, the atmosphere—the excitement, the feeling of being dressed up and out with you at such a public event, getting to introduce you to everyone and knowing you were *mine*." Her focus fled to her lap where her fingers were tucked between her legs.

"Then they called my name for that award, and I just knew. I couldn't accept the award without thanking you— both the you I had a relationship with, that I was... that I was falling for," she said, watching my face.

She must have seen my chest rise a little higher, my attempt at swallowing the gravel in my throat.

"And the you who'd inspired the song."

I shut my eyes against that moment, anger flooding

through me. I battled within myself, searching for the right words, something to dismiss her effectively and be done with all this. It was time to move on.

"Ben, please look at me."

I opened my eyes to find her a bit closer, studying my face. I shook my head, just slightly, one shake, but she saw.

"Please."

I wasn't even sure what she was asking for, but I couldn't stand it.

I shot to my feet with a frustrated grunt. "I don't want to do this anymore. I thought you'd come for closure, or... I don't know. But this isn't cutting it."

I stopped at the kitchen counter, straightened an already-neat pile of papers.

She was at my side before I'd heard her move.

"I don't know what to tell you but the truth." Her voice sounded low and strained.

I shook my head again, clenching my jaw to keep the words in. I felt them building, pushing against the roof of my mouth.

"I can't leave here until I'm sure you know what happened. You seem to have something in mind, and I don't understand what that is."

I whirled to her, the papers abandoned. "How about the truth? How about that you saw the window of opportunity and you took it. How about that you used me to get what you wanted, and I'm sure it worked, so good job."

Her mouth dropped open, a sharp inhale of breath, and then nothing but a look so hurt, I momentarily forgot I was the one who'd had his heart ripped out. Her lashes fluttered like she'd been punched in the gut, but I checked the urge to grab her arm and steady her.

"I wish it had been different, Whit. I wish you'd felt

enough for me for it to actually be real, and I wish even more than since you didn't, you would have just been honest with me. That would have made it better—would have made it suck, but it wouldn't have felt like a betrayal."

She forced her mouth closed and took a startled step back, then another. She pulled her keys from her pocket and turned to the door, but stopped just short of grabbing the handle.

When she turned back to me, she shredded me. Tears slid from the corners of her eyes, but she wiped them away fiercely and took three long steps until she stood right next to me.

"Listen to me right now, and believe what I am saying."

I waited, quiet, not a blink.

"I didn't lie to you about dating you. I didn't lie to you about caring for you. I didn't do it for a stupid stunt, and I didn't mean for it to hurt you." Her voice cracked as emotion swelled, but she swallowed it down and continued. "I had to tell you the truth that night because I'd realized I was in love with you, and I didn't want to fail you by lying, and I didn't want to miss thanking the person that inspired me originally, and who had inspired me so much since."

My hands were locked into fists at my sides—I couldn't move them. I could hear the words, but my heart didn't dare believe them.

But why not? She had no reason to lie at this point. *Did she?*

"I messed up, and I'm sorry. I didn't handle it well because I've never been here before." She held out her hands, palms up, like she'd emptied everything out. "I'm sorry, but you have to know that I didn't mean to use you that way—not the way you mean. And I do care about you. Very much."

CHAPTER FORTY-FIVE

Whit

I pulled at the door knob, fumbling, but got it open, my hopes crumbling and my eyes filling with tears.

Before I got it fully open, Ben was at my back, pushing the panel closed. He'd come at me so quickly, he'd knocked me forward, but grabbed my arm to keep me from running into the wall. He pulled on it until I turned.

I wasn't sure what I expected, but seeing him so close, even with all his anger and frustration directed at me, was no less affecting than usual. He had coarse stubble covering his cheeks and jaw, his hair was short, and his face looked lean, hard, and very un-Ben.

"Why would you say that to me?" he asked, his voice a low slice into the air between us.

"I—I said a lot of things, all of them true."

"Why would say you love me? What does that get you?" he asked, his eyes frantically searching between mine.

That look, that question, made me lose the reins on my tears. "It doesn't get me anything. I said it because I love you. Because it's true."

His face was so serious, so sad, all I wanted was to pull him to me and kiss him, calm him, make him know the way I knew.

"I'm so mad at you, I don't even know where to start," he said, his voice quiet.

"Tell me. Just... start." Because if he was talking, I could take it. Maybe we could take it.

"I hate that you told me in front of everyone. I hate that you didn't make me stay with you that night—pin me down or something and force me to understand. I have missed you so much."

He crushed me to him in a hug so tight, all air left my lungs. Then he drew back.

"I am frustrated that I don't know if I can trust you, and I'm mad at myself for wanting to be able to."

Hope bloomed. His perpetual honesty and his anger and all of it gave me hope, it being so much better than that blank defeat he'd given me in the hotel room back in LA.

"You can trust me. I haven't lied about anything else. Truly. Nothing. I avoided telling you about meeting before, and that was huge. I lied by omission, and it was unacceptable. But nothing else has been false between us, except maybe the attempt at being just friends who were fake-dating because that was ridiculous. But nothing else."

Adrenaline coursed through me as I watched his face, saw as his eyes moved over my features, hesitating on my lips, as his hands gently squeezed where they rested on my upper arms. I prayed with all my heart he would hear the truth in my words and believe me.

"I want to believe you," he said, stepping closer, like he couldn't help it.

My heart tripped in my chest, my breath unsteady in my mouth. He had to know this was all real.

"I want you to believe me. Ask me anything, I'll tell you the truth." His beautiful blue eyes were so intense, I couldn't look away.

"Did you plan on that speech at the awards all long?"

"No."

"Why did Nikki have me re-sign the confidentiality agreements?"

Alarm swarmed my chest. "What? I didn't know about that."

"I did it the last time I saw you before you left. I'm sure I told you—she asked me to stop in and talk with her that last night before you went to LA. That was it. And I was so distracted, I didn't think twice about it. But after... it felt like another piece to the puzzle I'd chosen to lose."

He watched me closely, as though I'd betray another lie with body language.

"She never spoke with me about it, but I can assure you I will be speaking to her." My voice was calm, sure, with nothing to hide.

"I believe you," he said, and a sprig of hope, of possibility, bloomed.

"Good," I said, giving in to the step closer I'd been wanting to take.

I put my hands at his waist, stopping short of outright groping his sturdy sides. Getting to touch him was both a relief and a kind of torture.

"Do you really love me?" he asked, his voice gentle, eyes searching.

"Yes." The one word rang ardent.

A whisper of a smile crossed his gorgeous lips. "Why didn't you tell me before?"

"I've never told anyone that—I really don't think I've ever said it to anyone, but certainly not a man. It was never going to be easy for me."

He'd slowly lowered his head so our faces were close. We were speaking lightly, softly, sharing space, breath.

"Will you tell me now?" he asked, his lips grazing my ear.

I shivered, almost laughed at the pleasure of it. "I love you, Ben."

He pulled back, a contrast of hunger and elation on his face. "I love you, Whit."

Finally, finally, our lips met, and the relief of that contact, of that seal on the moment, was immeasurable.

"I missed you. So much. Too much," he said between kisses, stepping closer, pulling me closer, everything in us working to get *closer*.

"Me too. I've been a mess," I replied, breathless and ravenous.

A few more quick, searing kisses, and he pulled back. "What do we do now?"

I chuckled, relieved at his next question. "Honestly? I have no idea."

EPILOGUE

Three years later
Ben

"What I experienced is something many men and women experience in combat. The loss, the fear, the pain, the depression, and the sense that there is no way to feel whole again. This organization is something dear to me because it, along with many other resources, has helped show that there is hope, there is wholeness, beyond the moments of pain. Thank you for joining us tonight."

Applause sounded in the ballroom, the wealth of Nashville's elite and much of Hollywood dotting the tables. Better yet, many of my old Rambler Battalion friends and leaders had shown up—my old company commander, Luke Waterford, and my first sergeant, now master sergeant, Harrison. And of course, Prince Charming himself, LTC

Reese Flint. Thatcher was overseas but had sent his best, of course.

I walked off stage, grinning to myself at what a strange thing it was for *me* to be the one on stage. But we'd worked for this for three years now, and this was a moment I'd never forget.

"You were perfect," Whit said, looking painfully gorgeous in a long silk dress in a color that somehow matched those blue-green eyes.

"You are perfect," I said, placing one hand at her back, and running the other over the swell of her belly. "This is surreal."

"Finally seeing this come to life? You've worked so hard, and I'm so, so proud of you." She pulled me to her and hugged me close.

I'd worked on this project for almost two years. When I left the Army, I enrolled in a Master of Social Work program. Through that, I began working with some colleagues and Whit, and in the end, we partnered with an organization that gave men and women dealing with PTSD and depression a creative outlet to expand its reach tremendously.

Funny enough, it was one of the organizations I'd looked at with my therapist while recovering in the early weeks. I was happy to be working for them now, bringing my perspective and frankly, Whit's fame, to their table. Their budget for the year would be fully funded by the end of the night.

"Yes. That. Feeling like I've found my purpose for work —" I glanced back at the stage, "—and I'm glad I managed to talk you into marrying me, and having my baby, and making me the happiest sap on the planet."

"I love you, Ben Holder."

"I love you."

Thank you for reading Whit and Ben's story! If you're ready for more sweet military romance, check out The OCONUS Bonus Series, set at a small military base in Germany. You'll even find some familiar faces in the series, including Bec Jones and Thatcher Wild, who get their own book in the series. Grab your next sweet military romance read today!

There's really no way to depict the realities of military life without addressing, at least in some small way, the loss, trauma, and resulting realities for our service members and their families. In the aftermath of Dillon Jones' death, Ben, Thatcher, Reese, and Bec all struggle to varying degrees, both in this and future series. And it's different for each character—they don't all experience PTSD, of course.

For Ben, who has the most obviously difficult time, he used resources—sometimes at the requirement of his superiors— and he worked daily to maintain his mental, physical, and emotional health. We see a glimpse of that in this book, and I hope you'll forgive the imperfections of the portrayal of his journey through grief and toward mental health.

While soldiers are certainly not the only people who deal with PTSD, I'd like to share a small contingent of PTSD resources for soldiers specifically and the people who love them. Here's a short list, should they be useful to you or someone you love, or be something you'd like to support.

National Alliance on Mental Health's resources for those with and supporting those with PTSD

PTSD Alliance: Supporting those with PTSD (and lots of great info)

Cohen Veteran's Network — information and direct care via an amazing not-for-profit philanthropic organization.

ACKNOWLEDGMENTS

It feels like each book is at once a more and less isolated thing to write. For this book, I probably have fifty people to thank in some way or another, but if anyone actually reads these things, you'll probably see a pattern of the same people emerging. Without these friends, mentors, partners, peers, and of course, the family too, I would still be wondering how to finish Luke and Alex's story.

To my beta readers Allison, Christy, and Emma. Thank you for your extremely helpful thoughts, your quick turn-arounds, and for rooting for Whit and Ben. Thank you to Julie for listening to me whine, cry, and verbally process every aspect of this book and this career (and this life, let's be honest). Thank you to Denise, Karen, and Monica, for cheering me on, sharing opinions, and having my back.

Thank you to the LVN book club, who came along at such a wonderful time. Your support and encouragement has meant so much, and your avid readership of all kinds of books has helped me find inspiration more than once. I'll treasure the months we spent together, and probably always hope for a reunion!

Thank you to Jamie, for your daily phone calls, your practical advice, and your very welcomed commiseration. So happy to be on this journey with you! To Alyssa, my new friend—thanks for helping me feel anchored here (even if you didn't realize it, hah!) and sharing the passion for writing.

Thank you to Zee Monodee, my amazing editor, for your relentless pursuit of a stronger POV and more heart—I am learning so much from you and can't thank you enough for your beautiful brain and persistent comments.

Thanks to Rainbeau Decker, for creating the cover images and design for this and every other book in The Rambler Battalion Series. Thank you for getting in the water, both metaphorically and literally, and for finding just the right shot every time. You are a marvel.

Thank you to my parents, who continue to be my biggest supporters and advocates. Thank you to my kids, Annie and Wesley, who each bring a measure of wonder and madness to the days. Thanks to our third and forthcoming baby, for teaching me (already—Lord help me with what happens when she's here) how to slow down and adjust my pace to care for myself and you and still accomplish goals.

Thank you to God, whose love is never foiled by misunderstandings, bad timing, grand gestures gone wrong, or anything else.

Thank you to Matthew, my beloved, who cheers me on as I write these books, who patiently helps outline the soldiers' backstories so they make sense in a realistic timeline, and who works reading them in between war histories and autobiographies of Generals as a show of support. You'll always be my favorite hero.

Finally to you, readers. Thank you. I still find it fairly astounding anyone reads my books, and to have readers who stick around and read more than one, and then reach out and tell me about it—wow. Thanks to those who've been in touch to share your thoughts, and thanks to those who read and share the books. It's no exaggeration to say I can't do this without you, so thank you.

ABOUT THE AUTHOR

Claire Cain lives to eat and drink her way around the globe with her traveling soldier and three kids, but is perhaps even happier hunkered down at home in a pair of sweatpants and slippers using any free moment she has to read and cook. Or talk—she really likes to talk. She has become an expert at packing too many dishes in too few cabinets and making houses into homes from Utah to Germany and many places in between. She's a proud Army wife and is frankly just really happy to be here.

You can join Claire's facebook reader group for exclusive content and fun: https://www.facebook.com/groups/clairecain/

Website: http://www.clairecainwriter.com

E-mail: Claire@ClaireCainWriter.com

Newsletter sign-up for new releases, exclusives, and freebies: http://www.clairecainwriter.com/newsletter

Grab the other books in **The Rambler Battalion series!**

Where You Go: The Rambler Battalion, Book 1

As You Are: The Rambler Battalion, Book 2

Don't Stop Now: The Rambler Battalion, Book 3

Home With You: The Rambler Battalion, Book 4

The OCONUS Bonus Series

Sweet Military Romance Overseas

The Problem with Planning Love, Book 1

Finding Happiness in a Hoax, Book 2

Learning to Fight after Flight, Book 3

The Bright Side of Brooding, Book 4

Holding On to Hope, Book 5

The Silver Ridge Resort Series

Sweet Small Town Romance

Unexpected Love at Silver Ridge, Book 1

Second Chance at Silver Ridge, Book 2

Patrolling for Love at Silver Ridge, Book 3

Fire and Ice at Silver Ridge, Books 4

Back to Silver Ridge Series

Almost Perfect, Book 1

Almost Real, Book 2

Almost Sure, Book 3

Almost Home, Book 4

SNEAK PEEK: THE PROBLEM WITH PLANNING LOVE

Livie

The-five-year-old boy in front of me took my hand in a firm shake, the wild dark curls on his head shaking with his enthusiasm.

I nodded toward this pint-sized little man. "You must be Robert Wolfe."

The giant smile that greeted me told me I was right.

"Yep. But call me Robby. You must be Mrs. Manderson."

I grinned. "I am *Miss Anderson*, yes. I'm so glad to meet you, Robby."

"I like this room," he said, surveying the large, colorful space he'd spend the next nine months of his kindergarten year in.

The uniformed soldier who'd come in behind him ducked out the doorway before even fully stepping in, cell phone to his ear. I shook my head softly—first strike against that parent, though I tried not to think it. But really, could he not take ten minutes away to meet his child's teacher and make sure his son was comfortable? Some kids would absolutely freak out if their parent stepped outside the classroom when they'd just been introduced to a new adult.

Add to that, this was Kugelfels, Germany. Granted, it was a DODEA—Department of Defense Education Activity—school, so still basically a US public school but run by the DOD rather than a state. Many kids had just moved across the world to come to Germany with their military parents during the summer PCS—Permanent Change of Station—cycle, so this guy abandoning his son with a new teacher at a new school in a new country?

Not great.

I smiled, all practiced warmth and comfort. "I'm glad. There are a lot of fun things to learn and do in here, that's for sure."

He crossed one arm over his chest and brought the opposite hand to his chin, then tapped his cheek thoughtfully as he looked around. "Yes. I can get used to this."

I tucked my lips between my teeth to stifle a laugh. Five was the absolute best age, especially when it came in this kind of little package—one clearly unafraid of his new surroundings. Maybe his father knew he wouldn't have any trouble with me.

"Did you go to preschool, or did you stay home with your mom or dad?" Either was fine, but I'd put my money on this kid being used to leaving home every day.

He turned and shot a thumb over his shoulder at his dad —or where he would've been. "I went to the CDC for everything. My mom is gone and my dad is in the order of the silver leaf so he has to work and can't do school for me. Grams and Ari trade off helping with the driving."

"The order of the silver leaf? That sounds really important." I already loved him.

The glut of information gave me the familiar pang that hit with certain kids. I loved all of them in the end, but some naturally wormed their way into my heart from the get-go. The tendency to over-share was one of many things I loved about teaching kindergarten, though sometimes it led to uncomfortable revelations.

He nodded, eyes wide, a serious wrinkle to his brow.

"It is. He has lots of people to learn from every day, just like I'm gonna learn from you every day." His eye caught on a basket of magnetic tiles in a cubby next to where we sat. "Can I play with those?"

"Sure you can. I have some things to go over with your dad, when he comes back in, and then you can go and I'll see you next week."

He plopped down into a tailor sit, or *criss-cross applesauce* as we call it in class, and dove into the basket with both hands.

I watched him a moment, then movement out the corner of my eye caught my attention and I turned to see...

Wow.

I swallowed down that reaction, pasting a professional smile on my face as I stood, extending a hand. "Olivia Anderson."

His giant hand engulfed mine, dry and warm and a little rough.

"Eric Wolfe. Nice to meet you, ma'am. I apologize for taking that call—I normally wouldn't but it's a bit of a time-sensitive issue."

Ah, manners. The unexpected manners were maybe more lethal than his physical appearance, though that alone was enough to tell me I shouldn't look him in the eye again until the year was over. This kind of reaction to a child's parent was oh so so *so* not appropriate. I'd never had it before—not like this, not even close.

"Well, Mr.—er, uh—" I shot a quick glance at the rank a little below eye level on his chest—ah, the silver leaf, signaling he was a lieutenant colonel, but I reminded myself not to actually say the *lieutenant* because the Army liked to be confusing, or so I'd learned after years working on military bases and learning the conventions, "—Colonel Wolfe, thanks for taking some time to meet with me. If you don't mind taking a seat..."

I gestured to a chair at one side of my teacher's table, a low half-moon shape, and took a seat opposite him.

Then I realized the chair was one of the children's sizes, and this fully grown man in no way fit, but he tried. His knees came up above the table, but his body sat low, only a foot off the ground. Ideal for little kids to sit on and scoot under the table, but for a man who had to be at least six feet tall?

A giggle escaped before I could stop it.

His brutally handsome face didn't crack. "Is something funny, ma'am?"

I blinked rapidly, trying to blur my vision and avoid noticing any of the things that made him so ridiculously attractive. "Uh, um, of course not, I—"

Then he smiled, all friendly humor and co-conspiracy.

And he has a sense of humor.

No. Nope. Not noticing anything. Not the cut jaw. Not the features that easily qualified him to be a model. Not the straight, white teeth behind really nice-looking lips.

"I'm so sorry. I didn't realize I still had the children's size chair there—you're my first parent meeting this year."

And the fact that I hadn't prepped the room would've made a normal teacher's head explode, but not mine. I didn't mind a fly-by-the-seat-of-your-pants approach as long as I got the job done, and especially if my lack of double-checking chair sizes came on the heels of a summer so full of travel, I'd be living on the highs for weeks. Months. Honestly, probably years to come, especially when I moved back home.

"I spend a great deal of time in like-sized chairs, actually. Robby and his sister Delia have a little table they make me sit at with them. I'm pretty sure it's one of their subtle methods of torture." He shifted in his seat, easing forward so he could rest his elbows on his knees and set his chin in his hands. "Please, do go on."

I laughed freely then. "No, this is insane."

I hustled over and grabbed a larger chair and slid it next to him as he stood, then returned to my seat before I could give into the temptation to smell him.

Not. Okay.

"Thank you. I probably wouldn't have been able to get out of that seat after another couple of minutes." He set a portfolio-type folder on the desk, opened it, and took out a pen. "So, tell me everything I need to know to make this a great year for Robby, and for you."

Resisting the urge to sigh, and ignoring the little leap in my chest when I noted he didn't wear a wedding ring, which confirmed what Robby had declared in saying his mom was gone... divorced? Or widowed? Whatever the case, not my business, so I began my spiel.

Ten minutes later, I'd given him all the information he needed, and he'd nodded, asked two intelligent questions, gathered his items, and then stood.

"Thank you for being here and teaching. I know kindergarten isn't easy. I have to apologize now because I'll be in rotations almost non-stop until Thanksgiving, but my mother and sister will be stepping in to help when needed."

My mouth opened like I'd say words, but none came. How did this man know to say these things? I mean, I knew how—his older daughter Delia would've already been through kindergarten and so must've been familiar with things, but...

"Wow, I'm sorry. People don't normally say that kind of thing, especially not..."

Hot, possibly available, officer dads.

A single dark brow raised. "Especially not...?"

"Uh... hah. Dads, I guess. The moms tend to be a bit more in tune with what teachers need. Around here, half the spouses are teachers as it is. Anyway, I'm sorry, I'm babbling. Thank you."

"Well... you're welcome. I'm sorry I can't be of more help in the near-term." His cell phone buzzed and he pulled it out, silenced it, then returned his attention to me. "I've got to get Robby back before I head to a meeting. Forgive me."

"I understand. My next student will be here any minute anyway. Thank you for making time to come in."

"It was nice to meet you, Ms. Anderson."

He extended his hand, which I took, my stomach dropping to my shoes at the contact, which would've normally made me roll my eyes because talk about off-limits, but then he said, "I look forward to seeing you again."

I sputtered a little, thrown. "Uh, yes. Yeah. Thank you... me too."

Mercifully, Robby appeared next to me and hit me with a large smile as he grabbed his dad's free hand.

"See you soon Miss Anderson."

"See you Monday!"

Start The Problem with Planning Love today!

Don't miss release news and exclusive content. Sign up for Claire's e-mail list: http://www.clairecainwriter.com/newsletter